Over Cast

Over Cast

K.W. Benton

To Ana & Kat,
These adventures pale
in comparison to yours.

xoxo
K.W. Benton

Printed in the United States of America

First Printing, 2014

ISBN 978-0-9915662-0-4
Benton Books L.L.C.
Leesburg, Virginia, U.S.A.
www.kwbenton.com

Edited by Kelly Hashway
Cover Art and Interior Design by Raven Tree Design
www.raventreedesign.com

To Ryan, Tucker and Zoe,
your love is what supports me so I can reach for the sky.

Acknowledgements

Thank you to Mom, Kirsty, Kak, Amy, Kathy and Dickie for all your love and support.

A huge thanks to Brenda and Jodie for the advice and help along the way.

Contents

Chapter One

"Do you have a response?" Principal Decker asks, his face stern.

Sitting quietly, I wonder for the fiftieth time in the last sixty seconds why I am in trouble again. Like dropped ice cream draws ants, I don't mean to cause problems, but if I'm around enough, they will find me.

I guess I am quiet for too long 'cause Mr. Decker asks again, "G.J., do you have any idea how Icy Hot ended up in Miss Ackers' undergarments?"

This I can answer with at least a half-truth. "No sir. No sir I do not."

"It was has been reported that you and Miss Ackers had another confrontation, and then after gym class she had the um… reaction to the ointment. So, I am going to ask you again. Did you put Icy Hot in her underwear?"

Well, now we are back to what I cannot answer without getting into trouble. It isn't as though I went and swiped her undies through the Icy Hot tub. *Ew, who does that?* I wouldn't be the one to play grabby panties with some girl's used undergarments. But, Sara was at me yet again, making up more nonsense about my family. And well … in trying to ignore her snotty remarks, I did recite, "liar, liar, pants on …" under my breath, and then … well they *were*. Just with Icy Hot. However, there was no way Mr. Decker was going to believe I'd just said, "pants on fire," and poof her privates were perspiring.

"Miss Gardener, what do you have to say?" The wings of gray at his temples and full set of luggage under his eyes make Mr. Decker appear way older than his early thirties. Some of the responsibility of that premature aging may be mine since it has happened only since my arrival.

"Mr. Decker, I was raised better than to play with other people things without asking, and I can assure you I did not touch Sara's panties—I mean undies … or, um, underwear." My face pulls in an "is that okay?" kind of way since I'm not sure exactly how to approach the subject of underwear with my principal.

Mr. Decker gives me one of those long silent stares that people do whenever they want you to confess. I resent him for presuming my guilt. It doesn't matter that I *am* guilty. He doesn't know that for sure. My chin shoots up a little in defiance of that baleful glare, indignant that he thinks I would do such a thing. Guilt sinks in. My gaze lowers to the floor like it does whenever I lie.

This must be why people use that stare, because Mr. Decker takes it as my admission I have done the deed and says, "I expect you to apologize to Miss Ackers."

Slack jawed in incredulity I stare stunned. In no way can I imagine saying any form of an apology to that horrible twit.

"Mrs. Ackers has requested you do so at the assembly on Monday, in front of the student body." Mr. Decker is now the one to glance down in, what I presume is guilt.

It is better he does, because to describe the look on my face would probably require using some curse words. Gulping air in to shove my pride into a space meant for much smaller things, I swallow my voice back down my throat. Speech returning I babble, "Mr. Decker, I really cannot talk in front of the whole school. It's just about the worst idea I can think of. Well, no it's not…but I really can't do that. Please be reasonable." I'm pleading. No way should I let my mouth loose on the whole student body at once. I have no idea what is going on with my abilities.

"It's either that or you are on suspension for a few days. And a suspension would pretty much preclude you from any scholarships you might have been hoping for. I know you are in the running for the governor's science award. Please do not make me have to remove you from the event because of such a childish prank. Mrs. Ackers is quite active in the community and does have some sway with the parties who will judge you. There are consequences to every action, and you need to pay these if you are going to have a shot." Mr. Decker ends with his eyes softening, painting genuine concern on his once stern face.

Understanding dawns, whether I was guilty or not, I was going to take the fall for this. Mrs. Ackers must've called up poor Mr. Decker and yammered in his ear till he caved. The *new girl*, played by me, is about to learn right quick whose booty needs to be smooched in order to get by in this town. I thought leaving small-town Louisiana would've ended the fish-to-pond ratio, but apparently, there are more big fish to contend with here.

Moving to Spokane, Washington, was quite a shocker. I was not used to being around so many people. Before my world had changed, we actually lived surrounded by a state park on Rt. 10 between Franklinton and Bogalusa, which sits right on that windy river of Huck Finn fame. While the trees cooled it down some, living near the border of Louisiana and Mississippi, you knew what hot meant. Sometimes we would walk outside and an instant shine would just cover us. Mama always called those our sparkly days. She always did have a nice way of putting the less pleasant things in life. But one thing you do when it's too hot to move is visit your neighbors. "Visit" in the South means gather all the intel you can on who is doing what to whom, so you can share that with the next neighbor in order to take everyone's mind off the fact that they're all melting. In Washington, it's called gossip. But if you were out visiting and you happened to hear about the powerful people doing what to whom, well you just did not carry that on to the next folks you visited, and if you did and they found out about it, they would make sure you were not welcome to "visit" anyone for a while. Basically, you were made to feel as though nobody on this green earth loved you but your dog. I miss Mama and our small house just off Rt. 10 with the miles of woods for our backyard. Blinking back the shimmer in my eyes, I nod, giving Mr. Decker the agreement he seeks.

Mr. Decker gives me a sharp bob of his head and says, "Good," a might louder than he should have, as if relieved the conversation is coming to an end. "Now which class were you headed back to? I'll write you a pass."

I glance at the clock, and in a distracted small voice I answer, "Lunch, sir." I wonder if I should advise Mr. Decker to have the fire department, the ambulance, a horde of psychiatrists, and/or the SWAT team available should something go wrong with my apology on Monday.

As he writes up my hall pass, my mind floats through all the events that have happened to bring me to this point. I had only been up to Washington once before. I had been about eight years old, and Aunt Celia had been marrying either her third or fourth husband at the time. I honestly can't keep track. She had stopped moving all over the country and found a home near Nine Mile Lake. It had been July, and I had loved the area around the lake. We'd played in the water, and my new "uncle of the moment" had taken us out fishing in his boat.

On that trip, Mama and I had gone hiking in one of the local conservation areas and we had seen an actual wolf. It was one of the most memorable experiences of my life. We had been climbing up a trail through the sparse woods. The sky was that color blue that made your soul feel good. I had been watching my feet, so I would not trip on the roots and rocks in our path when I'd gotten that tingle you sometimes get when there are eyes on you. Lifting my gaze up from my feet, it had locked on to the most haunting golden eyes I had ever seen. It had frozen me in place, and as Mama followed my stare, she'd gasped and drawn the wolf's attention. It moved off but had looked over its shoulder as it had loped away.

You know how sometimes things happen that stay tucked in your mind and you pull it out like a picture you can look at? This is one of those moments. I pull out memories and relive them whenever I need to find some peace. I am a nature baby, and that wolf had been a connection to something primal, nature in its purest form.

Needless to say, Mama had come away from the moment with a different tale of a near-death experience. We didn't have wolves down south, and it disturbed her we had come so close to a wild carnivore. She hadn't given much thought to the gators and snakes I had played around with every day of my life.

We never went back to Washington before Mama died. So, to move to Aunt Celia's in the middle of January had shocked me. We did not get much snow in Louisiana. In fact, I had never seen snow accumulate on the ground. Sure a dusting from time and again, but when our plane touched down at Spokane International Airport there were huge piles of it pushed from the runways. It looked like small mountain ranges had popped up at the edge of the cleared area. And cold—*brrr* does not even begin to cover it. Aunt Celia had to take me from the airport to the mall so I could get some layers of clothing to hold out the chill. Nothing I had could keep my body from trying to bring up my core temperature by shivering.

It took a little over a week for Aunt Celia to set me up at school. I had to test in and actually tested higher than ninth grade, but the school counselors thought, with everything that had happened, putting me in with an older group of kids might be too much. I agreed. So, into the new pressure cooker I went, not knowing a living soul. The cliques were established. If I felt like an outsider before, I am now a curiosity. I'm not sure which is worse.

The very first day, as I left the front office to try to track down my class, I opened the door and ran straight into the chest of one of the most incredible looking boys I have ever seen in my life. As Brad Pitt has ceded his title of world's hottest man to Channing Tatum, Channing will be handing that crown over to this guy—should the two ever meet up. Now, I'm five feet and eleven inches tall, and I was eye level with his collarbone. He was solid. I mean the sleeves of his green and white letter jacket could not contain the swell of his biceps. In order to balance myself after our collision, my hand hit his shirt where I felt the bricks stacked under the cloth to make those insane ridges of truly fabulous abs. My gaze meandered past his strong jaw and full lips to meet his intense green-gold eyes behind those incredible sable-like lashes. I drew in a breath to sigh in acknowledgement I was in love. Then he opened his mouth and love went out the window.

After he grabbed my elbows and pulled me slightly closer he said, "What is that strange smell?" He said it so loud that the people around us all turned and stared at me. I had taken all of two steps into the halls of my new social atmosphere, and I was the girl who smelled weird. I wished the guy had just shut up. Who says that to a person they've never met? The look on my face must have willed him to run away because he took a step back.

The giggles and smirks from the on-looking kids, flowing into school past the front office at that moment, were to be expected. What I didn't expected was for Hottie Mc Hot Hot to then lose his ability to speak. He stood there moving his mouth, but nothing came out. I murmured, "Excuse me," and walked around him.

A short girl with jet-black hair and the craziest outfit I had ever seen popped up next to me as I desperately tried to fade into the crowd and escape the grinning oglers. Over her shoulder, she called louder than I would have thought possible, "You're an idiot," to the now mute beautiful boy. She turned to me. "Welcome to Lakeside, home of the obtuse. I'm Nat."

"G.J.," was all I said back to her.

"Don't mind Hamilton." Gesturing behind us, she went on. "You can't have that much animal magnetism and not have some flaws. Verbal skills are where he gets marks off."

I smiled at her and said, "So he's not the welcome wagon?"

"No, our version of the welcome wagon happens at lunch where we will shower you with tater tots and crappy pizza while you walk the gauntlet of trying to locate me," she did a presto move with her hands, "at my table under the Eagle Spirit Banner," Nat said, openly inviting me to sit with her at lunch.

I grabbed the invite with both hands. "Are those tots with or without ketchup?"

"It's BYOK," Nat zinged back. "I'm in your first class. Come this way." And she started down the hall that T-ed into the one we were walking down.

"How do you know my schedule?" I asked, unsure if I should follow her.

"I'm psychic." She smirked, walking backward and waiting for me to follow her. "And I help Mr. Decker in the office for extra credit, so I was the one who printed your schedule."

I followed her to our homeroom; looking at the locker numbers until I came across the one I'd been given. I stopped to work the combination and told Nat I'd be right there.

She stared at the locker I'd stopped at. "That's your locker?" A little something like fear moved through her eyes.

"Yep, 2141. This here is me," I said, unsure what caused her to go so still.

She bobbed her head quickly and muttered, "I'll catch you in class." Faster than I thought possible, she ducked away into the traffic of kids headed to their destinations.

As I turned back to my locker to work the combination, I jumped about a foot in the air. Right behind me was a lean, handsome young man. He had maybe three inches on me and seemed to have the world in his palm. The grace in which he slid next to me and worked the lock on the locker next to mine made me feel like I was trying to do my own combination with my toes. I got my locker open, with a triumphant grunt, as he finished getting ready for his first class. As he closed up, he turned to me and said, "Drake Aldrich."

Fumbling to get my things organized I responded, "Um. Hey there. I'm G.J.."

His eyes narrowed. "You don't sound like you are from this area."

"Well that might be 'cause I'm not." I sorted out what I needed and closed up to make my way toward my first class.

"Are you headed this way?" he asked, tipping his chin in the direction Nat had bolted.

"I believe I am." I noticed my Louisiana speech pattern more than I ever had in my life.

"Where do you hail from exactly?" Drake asked in an old-world way of putting things.

"Down south," I replied, looking up at the numbers above the doors. I stopped to enter the room stated on my class schedule, which I was clutching like any newbie would.

Drake stopped too and said, "Welcome to Lakeside. Tell your little friend I said 'hello.'" He smiled, raised one eyebrow, and backed into the classroom across from my homeroom. All I could think was Sade must have met his daddy when she wrote "Smooth Operator."

I walked into class and a hush covered the room as if I'd stepped too close to a bush full of crickets. Nat pointed to the seat next to her in the back with the eraser end of her pencil. As I passed, I heard hushed whispers pick up behind my back.

Nat's face was grim. "Hey, all right if I sit here?" I asked not understanding her mood.

"What? Oh yeah. I saved it for you. What did Mr. Wonderful have to say?" The sarcasm of her reference to Drake caught me off guard.

I was just about to tell her that he'd said to say hello, but as I started to form the words, she cut me off.

"Ugh, I can't get a read on that guy. I don't like it when I can't read people." Nat's made it clear Drake bothered her.

I would have asked her more but a lumpy gray-haired lady waddled in and wriggled behind the desk at the front of the room. In a singsong voice she called, "Good morning, people. Settle down and stop talking. Looks like someone has joined us today." She perused her attendance sheet. Looking up she spotted me. "Am I correct that you are Glory?"

Laughter bubbled from the other people in the class.

"Yes, ma'am, I sure am, but if you wouldn't mind, I prefer G.J.."

"G.J. it is, Miss Gardener. I'm Ms. Stontz. Let me know if you need anything to get up to speed. We are currently working with Mr. Shakespeare. I have no idea what you know and what you don't, but if you would like to pick up the syllabus on your way out, it might help get you caught up to where we are now."

Ms. Stontz finished attendance and so went my first class in my new school. I liked her, and she made the ebb and flow of the world's most famous author seem as natural as the tides. After class, Nat headed off to science, and I made my way to PE. Looking over the crowd of polyester covered youths in the green and white uniforms, I saw the spectrum of your basic teen assemblage. From the beautiful tiny blonde who ruled the minions around her to the kids who most likely only showered when their parents made them and wore gamer t-shirts without actually playing said games. Again, I found myself not knowing another being, with one exception that made me want to crawl under the bleachers and die. That boy Nat had referred to as Hamilton was there in all his glory. His body looked like that of a man, not a ninth grader. It was simply not right, and I guessed he must have failed five or six grades to be in our class. As I narrowed my eyes and pondered why his mother had bought him a shirt that made her boy look like he had been shrink-wrapped, the hubbub over my mama's choice of names played out the same way it had before. Only this time someone was kind enough to add "nice name." Rolling my eyes, I could tell this class was going to be one of my favorites.

Now I don't know about you, but I truly believe dodge ball is a sadistic form of torture that must have been created by a mind like Attila the Hun's. The fact that every PE teacher in the nation has foisted this barbaric game on the youth of America is one of those conspiracies that the likes of Oliver Stone or Mr. Michael Moore should look into.

One of the worst things that can happen to a new person in high school is for them to catch the ball. See, if you catch the ball, you have to throw the ball. If you do not throw the ball at someone actually on the opposing team, your team gets mad at you, and if you do throw the ball at someone when you have no idea who they are, well you might commit one of those social sins that no mea culpa will correct. Of course, I caught the ball. Looking across at the other side, there was only one person I knew at all. So, I slung that sucker at that all-too-well-defined chest so hard that I had hoped Hamilton would think twice about trying to catch it.

Now if you recall from my earlier observations of this boy, you might have put together what I hadn't in this eager moment of petty revenge. He's an athlete. He did not get all those glorious muscles by playing X-box seven to ten hours a day. And you might recall the name of the game, which was what he did. That rat bastard dodged the ball. And with his poetic twist of lithe muscles, he'd ruined my chances of getting along at Lakeside High School. How you ask? Because hiding behind his impressive chest muscles was the petite form of the girl I would come to know as Sara Ackers. And that wayward instrument of my destruction—the ball—smacked her right in the kisser.

I swear it was like a *Brady Bunch* re-run. Sara held her face and nasally screamed, "You broke my nose."

Horrified, I broke into every form of apology I could think of, but the full-on belly laughter of the beefy man, who had with one dodge of a ball, ruined my life drowned me out.

Now that it is clear that I hate her, with very good reason, I can laugh about it. But at the time, I really had felt bad about breaking her nose and giving her two black eyes. It had looked like half the blood was falling out of her nostrils and the other half of the hemorrhage was flooding the skin behind her eyes.

Since that was the start of the relationship between Sara and me, you can see how things might have begun poorly and have had some trouble getting straightened out. It did not help that on my way to sit with Nat in the lunchroom that day, Hamilton had grabbed my bicep and squeezed it saying, "You have a hell of an arm there." His friends, all wearing the same letter jackets, had broken into laughter and mimicked noses breaking, complete with finger explosions and sound effects.

As I stood immobile under the weight of the whole lunchroom giving me the stink eye, Nat had pulled me away and yelled in Hamilton's face, "You are an absolute moron."

And since that auspicious moment, things have just gone downhill like box cars with no brakes set at the top of a snow-free K-2. See while I was busy feeling just awful about Sara's potential need for reconstructive surgery, she was busy telling anyone who would listen, in her broken nose twang, that I was an escapee from an institution, prone to violent spasms that would send spittle at everyone around me within a five to ten-foot radius; I had a rare skin disease that was so contagious I had to get cleared by three doctors and rechecked regularly to be sure it would not spread to the other kids in school—That one is the most inventive form of cooties I have ever heard—, I bit a former teacher for giving me a poor grade, and, last but not least, I had killed my own mama.

One through four I could laugh off. And her writing the phrase "Large Marge" on the back of my shirt, I could get past. Sara and her friends making rude coughing comments as I went by is... easy to ignore. Mr. Decker had to step in on a few occasions, when they actually vandalized my locker, and somehow my gym clothes ended up in the toilet. But number five on her list of nasty gossip, well that was a lie I could not let slide. So after a week of conniving whispers behind my back, she had been emboldened enough to say such a thing to my face. And that was when, in order to keep my cool, I recited the rhyme ending with "pants on fire" under my breath and ended up having today's chat with Mr. Decker.

Chapter Two

Grabbing the pass from Mr. Decker I head to lunch to meet up with Nat. She really seems to get me and is fast becoming my best friend. It doesn't hurt that she takes guff from not one soul in that school. People seem to actually respect her and try their best not to make her mad. Sadly, her cone of cool is not big enough to include me when she isn't around, so I have to fend for myself when not in her proximity. Since I'm late to lunch, I grab an apple and a soda and start toward Nat's table. On my way, the table full of letter jackets stuffed with big-necked boys all stop what they are doing; Hamilton starts to sniff the air as I approach. The rest of the pigskin-chasing mental giants all do the same thing. I assume this is Hamilton continuing to perpetuate that I smell bad. Looking away, I see Nat rising, ready to rescue me. Just before I make it past his table, Hamilton once again grabs my arm to stop me.

"Where's your lunch?" he asks, looking at my apple, soda, and then back to me.

"This *is* my lunch." I wiggle the items in my hands.

"You're a big girl. You need to eat more than that," this hateful boy says right to my face, in front of the whole cafeteria. I swear, when he talks, it is like he is related to E.F. Hutton. Everyone stops just to hear the next thing he says.

I just blink. This horrible person could *not* possibly have just said that to me. Before I can form a word, Nat gets to us.

"Truly, Hamilton, you are just plain dumb," Nat says, pulling my stunned form away.

The boys at his table all grunt in laughter, and it spreads like wildfire across the echoing room. After that wonderful experience adds to my meeting with Mr. Decker, this "big girl" did not even want to eat the apple.

Nat shakes her head. "You'll be hungry later if you don't eat something."

I open my soda and try to get liquid down; swallowing slowly to be sure the drink doesn't use my tonsils as a trampoline. I take a deep breath. "It is rare to come across a person who can be that rude on a regular basis."

"I've known Hamilton since we were little. He just doesn't understand how people will react when he says that wild stuff. Ignore him. That will be best for you both in the long run." She is watching me intensely as she asks, "So what happened with Decker?"

"Well, I guess I'll be working on either my public speaking or puking come Monday, 'cause I have to apologize to my other tormentor in front of the student body. Is that a thing here? Was there a typo on a brochure and instead of a 'mentoring program' they went with a 'tormenting program' for new students?"

Nat smiles, shaking her head. "Are you going to do it?"

"I have to. It was not so subtly indicated by our fearful leader that Miss Ackers' mama either gets what she wants or I lose out on the science competition I have not even completed my project for yet. After all the uproar in my life, I really need to start logging some serious kudos for brain function if I am going to be able to apply to the top schools. And no way would any of the really big academic houses even think about a scholarship for someone who has a suspension for 'Icy Hotting' someone's privates." I finish and take another sip of soda.

Nat's smile is brighter than the sun on July the fourth. "That was rock star. I don't care if or how you did it. That is a classic. That will be legend at Lakeside High for years to come. Generations will pay homage to the mind that spiked an Ackers' undies."

"That's just it, Nat. I don't know how it happened." I deny while mentally reviewing the nursery rhyme I had quoted.

Nat full out laughs and says with a snort, "Classic." Her laughter is musical, and she doubles over, wiping tears from her eyes when Drake sits down at our table. Nat reduces herself to a giggle and clears her vision by running her fingers over her eyes. When she sees Drake there, it is as if a switch flips and her humor gets shut off.

"Hello, G.J.," he says in greeting. "Natalia." He dips his head to Nat.

Nat just stares at him as if she wants to break his skull with her laser like glare.

"Hey there, Drake. I didn't know you were in this lunch," I say in my usual southern friendly manner.

"I just changed my schedule around, so I'll be in this lunch from now on." He shoots Nat a little grin at her growing expression of frustration.

"Oh well, you will have to join us for lunch." My southern hospitality takes the lead. "OW." Nat's foot shoots out and about cracks my tibia. "That is to say sometimes." Nat glares at me. "On a rare occasion?" My voice peters out. There is no graceful exit for the fourth most awkward moment of my day.

"Why I would love to join you gorgeous ladies for lunch… daily. I can't think of a better way to get to know more about each other." Drake smirks at Nat. "Can you?"

If Nat was trying for lasers before, her eyes turn to nukes now. My eyes are bouncing between my two meal companions, and I wonder what in the world I'm missing. Slamming her hands on the table Nat rises, which would be more impressive if she had farther to go to reach her full height. "I gotta go. G.J., I'll catch up with you later." She leaves me alone with Drake, and his eyes follow her while she exits. His intensity makes me feel like I'm watching *Animal Planet* and not an episode of *Too Cute*.

Focusing on Nat's still retreating back he asks, "So you like playing with fire?"

"Pardon?" I ask.

"I heard you set Sara's pants aflame today in PE." Finally, he turns his cool gaze to me.

"That's not exactly what happened." I really don't want to go over this again.

"What did happen exactly?" he asks.

"Well, I am not rightly sure. Sara said something awful about my mama, and I tried to brush it off. Next thing you know, my butt cheeks are getting personal with one of Mr. Decker's office chairs." That is about as Cliff's Notes as I can make it.

"Where did the fire come from?" Drake asks, his eyes squinting, like when you try to see something a little more clearly.

"There was no fire," I say, my gaze deciding to inspect the lunch table right now.

"So why is every piece of gossip relating burning to this story?"

"Go ask the gossips."

"I prefer to go to the source," he shoots back.

"There was no fire." I try to give the impression that we will just leave it at that, but for some reason I continue,

"There was Icy Hot."

It is now his turn to say, "Pardon?"

"Somehow, and I really don't know how, Sara's undies got swathed in Icy Hot," I mumble.

Drake laughs, a rich laugh that makes me smile, and burbles of laughter escape my attempts at suppression.

A low rumble sounds in the room. The vibration so fear-inducing I just know something awful is happening. I look at the ceiling to see if it is coming down on our heads. Drake glances over his shoulder. When I turn back to him and ask what on earth is happening, the noise stops. I still feel as though the world just changed, but I have no idea how. Every particle of air seems like it holds its own personal lightning bolts. Still upset I ask, "Was that an earthquake?"

Drake laughs again. "Nothing that dramatic."

"What was that then?" Fear still controls my voice. The charge in the air is very real.

"You'll get used to it. Trust me. Bell is about to ring. Let me walk you back to our lockers."

Drake takes my elbow as we head back to book up for our afternoon classes. When we're all set I say, "Thanks for lightening my mood. It's been a tough time. I'll see you around the old lockersted."

"I think we have science together now that my classes changed." He moves me off to my class.

I like to think of myself as a fairly independent person, but Drake just takes control. It is rather unnerving for someone whose will is as strong as mine is to just hand it over to someone else. Worse yet not to realize it's happening. It's almost like we're dancing, and he's taken the lead. He isn't bulldozing me. He's just making "being in charge" his job and not mine. He seats me next to him at a lab table without me even having to choose which way to walk around the table.

After the week of fabulous press I have been getting, the Sara minions and the people scared of Sara and her minions are all unwilling to be my lab partner. That leaves only a few of Hamilton's think tanks in their leather-armed warrior garb as my potential lab partners. And throughout "shiny happy fun week" as I was paired with one then another of them; they seemed to sit farther and farther away from me looking as though I would bite them if they responded to anything I said. But as easy as Drake assuming the unwanted roll of lab partner makes my life, I'll have to say I don't care for my Stepford moment.

My face must register my displeasure because Drake looks at me and asks, "Something wrong?"

Now how do you say to someone "I don't like how you very politely walked me to class"? Or ask them, "Do you practice some sort of mind control?" Or "Why would you want to be my lab partner?" So, I just shake my head, which for anyone who knows me better, would have been a tip off that the real answer is yes. Because one thing I use whenever possible are words. I change the subject by looking up at the board and flipping to the page for the experiment we're doing today.

Nobody looks cute in protective science goggles, so for Drake to watch my face and not our measurements and charts bugs me. He also chats and distracts me, which is annoying. A couple of times I have to pull on my power to adjust the pour I'm making or lower the flame on the Bunsen burner, so a reaction won't blow up the science lab as the topper to my delightful day. I never see him do it, but I swear he is turning up the flame. The fourth time it happens, I reduce the heat with a little tweak of my abilities. Drake smiles and says, "Huh."

I sharply whip my eyes to his through the scratched lenses keeping them safe.

"You, my dear Miss Gardener, are something new entirely. I am going to have a blast working with you." And the flames again leap up from our burner on their own accord before going back down.

I take my attention from the lowered flame and focus on Drake. "You too, huh?" I ask.

"No, I think you are one of a kind," he says in his cryptic way that makes me want to get it, but I know he's holding some of the pieces back, so he can have more fun watching me puzzle it out.

"This is not a sharing topic," I warn him, "although, should you choose to, people would just think you were a nutball. People believe what is easy. So unless you want to be put on a prescription for instability, don't blabber."

"Would not dream of it." He lowers his voice and continues, "But I do think young Miss Ackers should kiss your feet that her pants did not actually go up in flames."

I dart a look around the room to make sure no one is listening. "I don't do things like that. My mama raised me right." My whisper fills with intensity. "Never in my life has my ability just whipped out like that."

"I have news. It happened." His cool retort deflates me like an ice pick to a balloon.

"I know, all right. I know it did. Happy?" My misery fills up my words.

"G.J.," his hand finds my shoulder, "don't get caught up in the guilt of having done it. What's done is done. Could you do it again?"

"Of course I can, if I try. The problem is I wasn't trying. Not consciously anyhow, but stars above help us all if my subconscious can now make things happen. All I'll need is one late night run through a Taco Bell, and my dreams will have dragons wearing hot pink bikinis chasing unicorns to the mall, so they can play in the World Series of Poker." My nervous yammering is on the loose again.

For once Drake appears decidedly uncomfortable. "Don't even say such a thing." He adjusts himself in his seat, trying to resettle into his calm persona. "How hard is it for you to do what you can do?"

"Not hard at all. I usually just... do it. I mean, I have to think about it, but all I have to do is add my will behind the thought and..." I stop talking.

Drake narrows his eyes at me. "Nothing else? No ritual or rites? You just make it happen?"

"What? No, I am not some kook who has to gather bat brains and eye of newt. Who does that really?" I waive my hand and dismiss his statement as sheer poppycock.

Again Drake laughs. "Life is going to get interesting with you in town, G.J. I can't wait."

Science ends and we part ways. I don't catch up with Nat until I wade through the throng trying to find their buses. Somewhere in the hustle bustle I'm stabbed with a pencil tip, and I guess my hair gets caught in a binder because it rips out of my head like someone from the "Bad Girls Club" is snatching a weave. *Seriously, people, we all have places to go. Let's do try and get there without sending someone to the emergency room, for heaven's sake.*

Nat lives in the neighborhood after mine on our bus route, so she's on the bus when I get on in the morning but gets off after me on the way home. Even though she seemed mad at lunch, she apparently has gotten over it because she's saved me a seat.

"What happened to you?" she asks, observing me rubbing my wounds.

"Apparently, I need to brush up on my WWE in order to make it through the halls at the end of the day," I grumble.

"What did you and the infamous Mr. Aldrich have to chat about after I left?"

"What else does anyone have to talk about today?" I roll my eyes, still dismal about what's to come on Monday.

"Did you tell him?" She looks horrified.

"Tell him what?" I ask, thinking about the not-for-public-consumption things Drake now knows about me.

"Wait a minute? Do you trust him to know things you won't even tell me?" Her eyes grow round, and her lip gets that little sneer showing either hurt or disgust.

"Of course not. Look, I've been a very private person most of my life. I haven't had a ton of friends, and opening up is hard for me. Drake seems to know about what I'm going through." I'm trying to figure out what I can say on the bus that will make Nat understand Drake only guessed I could make things happen with my mind.

"Okay, that's fair. I guess now is not the time to let spill all your secrets, but would you be willing for me to know?" she questions me with force in her tone.

I think about her question and realize Nat has my back, but if she knows what I can do, will she trust me? So out of my mouth comes the answer I hope will put her at ease. "I do trust you, Nat."

She connects her gaze with mine. "You can tell me anything. I am better than a diary. And I trust you, too."

"Thanks, Nat. That means more to me than you could possibly know." I really like having Nat as a friend.

She asks me what I am up to tonight. Rain fell steadily over the last week, and the temperature has warmed up a bit, so the snow is virtually gone for the moment. "I have stuff I need to work on, but I'm going to take a walk in the woods. I used to do that every day back home. I would spend hours wandering in the woods around my house. I wouldn't come home until

the evening chorus of frogs and night bugs were singing their
farewell song and sent me in to read or watch some old TV show
Mama loved when she was younger. Mama shared all of her
interests with me, which is why some folks say I'm an old soul.
Mama loved to work in the garden and raised me to. Her love
of all things green was where she got my name. Glory Juniper,
I think it is a bit much, so I just go by G.J..”

"I think that's a good choice."

“Thank you. There was not one day I can remember where
we were not at least two knuckles deep in the soil. There is
a picture Aunt Celia took of Mama and me making mud
pies. We're laughing and covered head-to-toe in dirt. That
is one of my most cherished possessions.

"Aunt Celia, that's my family I came here to live with.
She doesn't grow much. I know this area is different, but
every one of her indoor plants is polyester. I have not spent
more than twelve hours before without touching mud. It's
strange, I know, but I miss it."

Nat smiles as if she is enjoying my ramble. "No stranger than
anybody else in this town. Do yourself a favor—take water, a snack,
pepper spray, and your cell phone. And call me when you get home."

"Why? Are you worried I'm going to get lost? Honey, you
don't have half the trees in this area I used to have back home."
I'm confident in my communing-with-Mother-Nature abilities.

"Have fun, Jane. Let me know if you find Tarzan out
there," she quips as we come up to my stop.

"Don't worry; you'll know if anyone teaches me the call of the
wild," I shoot back and wink at her as I ease past yet another giant-
shouldered boy in a letter jacket in order to make it off the bus.

****

I write Aunt Celia a note and grab the supplies I have of
what Nat listed—everything but the pepper spray. I start

my adventure up the hill that is my new backyard. The climb is steep and the air seems thinner, but I find a good rhythm and keep moving up the sparsely-wooded rocky terrain. Everything is different here. The texture of the dirt is foreign, and the air is cold, but the fact that I'm in the woods with the smell of pine filling my lungs makes me not care that my fingertips are icy. I explore for about an hour when I come up on a clearing. In the middle of it is a circle that has to be twenty-five feet across. It looks as though all the vegetation in the middle has died out. Puzzled, I walk around the area; something makes me not want to cross it.

Like walking up to an empty house where your friends once lived. You know life should be there, and you want it to be again, but for some reason the house doesn't have new occupants. I squat, inspect the ground where the circumference meets the outside space, and see a clear scorching of the earth. I glance up. I've seen one too many movies along the lines of *Fire in the Sky* and *Close Encounters of the Third Kind,* to not have the heebee geebees. This place is giving me the strongest feeling that someone else has their eyes on me. Peering around, I stand up and back away from the edge of the circle. Now I swear I'm not trying to end up on one of those Sy-Fy shows about the unknown—although I would not mind having a chat with Josh Gates. I do love a good give-and-take conversation, and he can banter with the best of them. I do think, however, he uses *Destination Truth* as his way to pick up chicks. This circle does make my brain have a mini flash of chitchat with the Sy-Fy host.

I walk around, taking shot after shot with my cell phone. When I hear a noise behind me, I scream like the girl I am and run. Forget wilderness 101, running makes you prey; I don't care. Something is just not right about the place, and the adrenaline in my body goes right for flight, like fight is not even on the menu.

I calm myself down to an intermittent squeal from full-out bloody murder noises and slow down to catch my breath. What in the world just happened? What was it that made me freak out so badly back there? I don't get scared in the woods. Well, I didn't until now. The breaths my lungs are insisting on make me sound like the little engine that could. With little energy left, I'm not sure what to do as the next twig snaps near where I am standing. This time I have to find the source. Searching, I find a matching pair of those golden eyes that have stayed with me from that time when I was eight. This wolf is bigger; if you were playing Super Mario this wolf would definitely have the given name of Super as opposed to the just plain Mario version. He looks at me, and I stare straight back at him. I knew if I tried to run, I would be a perfect lunch for him and his friends. So, I do what I do best. I talk to him.

"Hey there now, puppy. How are you, good boy?" There is no denying this was a male wolf.

The animal lowers his head as if annoyed with something I'm saying.

Mulling over any possible 'faux paus' in my first attempt, I adjust. "Hey there now, big wolfie. Gooooood wolf. Nice wolf." I hold my hand out in a sign of peace. Yes, I'm making peace with a huge wild animal. I start rethinking the snack Nat told me to pack. Does this king of all he surveys want my Kashi bar? Maybe it would distract this fella long enough for me to make it home. Do wolves like "seven whole grains out on a mission"?

The gigantic ball of fur decides to take several steps toward me. Air whooshes in my lungs, and I am sure my irises are showing all white around the edges. He lowers his body and scooches forward. The big animal shows submission as he makes his way toward me. I'm not sure how much to trust what I've learned from my Saturday mornings with Jeff Corwin, but I decide to go with it. I sink to my knees and invite this wild beast to come closer.

The wolf stops and looks at me, tilting his head as if to say, "Hey, lady, are you nuts? You do know I'm a wolf, right?"

It's nice to know we both think my brain has just gotten two free tickets to Aruba and took flight. I sit still, holding the animal's gaze as it moves even closer, its head slightly jerking as it sniffs again and again. When the wet rough tip of his nose finally makes contact with my outstretched hand, it's like an electric charge jumps up my arm. The huffing noise the animal makes grows louder, and his muzzle starts to get more and more invasive. He circles me, sniffing my hair, the strands tangling with his fur. I bring my shoulders up to protect my neck. He explores up and down my back and torso, breathing every part of me in. He shoves up the back of my jacket with his nose. When his cold nostrils touch skin, I yelp and start laughing. He jumps back skittishly.

Giggling I say, "Sorry, but that tickles. I have always been ticklish. Mama said 'Tickle me Elmo' had nothing on me. We would have tickle fights all the time growing up. She always won 'cause I would be laughing too hard to tickle her back." My chest tightens, and I take a deep breath to ease the pain. I rub my heart and look up through the trees. "God, Mama, I miss you so much. I don't know how to get through this without you." Tears fall from my eyes. The adrenaline of the past twenty minutes robs me of the brave front I have put up and leaves me exposed. Somehow, I don't care what the wolf does. I just need to release the pressure of my grief. What starts as quiet tears moves on to full-out racking sobs. The wolf whines. Men, no matter the species, apparently can't stand when a woman cries.

This total meltdown goes on for… I'm not sure how long, and the canine tentatively comes back and just sits next to me. Running out of steam, I raise my face and meet the wolf's golden eyes. "I don't normally break down. I guess I don't make the best first impression, huh, big guy? It's been a tough few months. I had a bad time at my old school, and my mama was killed, so I had to move here." I unload on the poor animal. "I was raised in rural Louisiana, and while there were plenty of places to go see around where I lived, we didn't. Mama and I kept to ourselves, with the exception of visiting with the people around us. Our small house was set in a clearing in the Dean Lee State Forest. One thing about that area is any way you turn, there is a cemetery the direction you are headed. The towering trees around our little cleared patch of earth walled my childhood in and kept the world from seeing the strange things I can do.

"I honestly can't speak to who my father is. Whoever or wherever he is, he has had nothing to do with Mama or me. Mama made sure I didn't miss him much. She raised me not to speak poorly of people I didn't know, and since I don't know him… I have nothing to say. Raising anyone by yourself is hard, but raising me has extra challenges poor Mama wasn't sure how to handle. I was very lucky I had her for the time I did. From what Aunt Celia says, Mama almost didn't make it through carrying me. She was actually in a coma when she gave birth. The doctors said I was a miracle. While no one can say what was wrong with her, Mama's body was on its last leg by the time I popped into the world. Ms. Clem, our nearest neighbor, dropped by for a visit and found Mama on the floor. Ms. Clem called the ambulance, and then Aunt Celia came and took care of me until Mama recovered. She just dropped everything in her life and came to stay with us. Aunt Celia is like that. But once I was born, Mama started to recover.

"I feel guilty that somehow I overburdened her small body. Mama was five feet two inches tall and had the tiny frame that makes those Lilly Pulitzer patterns actually look cute on it."

The wolf tilts his head as if he has no idea what I'm talking about. I can tell because I get the same look from time to time from people.

"I was about the healthiest baby you could find. At ten pounds thirteen ounces and twenty-four inches long at the time of my birth, I was literally 10.297 percent of her normal one hundred and five pound body weight. Not counting all those extra things a woman has to carry when they are pregnant. I was also 38.7 percent of her height." I eye the wolf as if to see if he likes facts as much as I do.

Panting is the only reply he gives.

"Aunt Celia said the nurses had not seen a baby my size come out of a woman that small in they didn't know how long. Once Mama was up and around, Aunt Celia headed back to her then nomadic life but came to visit pretty often in her travels. She floated in and out as I grew up and was always great fun to be around."

The wolf lies down as if he can sense this is going to take a while.

"That was just the start of the trouble I gave Mama. I know it sounds strange, but I can do things sometimes that people shouldn't be able to do. Being in such a remote place, I played in the woods a good bit by myself. It was probably for the best. I have always been unusually good with animals, too. So this is not as strange as you might think." I gently put my hand in the hair around the wolf's ears, his head pushes back into my hand demanding the pressure he likes.

"If I wanted something, somehow I got it. I don't mean if I wished for a pony, one would show up at my door. Although that did happen once when I was five, but I'm not sure if that was me or Mr. Lafontaine's bad fence from down the road. If I wanted a ball or a toy, it would roll to me. You might think that is just a coincidence, but building blocks don't normally roll.

"As I grew up, while teaching me all of the normal stuff you would a child, Mama had to learn how to teach me to adjust to things she herself had no knowledge of how to control. While some kids had to learn proper table etiquette, I had to learn not to float the second helping to my plate, but ask to be served; or to actually go to the door to open it, instead of swinging it wide from the other room. Mama took on the challenges we faced by being strict on manners. Courtesy was the best approach to tamping down my odd abilities. As I got older, it became easier to take the sense of decorum Mama has raised me with and apply it to control the 'over reach of my will,' which was how she like to put the way I can make things happen with a thought."

At this, the wolf raises his head and tilts it at me in what I assume is an "are you crazy?" expression.

"This is not to say Mama was strict or to imply that I did not have fun growing up. That is simply not the case." I look at my companion and continue, "I love school. Learning everything someone is willing to teach me. I would come home and play the "did you know" game with Mama until she said her brain was getting too full. Then I ended up in high school. Don't get me wrong. I still love all facts and high school is full of them. But what also comes with all that lovely knowledge is the ticking time bomb of hundreds of kids, whose hormones are raging, swinging their moods from one extreme to another. This terrifying cocktail of angst confines itself in one building from seven forty-eight am until three twenty PM with no relief for five days a week.

Girls bodies are doing the craziest things, and boys want to explore as many of those things as they can." I peer at the wolf rolling his eyes to meet mine. "The boys are figuring out where they are going to end up in the hierarchy that is male dominance. You probably understand that better than most, huh, big guy?" My scratching behind his ears intensifies. He makes this half-yawn, half-squeal of delight and shivers from his head down to his toes.

"Human boys beef up or not as the case may be. They lift weights; get in fights, play sports to expel some of those crazy hormones, and to prove to themselves, their friends, or their daddies that they will make a mark on this world. Girls, on the other hand, are using their God-given abilities to sway or manipulate anyway they can. In sorting out how to do this, they do find some vicious ways of dealing with each other.

"Boys are playing football, whereas girls are playing chess. By this I mean, boys have a playbook and set rules in order to get to a physical goal. They take each down as its own moment in time, and depending on what happens in that down, they make decisions as to how to accomplish their ultimate prize. They will knock you down, throw you, outrun you, or outsmart you, but they usually cannot make a decision about the next move till they know how the last play ends."

The wolf sits up and licks my hand, almost like he's excited by something I said.

I go on. "Girls are usually thinking at least four moves ahead if not twelve. In their minds, the 'if-then' scenarios play out ahead of time, so far in advance, it's mind-boggling. From the start of their day, it begins: 'If I wear this, so and so will react this way and that will cause...' And so forth. This does not even take into account their long-term machinations. They do this thing they learned growing up. We used to call it 'visiting' but round here, they call it gossip. Some girls use that skill along with a vivid imagination to turn the herd faster than a pack of wolves. Pardon the expression, but I thought that was a reference you could relate to."

I think the wolf just rolled his eyes, which makes me smile a little.

"Okay, okay. I will skip the wolfie references from here on out. Not all girls are like that, by the way, but the ones who would be queen sure are. I happen to be of the opinion that I am just fine somewhere in the middle. I have no need to be royalty, but I am not interested in ending up someone's pawn either."

The wolf makes a weird chuffing noise.

After making sure that isn't an "I'm hungry enough to eat you now" gesture, I keep pouring out my life story to this animal. "When in the lower grades this was not a big issue because everyone knew who you were and where you stood. But high school changes that by bringing several established hierarchies together. These kids have already found their places in adolescent society and now are squished into so many square feet with the same level members from other environments or schools. I was the tall girl, a peripheral person at my lower school. I was the kid from a respected single mother, which was hard for Mama to have been in the rural south, but she managed it with generosity, manners, and kindness. I was the go-to kid for most facts, like a walking encyclopedia. I preferred to be alone, and the people who knew me were fine with that.

"High school has changed the description of me. I became the geeky, giant bastard. Not much I can do about being five feet eleven inches in the ninth grade. To be a girl reaching those heights when most of the men in my parish would not hit the six-foot mark in their lifetimes made me a bit of a target. High school has taught me not to correct the people around me and never to raise my hand. If I have an answer, I keep it to myself. If anyone draws attention in anything but the established protocols for becoming popular, they'll find themselves in the crosshairs of every social-climbing callous youth that wants to catapult themselves to new heights by stepping on my broken soul."

The wolf lays his head on my leg and nuzzles me. I take it as support.

"I am telling you it took me pointing out, in a class, to one girl in the homecoming court that Peru was in South America and not near Iraq to have the social harpies swarm me like a battalion of flying monkeys. I find it somewhat ironic that the school mascot at this local 'pleasure dome' is, and I am not kidding you here, a demon."

The wolf puts his paw over his eyes.

"That one act secured me as a pariah, which was why when basketball season started and the forward on our team asked to be my study partner, I was surprised."

The wolf moves his paw and lets out a soft growl.

Deciding to ignore him, I keep rolling. "Even more stunning was we had a lot in common and enjoyed the outdoors. I would help him out in math and social studies by quizzing him while we went fishing or took a hike in the park around my house. We had fun and I considered him a good friend. When he asked me to the winter school dance…"

The wolf sits up and barks.

For some strange reason I feel the need to clarify, so I quickly add, "As a friend, because he did not want to get stuck asking the previously mentioned HC princess."

Oddly, this settles the big guy down, and he lies down, resting his head on my leg again.

I stare at the wolf, not sure what that was all about. "Well," I continue when my thoughts come back to me, "that was more than the popular crew could allow. So, someone had the bright idea to get a beehive and put it in our car. I'm not sure how they did this, but somehow they were able to get a hold of the accidental creation of biologist William Kerr. If you aren't sure who he was, look him up."

The wolf rolls his eyes back again as if to say I am nuts.

"Okay, you can't, so I'll tell you. In 1957, he was trying to create a heartier bee in order to have them produce more honey. Sadly, when a substitute beekeeper let loose the wrong bees, they crossbred and let loose on Sao Paolo, Brazil. The little buggers that became, what we know as Africanized honeybees, aka Killer Bees. These unfriendly creatures have migrated north to the southern parts of the United States.

"The little prank did not work the way they intended. See, the bees stayed hidden in the back of the car until Mama got in and slammed the door. Then they swarmed her. She tried to get away, but they just kept after her. And, in her attempt to escape, she left the car door open. There were so many things that could have saved her life. So many 'if onlys' that could have made a difference. But the fact was none of those other scenarios had happened." I start to cry again.

My wolf whines and wraps his paws around my neck from a begging position. He gently licks my face until the tears stop falling. Pushing his nose under my chin so I will meet his eyes, he takes his paws down and nods as if telling me to continue.

"Aunt Celia came down, and we laid Mama to rest. I can't quite get my head around the fact that she's gone. Sometimes the grief is so overwhelming that I can't seem to put my thoughts in a functioning order. Now I know I said I have special abilities, but I swear I had nothing to do with the series of tornados that touched down near Franklinton. The total devastation of the homes of those kids, who were suspected but never charged, happened of its own accord. I truly do not know how those twisters only hit their houses. In order to get me away from everything, Aunt Celia packed me up and moved me here."

The wolf licks my hand resting in my lap near his head, as if giving some kind of approval.

"Please don't take offense, but I hate it here."

The animal makes a chuffing noise as if he's indignant.

Now I know I seem ready for the loony bin, but I go on anyway. "My Aunt Celia is great, but her life doesn't match up with anything I am used to. School is the kind of awful and that makes some people turn into a hermit or get one of those bunkers like on *Doomsday Preppers*. I accidentally wacked this girl in the face, and she put a social hit out on me. I swear if Mr. Coppola is interested in any tips—should he make another *Godfather* film—he should look her up. There is the rudest boy in the world there, too. I have no idea what makes someone as sadistic as he is. And something wonky is happening with my abilities." The wolf gives one of his now familiar head tilts, but I keep going. "Nat is about the only good thing. She is the first friend who really seems to get me." I expel a deep lungful of air and look down at my companion.

The wolf stares back as if asking if I am done.

"I have, at fifteen, now had my very first mental breakdown. What wonders await me in my future? Here I am on the frozen ground, in the woods, telling my woes to a strange dog."

The animal growls again.

"Pardon me, wolf."

The wolf sits up, turns its nose to mine, and licks the rest of the tear streaks from my face. He moves closer and closer, pushing his body into my space. Losing my balance,

I fall over. He continues slurping at my face and nuzzling my neck. "Hey, cut it out. I'm not that kind of girl." I squeal and laugh as he continues his barrage of spit bathing me. Having enough, I pull on my will and push the beast back, so I can catch my breath.

The wolf lets out a whiny squeal I would normally attribute to a little girl having her lollipop stolen. He takes a wary ready stance, unsure of what just happened. He seems terrified.

"I'm sorry. I just needed some space. That is the kind of thing I was telling you I can do. Oh for heaven's sake, you don't know what I'm saying."

He lowers his head and watches me warily. I've ruined the moment, and the animal cannot trust me. "I'm sorry. I'll just go." Picking myself up and dusting off, I walk away. The animal barks, and I glance back at him. He stands still for a moment and wags his tail. I smile back before making my way home.

Chapter Three

I call Nat and tell her I'm alive. To avoid hearing a lecture about the wolf, I edit the encounter. When Aunt Celia makes her appearance for a quick change into eveningwear, she is a woman on a mission. She gave up on marriage about two husbands ago, and now I'm guessing she is doing her best to date every single man in the greater Spokane area. She goes out almost every night, although she never says with whom, which I think is a security issue we will have to address some time soon. When she is in, she must spend her time on the various singles sites, if the number of mailers we receive about finding love is any indication. While she is primping this time, I ask if I can set up some planters this upcoming weekend. "I really need to grow things," I explain. Getting her consent, I make a list of what I want to grow. "I thought an herb garden and a couple easy plants to start off with."

"Sounds good kiddo. Whatever helps you settle in." She smiles and kisses my cheek as she heads out the door.

Homework takes about three hours, and I spend another hour researching on the web for my science project. Do you ever think about how older people used to have to find information? I do. I can't imagine knowing all the things I do if I had to rely on encyclopedias, microfiche, the Dewey decimal system, and the local library's hours of operation. Half of my homework is done after nine at night. I'm impressed when older folks know stuff without knowing how to use a computer. It's as if they earned it the hard way. I fear knowledge is going to become disposable somehow. Like people will not actually remember anything because they will have their smart phones and not need to take up the space in their own heads. Kind of like never knowing someone's phone number anymore because it is in your cell. What else is going to make those brain cells useful?

****

I trudge back to the place I am forced to go by state law. It's Friday. Nat and I run over a few sonnets on the bus to prepare for our quiz first period. As I get to my locker, one of the letter jacket gang is leaning on it, chatting with a girl from my Spanish class. It takes several attempts to interrupt his pathetic attempts to woo the fair maiden. Listening in, I can't believe the hokey lines work. But sure enough the chick agrees to see him after the basketball game. I truly feel that this is why the gene pool is suffering.

Finally getting to class, I sit down just as Ms. Stontz is passing out the quiz. She gives me one of those teacher looks that says, "Don't be late again." I nod. This day seems to be par for the course. I have no trouble with the quiz and finish it zippy quick. Nat turns her head and glares at me, seemingly surprised and a bit upset. She peers around the room for a minute and goes back to her quiz. Ms. Stontz has a smile on her face as I hand in my paper. I get the strangest feeling, as if she thinks I've just thwarted a criminal mastermind.

We split up after English, and I don't see Nat again until lunch, as usual. P.E. proves to be as fun as always. Hamilton enjoys spiking the volleyball at me, and somehow I manage to bump it back. I swear that boy just likes to cause me pain. Sara spends the time oohing and ahhing at Hamilton's ability to slam the ball down, slamming it so hard that I think my arms will break when I send the ball back. She also touches Mean Muscle Boy so much I would swear she is his personal masseuse. I bet half the kids take showers after this class to get the ick of that flirting off them.

****

Selecting the lesser of all evils as far as meal options go from the ladies with the fabulous hair nets, I walk up to Nat's table at lunch. About halfway there I freeze. Sitting with Nat are three boys. One of which is Hamilton Calhoun. What *ever lovin'* reason does this boy have to ruin every moment of my life he is capable of getting his giant hands on? Looking around, I desperately search for another seating option. After Sara's full-on war of lies, there are no other tables available for me to sit at. It is almost like the kids at each table put up a shunning wall as I glance from one empty chair to another. Oh so very reluctantly, I move in Nat's direction. Maybe Mr. Calhoun is only stopping to chat with her. As I walk up, I catch the tail end of something Hamilton is saying, "…fine."

Nat glares him a warning and says, "Bad idea."

I stop next to Nat and bravely chime in, "Hey there, Nat. Mind if I sit?'

"No, of course not," she replies and turns to give Hamilton a dirty look.

"You sure there is enough room over there for you?" Hamilton asks.

I take in the side of the table, which is empty with the exception of Nat's petite frame. Then I fix my eyes on the complete jackass that has just thrown me one of those insults

I have grown to hate him for. "Hamilton, you are a true idiot," Nat says in a tired voice.

I am about to sit down when a hand takes my elbow and steers me slightly farther away from Nat. I find Drake easing between Nat and me, intending to sit down. Over his shoulder, the expression Nat gives me makes it clear she really does *not* want Drake anywhere near her but, in particular, doesn't want him close enough to bump elbows. "Hey there, Drake. I was just about to sit down. Are you joining us today?" I ask while pleasantly trying to get back next to Nat.

Sliding between us Drake says, "Of course. This is *our* table, isn't it?"

I maneuver back between Nat and Drake . "What a nice way to put it."

Drake does a little step and moves toward Nat again. Someone should put on some two-step music for all the dancing we're doing. Hamilton and his two cohorts stand up and move.

Relieved that they are leaving, I indicate he take Hamilton's spot. "The boys over there made room for ya. Now let's all enjoy lunch."

Persistent as he is, Drake pulls his foot up in order to take the seat next to Nat instead of the now vacant spot across the table. So, I use my will to scooch him down so I can slide in next to her. Only my scooch sends him flying down the table, knocking over the three boys rounding the end of the table and are heading right for us. They all go tumbling down. I'm sure you are going to think it's inappropriate, but the very first thought that crosses my brain is a little cheer at my perfect strike. Those boys go down like bowling pins. My next thought is "uh-oh." The whole room is staring at the young men tangled on the ground. Now the rest of the letter jacket clad young men head for the ones on the ground with Drake. An ear-splitting squawk sounds from the intercom system, and everyone's hands shoot to their ears. Nat grabs my arm and jerks me into my seat. When the noise stops, Mr. Decker's voice comes on the line and directs Hamilton, Drake, and the other two boys, who are apparently named Adam Wyfle and Chris Sanders, to come to the office.

They make it to their feet and head toward the front office. I stare down at the fenced-off food on my tray. When Nat finally speaks, she whispers, "What just happened?"

Dumbly I say, "I don't know."

"G.J., what was that?" she asks again.

"I don't know. I don't know." Panic is starting to make me tremble.

"G.J., did you—?"

"I have to go." I stand up so fast my knees knock the table, making a banging noise that calls attention to us again.

"Wait," Nat appeals, but I keep walking, dumping my tray, and stacking it as I leave the cafeteria.

I spend the balance of my lunch period trying to calm down in the girl's bathroom near my science class. What should have been a little push to slide Drake down just picked up a six-foot two inch, fairly muscled young man and slammed him so hard into three huge boys that they all hit the ground. Why in the name of all that is holy is this happening to me? I know how much power I have. It's almost like, if I thought a plastic cup were made of glass and I was lifting it with the amount of inertia it would take to raise the glass. That happened one time, when Mama and I went to a pizza place out by our house after Church. The joint had birch beer, which I just love. The waiter brought it to me in one of those mugs that look like the beer mugs adults use. The kind with the handles that have the little thumb rests on the top to help balance the weight. Like the big girl I wanted to be, I lifted that mug, so caught up in the idea of acting like I was drinking an adult drink. Only it wasn't a glass mug at all, and I sent that birch beer all over my Sunday dress and dripping off my nose. Mama laughed, but she never could get the stains out of the lace on that dress.

Mentally rallying, I head to science, bursting with apologies for Drake. I'm sure he must know I'm responsible for tossing him like a hot potato after our little chat yesterday. When I walk in, Drake isn't there yet, so I sit at the lab station we shared the class before. The boy who proves to be Adam is back from Mr. Decker's office but not Drake, and I wonder why. Adam gets up from where he's sitting and, without saying a word, sits in the seat I wanted Drake to take. I am just ready to tell him the seat is saved when the bell rings, and Mr. Alberts starts class. Again, like all the boys who wear the letter jackets, Adam tries to sit as far from me as the lab station will allow. Now, I don't know about you, but it is hard to do an experiment without any physical contact between you and your lab partner. Inevitably, you will need to pass something, hold a solution, peer closely at some reaction together, or at the very least say something. For me, the latter is more likely to happen than the rest. We're at least five minutes in before I break the silence, and I think that may be a personal record.

"Hey, Adam, if you would be more comfortable working with someone else, I don't mind if you switch," I say, trying to give this uncomfortable boy an out.

Startled he looks at me. This might be the first time he's stared me right in the eye. Almost as quickly as it happens, he glances away. "I'm good."

Now I'm a bit taken aback. His eyes are so light brown they appear to be gold. He is built very similar to Hamilton, only not quite as big. Adam is none too shabby in the looks department. He is fairer than Hamilton. Silence reins for a few awkward moments; then the mouth from the south springs wide again. "If you're good, would you please stop acting like I smell like something you found on the bottom of your shoe after walking through a dog park?"

"What?" he asks, pulling his head back like I'm a venomous snake about to strike.

"You and all your buddies act as though I reek like the perfume department at the mall. Just stop. You are the one who moved to this table, and you are the one choosing to stay here. So be my partner or scoot," I say, flipping my hands in a shooing motion.

"I don't think you smell bad. What is it you want me to stop doing?" he asks with a serious expression on his face, but from where he's sitting, he's practically the full table length away from me.

"Adam, take a look around. Do you notice anything different about your body posture and the rest of the partners in the room?"

He glances around and shrugs.

I am so annoyed with this boy I think I'm going to smack him. Sometimes, but not often, I let my face say what my mouth is too polite to mention.

Turning his head to take in our surroundings, Adam then looks at our seating arrangement. Then he does the strangest thing. He pulls his chair around and sits right next to me. That isn't the strange part. The strange part is when he leans over and inhales like I'm a batch of cookies right out of the oven.

I turn my face toward his and am nose-to-nose with him. He has this happy smile curving his lips. Like one whiff of me is his moment of Zen. I blush and can't help smiling back, and a giggle burbles up.

"What in the world?" I ask.

"I definitely don't think you smell bad," he says with that goofy smile.

"Point taken." I desperately need the topic to go back to science. "How about you prove that you can be a good lab partner now?" I face the experiment and start working, straining my eyes sideways to look at him from time to time without having to fully face him again.

We work together fairly well. I have to explain some of the reasons why we're doing things, but I do know more than the average ninth grader about science experiments. Adam acts like nothing is wrong, actually leans in to peer through the microscope, and touches me several times. It is such a turnaround I'm not sure what to make of it. About thirty minutes into class, Drake appears. Mr. Alberts tells him to join a group, and Drake pulls a stool over on the other side of me. While he is still moving his seat, Adam stands up and grabs the back of my chair, with me on it. Did I mention I am not a tiny person? He picks me up, stool and all, and moves me to the other side of his seat. Adam scoots over, centering himself, and sits back down.

I decide right then and there that I am not the only person in Nine Mile Lake that has gone round the bend. Drake looks just as gob smacked as I am at the adjusted seating arrangement. He is too polite to say anything, but I feel no such compunction. "Adam, honey, what in the ever loving hell are you doing?"

He pats my knee. "It's all right. I got this."

Completely at a loss, I flip my gaze from Adam to Drake and back to Adam. Adam winks at me. I almost start to check the labels of what we are working with to see if there is a hallucinogen or some other narcotic releasing into the air. There is no way to apologize to Drake in front of Adam. Nobody else knows I threw Drake in the cafeteria. It all happened so fast it looked like Drake just slammed into them. I try to relate my apology with my eyes, but Drake shakes his head. It's unclear if he is not accepting my silent apology or if he is saying not now. When the bell signals the end of the period, Adam walks me out of class, putting himself between Drake and me until I've gotten to my next class; Drake heads to his. Adam says, "all right, you should be cool now." He leans down, sniffs me again, and runs off to make it to his next class before the bell.

I spend the whole rest of the school day trying to figure out what Adam's bizarre behavior means. Why has he gone from completely standoffish to over protective lunk in a matter of a few minutes? On my way to the bus, I am so caught up in my thoughts that I don't notice Sara until she's right in front of me. The bruising around her eyes is beginning to yellow a bit on the outside, giving her the odd look of a possessed raccoon. She still manages a pretty good snooty. "I hear you owe me an apology."

"So I have been told," I reply with boredom in my tone.

"Well?" she prompts. "Go on."

"You want me to apologize now? Does this mean I won't have to do it on Monday at a public flogging?" I answer.

"Oh no, you will absolutely pay for what you did in front of the whole school." Her evil little smirk makes me feel like there is going to be more than a forced apology happening on Monday.

Now see, I don't do well with threats. It might be that I have yet to really connect with my inner coward, but every time someone wants me to run and hide, it just makes me want to disappoint them. "Sara, darlin' you're only going to get me to do this once, so I'm saving what I am going to say till Monday."

"You are going to regret ever coming to this school," she says in the most cliché of all "you'll rue the day" voices I have heard since the last Lifetime movie I watched.

I just walk past her. What do you say to someone who wants to be your arch nemesis? It's like she has the second verse of *Say, Say O' Playmate* as her theme song. For those of you who don't know the words, they start off, "Say, say o' enemy, come out and fight with me…" Out of nowhere, Adam is right next to me.

"Sorry it took me a while to find you. What is your last class?" he asks as if I had plans to see him.

"What?" I ask, not done with running through all the "could of/ should of" things that I might have verbally slung at Sara in my head.

"Your last class? Doesn't matter. I should have waited at your locker. That would probably be best anyhow."

I stop and squint at him. "Why would you wait at my locker?"

"To walk you to your bus," he answers as if it were plain as day why he would be doing that.

"Adam, honey…"

"Please don't call me honey. You are going to get me mauled." His head pops up, peering around. "Oh, man." His voice sounds defeated like I've just ruined everything.

"Hey, Adam. You two seem awfully… cozy." Hamilton's voice is low and menacing behind me.

When I turn to face Hamilton, he's giving Adam such a look of disgust you would have thought we were dining on three-day-old road kill. Adam tries to defend himself. "I… I was just walking her to her bus."

"How 'sweet' of you. Does that make you her 'honey'?" Hamilton says "honey" like it's is the most foul and corrosive word in the English language.

"Listen to me, Hamilton Calhoun. You leave Adam alone. He has no control over my choice of words. I am from the south. 'Honey' is just part of our vernacular. So is 'sugar,' 'darlin',' 'sweetheart', and many other random terms of endearment that mean absolutely nothing but slide out 'cause that is how we are raised. If you knew anything about me at all you would know that—"

"Know you?" Hamilton's voice rises. "I know more than you think about you." His breathing is heavy, and he's crowding my space. His eyes are lit up, and my mind spins with how aggressive his stance is as he leans over me.

"You don't know me in the least." I shoot up right in his face. He isn't the only one who has some hostility to unleash on the world. My eyes narrow, and my jaw sets. "What could you possibly know?"

"I know what killed your mother." His face is just over mine as he stares down.

Somewhere in the crowd I hear, "See, she *did* kill her mom."

Those six words hit a mark that even the most advanced weapons systems could not have located. My mouth opens and all the air that has been heaving in floods achingly out of my lungs. The breeze it causes moves the hair around his face. It must distract him from his blinding hate because he eyes my mouth—I guess to find the source. The verbal blow could not have hurt more if it were physical. My chest seems to cave in, and I back up, hurt now owning the look on my face.

"Hamilton. You cannot be this stupid." Nat somehow has slid her tiny form between him and me, and the larger boy changes his gaze to her, confused.

Blinking, my eyes wander blankly around at the observing faces. Turning blindly, I somehow find my bus home and wait for it to carry me away from this awful place. Nat joins me but doesn't say a word for a while. She just holds my hand and lets me run through my thoughts. Just before the bus reaches my stop she says, "Let's do something fun this weekend. What are you up for?"

All my distracted head can produce as a response is, "I don't know. I'll call you."

"Hey, I'll come by later."

"I'm going to hike for a while. I'll call you when I get back," I say as she slides out to let me free from our shared seat.

"What happens if you run into the furball again?" she asks.

"I can't stay inside." If I don't get the comfort of the woods today, I think I'll die.

Chapter Four

I wander lost in my own head through the woods. My legs are as tired as my soul, so I find a place under a tree and sit down. Why is my life so screwed up? What have I done to become karma's bitch like I am? I'm so wrapped up I did not even notice the wolf. It is only when he moves very close that I focus my eyes and see him. He tilts his head to the side almost in question. "Rough day," I explain.

He moves even closer. Now that he's freed me from my thought coma I shiver. The temperature has dropped in one of those wild east Washington swings when the air pops in for an unplanned visit from the northern arctic region. My teeth chatter a bit. The wolf moves closer and sniffs me. He does that weird chuffing noise as if he's stifling a sneeze.

"I would give you a lesson on personal space but I'm cold." Carefully gauging his reaction as I move, I bring my hand up. His eyes follow my hand as far as they can, turning his head slightly until I place my hand tentatively into the fur on his back. He relaxes and pants. The simplicity of the creature makes me smile. I pet him, letting my fingers play in his hair. He's warm, and it feels therapeutic to sit contently cuddling this wild being. I shiver again from the cold, and he lowers his head, so he's covering my legs with the upper part of his warmer body. I can see why people brought dogs into bed with them before modern heating. They're better than an electric blanket set on high. The down side is that this blanket has to weigh in at somewhere past one hundred and ninety pounds.

I stay still, not wanting to lose this one moment of peace I have found today. But eventually I say, "All right, big guy, I am fairly certain my circulatory system would like to continue its very fine job of moving blood to and from my feet."

He rises up on his elbows, shifts so his weight isn't on me nearly as much, and looks at me.

For some reason I feel the need to explain why I'm ruining our moment of bliss. "As nice as this is, I let it go on too long and have now lost feeling in my toes. You have to get all the way off. I have to stamp my feet to get the prickles out of them."

Before he removes himself, he turns and licks my face.

"Does this mean I am forgiven?" I ask, referring to yesterday when I pushed him away with my will.

He licks my face with more urgency.

"Hey, enough already." I push him away with my hands and stand on my tingling feet. I stamp in place until I'm sure my feet will hold me. "Thanks for the snuggle. I needed it bad today." I walk away.

The wolf stays by my side. He's so large my hand can rest easily on his back with my elbow bent as we move. "You coming home with me?" I ask.

The wolf just keeps walking next to me. I enjoy the silence from my unusual companion. I decide to head straight back to the house and not take the winding route I had at the start of today's trek. When I'm almost back to the house, we come up on another clearing with a strange circle in it. I stop, and the wolf sniffs and growls, lowering his head. I take a few steps closer. Once again, I have the unsettling feeling I had gotten from the last circle. I muse aloud, "What are these things?"

The only response from the wolf is his continuing growl.

"I feel the same way, buddy."

Putting my hands up, I feel the energy change in the air, as I get closer. The wolf apparently doesn't like the idea of me getting closer to the circle, because he grabs my coat with his teeth and pulls backward, digging his paws into the ground. "I'm not going in it. I just want to see what it feels like around it."

The circle is simply wiped of all vibrancy. Not one speck is left. I peek down at the wolf, his jaws locked tight on the edge of my jacket. The look he gives me would speak volumes if I spoke wolf. But I don't, so I decide to do the talking. "Listen here. I have to fix this. You need to give me a minute."

He chuffs again but doesn't let go.

"I am going to play with that power I used on you yesterday when I scared you. Back up, because it has been doing some strange stuff, and I don't want you to get hurt."

He just holds on to my coat.

I throw down my final warning. "I warned you. And if you rip my new coat, I am gonna float you in the air till you make that little girl noise again."

He chuffs and makes a questioning whine.

"I have no idea how to do this." I put my hands up and just will the energy that had been taken away to come back to the circle. It takes a while; a wind picks up. This wind is warmer than the chilly breeze that had brought the cooler temperatures and is blowing in the wrong direction. Little eddies of nature's debris swirl as the two converse air currents meet around us. The wolf whines his displeasure. But soon everything settles back, and the vacant circle feels whole again.

The wolf lets go. He sniffs the ground around the former circle. He raises his head to me and barks, wagging his tail.

"I think it feels better, too," I say and walk in the middle of what had been a dead zone. "I wonder what causes these things."

Both the canine and I check the area until we realize it seems settled and right again. Having that wonderful sense of completion, I decide it's getting late, and I continue back to Aunt Celia's. The wolf stays with me until I reach the yard; it sits at the edge of the woods. "See ya around. Thanks again for the company." I go into the house, thinking my tentative relationship with this animal is odd.

I'm washing my hands at the kitchen sink when an enormous howl sounds from the woods. Now if you have never listened to a wolf howl in person, it is bigger than any recording you have heard. I imagine it's like taking a picture of the Grand Canyon. No photo will ever explain the moment when you are standing on the edge looking out. I have no idea what he is saying, because like I said I don't speak wolf, but he's definitely letting somebody know something really important.

****

I call Nat, and she insists we go out for coffee. I leave a note for Aunt Celia, and Nat's mom takes us down to the coffee house by the post office. I can tell where Nat gets her looks from. Her mom is just as lovely as can be, seeming more like Nat's sister than her mother. She heads off to run some errands and tells Nat to call when we need to get back home.

The coffee shop is in a small series of buildings near Nine Mile Falls. You might pass it right by 'cause it sits back behind a nursery; you know one of those places that sells the plants for your yard. Not the place where put your young ones when you can't watch them. Although, it would be a good idea to have a coffee house near a one of those kid garages. I mean, if you have to work all day and then you have to pick up a child who automatically comes full of energy and add to that them having the advantage of a nap in the middle of the day, you might need a cup just to keep up. It's a homey kind of coffee house. You know the ones with the little nooks of comfy sofas that you do your best to tell yourself the stains on are just someone's beverage spill and repeat over and over "just someone's beverage" as a mantra so you are comfortable sitting on them.

We walk in as the sun goes down behind the hills. Even though it's still light outside the dark paint colors and dim lighting make the shop seem as though evening has entirely set by the time the door closes behind us. The door seems like a time warp flashing us forward into full night. We pick the drinks that somehow define us and mosey to a seating group sitting farther back than the front door. We get cozy, and Nat wastes no time.

"Are you okay?"

"I'm not really sure how to respond to that. If you mean, are all my bodily functions up and running, short of a CT scan I believe all systems are a go. If you mean can I get my head around everything that has happened and has continued to happen to me, well I guess that is one of those 'time will tell' things a Magic 8 Ball mentions. I really can't see how all of these slamming doors are opening windows, even though Aunt Celia swears that's how it works." I take a deep breath. "What is going on with this town? Is there some kind of ordinance against being nice to people?"

"Hey, I'm nice," she challenges.

"Yes, you are. You are definitely who I can compare to when I say the rest of the people in this town are rude, strange, or downright mean."

Nat laughs. "Adam was nice to you this afternoon, wasn't he? And I thought you and the Drakester were super buds."

"Adam falls in the strange category. Did I tell you he sniffed me today? I don't mean he turned toward me and breathed in. He leaned over and took a big ol' whiff. And then he wanted to be my friend. Can you explain that? No you can't because that is S-T-R-A-N-G-E."

Nat's laughing, but when she regains her composure she says, "That happens a lot around here. You'll get used to it."

I look at her as if she has four heads. "What crack are you smoking? Who gets used to people wanting to be their friend because you let them invasively smell you? I've got it. Maybe Monday I should just stand at the doors to the auditorium and have people sniff me; then everyone will like me, and my little speech will go swimmingly. Hey, is that why Sara doesn't like me? I broke her nose before she caught my aroma?" Sarcasm drips from my diatribe.

"How on earth do you think that is weird when you pick people up and send them flying across the cafeteria?" she shoots back dry as the desert.

"Well, that's different. That was an accident."

She gapes at me like she will see my four heads and raise me eight.

"I didn't mean to do that. I was just giving him a little scooch, and it got bigger than I had intended." My voice is small.

"What's with the scooching? You think that falls under the *not* odd events category?" Nat asks.

"Well it's not... for me... Well this one was, but I still don't know how that happened."

"What do you mean? You can just do that?" She looks at me and blinks.

"Well, yes...I know it's something not many people can do, but I have always been able to do things like that."

"How about you sub in 'nobody' for 'not many' in that statement?" she suggests.

My eyes sweep the area before I continue. "I have not met everybody, so I don't know if 'nobody' is the answer or not." It's possible I'm pouting, but I am simply not going to admit to that.

Nat pins me with one of those "really?" looks people give when there is no need to dignify the response with an actual utterance.

"Drake can do something too, but just not the same *something*," I add defensively.

Out of the darkened shadows of the room a face appears. I am not ashamed to admit Nat and I squeak like church mice. The face moves forward, and I realize it's actually attached to a body. I'm pretty happy about that. The body is clad all in black from head to toe.

"Gus, you scared the crap out of me," Nat admonishes, slapping this person's shoulder as he gets close enough to give her a hug.

"Sorry, I wasn't trying to startle you." Gus indicates he wants an introduction by turning his attention to me.

"Oh yeah, this is G.J.. She's new, just started about a week ago."

"What an unusual name." He grasps my hand with his still-cold-from-being-outside one. "My name is Augustine Sanzar. Please call me Gus." He continues to hold my hand long past what I would deem the normal handshake amount of time. "Is G.J. short for something?" His eyes are a beautiful shade of blue. Like blue topaz when its facets catch the light and it blazes. His dark hair and pale skin just make the brilliance of his eyes that much more remarkable.

It takes me an embarrassing amount of time to realize his perfect lips have moved in order to communicate with me. And I respond with a breathy, "Glory."

His mouth twists in an arrogant smile like this happens to him all the time. "Pardon?"

Shaking my head, I speak a bit louder. "Sorry, my given name is Glory."

I try to pull my hand back, but with an effortless hold, he keeps it. "How do you get to G.J. from that?" he asks.

I'm still a bit flummoxed, and my ears don't want to turn the sound of his voice into actually words for some reason. So Nat, bless that sweet girl, steps in and pulls my hand from his saying, "Her middle name is Juniper."

I sit back, trying to figure how to get somewhere close to cool after that moment. It doesn't take me long to come to the conclusion there's no way back to the vicinity of cool.

This stunning boy makes himself at home by sitting right next to me. His leg is touching mine. So I feel obliged to try to scoot over to give him more room, which he promptly takes up by widening his legs. If I scoot over even more, will he follow me or end up doing a split?

Nat laughs and tries real hard to keep the cream and caffeine from shooting out her nose. Flattening her hand over her mouth, she pinches her nostrils closed with the crook of her first finger and thumb. I guess she sees what I see. Stretching his arm along the chair back, he makes me feel captured. I honestly am not sure how I'm responding to that sensation. Nat assures herself her refreshments are heading in the direction she intends. "Okay, Gus, turn it down or she'll head for the hills. I mean it."

"What am I doing?" Gus asks, the picture of innocence.

I'll give you three guesses as to what he does next, and the first two don't count. Yep, he leans over and sniffs me. I look at Nat in utter disbelief. I flip my face to his, which is all up in my space. As calmly as my voice will allow, I inquire, "Why are you doing that?"

"What?" With just that one word, Gus makes me feel foolish for asking.

"Smelling me?" I run through Mama's lessons in my head to see if there is a polite way of dealing with people who sniff you. And as far as I can recollect, there isn't.

"Why not?" His tone is so nonchalant it makes me seem like the crazy one.

"It's just that it seems a bit forward to do that to someone you have known for less than all of five minutes. You may want to hold off on that until... oh I don't know... NEVER." I glance to Nat for support at what I think is a perfectly reasonable suggestion.

"But you smell good. Why would you have a smell if others were not supposed to smell you?" Gus asks in honest fascination.

"I have a good number of opinions too, but I don't share..." Even I have to stop myself there. "Well that's a bad example, but there are lots of things people have that they don't necessarily share the first time you meet them." Looking back to Nat I say, "Is this a northwest thing I just don't get for cultural reasons, like how you all don't understand grits or that sixty degrees is cold outside?"

Nat smiles. "Gus, no more smelling. It makes G.J. uncomfortable. G.J., Gus goes to Lakeside, too."

I guess that is my hint to drop the smelling subject, which I'm happy to do. "Oh I haven't seen you around. What grade are you in?" This is a legitimate question for a majority of the boys in this school. As most of them who should have unruly pimples and bony shoulders actually look like they should be shirtless for a living on the cover of a magazine or a Times Square billboard.

"You aren't in any of my classes. Do you like plays?"

"I can't say I've had occasion to see many plays. I've read lots, but we didn't go out much when I lived in Louisiana." I answer him, trying to hold what the rest of the world would think of as a normal conversation.

"I like your accent," he compliments.

"Thank you." I make the mistake of looking him in his eyes, which are not far from mine.

"Gus works backstage for the school productions," Nat adds, breaking the intense eye contact Gus and I have made.

"Which, sadly, I need to get back to. Ladies, it has been my pleasure." He abruptly takes my hand and kisses the back.

You can think that is gallant if you want to, but I think he's trying to get in one last whiff. I don't feel too bad about it because he does it to Nat, too. "It was nice to meet you," I add.

"I'll see you at school." And then, with his black clothes and dark hair, it appears as though he just vanishes into the dark hallway.

"Seriously, is it me or are the boys around here just odd ducks?" I ask.

"Gus is a good guy. He's just a bit dramatic; I think it's a theater thing." She flips topics. "Speaking of the unusual…" She prompts me back to the topic we were on prior to our interruption.

"There's not much to say. I have always just been able to do things. The only problem is the things I do are now off somehow. Not all the time. Just sometimes. And I can't tell when it is going to be normal or abnormal."

"Huh." Nat sits back, thinking. "What can Drake do?"

Realizing I've spilled his beans I try and avoid her question, "Not for me to say."

"Come on, G.J. I can't read that guy, and it makes me crazy."

"What is with you two? Why don't you just speak to him?"

"It's uncomfortable." She squirms to prove her point.

"What?"

"Talking to someone I can't read." Nat crosses her arms and flops back sullenly.

"He's a nice guy—one of the few in this area that has not inhaled inappropriately around me. Give him a chance.

He's not bad to look at," I add, which just seems to annoy her more. "What could be the harm in getting to know him? Maybe you'll even understand him better."

"It doesn't work like that," Nat says absently.

"That is exactly how it works."

"How do you know? G.J., when I say I can't read him, I mean I can't *read* him." On the second "read him" she starts to gesture wildly from my head to hers and back again.

"Huh?" I ask as if she has just changed her primary language to Mandarin.

"I told you the first day we met. I'm psychic." Her tone is totally serious.

I close one eye as if shutting down some of the input from the world will help me process her statement without a syntax error. Then I think back to everything we have talked about and realize she's never lied to me. My brain just didn't believe her. "Well, isn't that a kick in the pants?" I marvel. "So you know what I am thinking all the time?"

"For the most part I have to be near you, but I can read anybody I want, except Drake. I don't know why I can't read him, and I don't like it." She's a bit morose.

"Good heavens. Who knows you can do this?" I ask.

"Most people know around here."

"Honey, you are in high school. That can be dangerous," I say, my eyes wide.

"Nah, people trust me to keep their secrets." She shrugs as if it's no big deal.

"Are you sure other people aren't worried about what you know?" I'm sure this is a problem for somebody.

"It's because of what I do know that it's not dangerous." I have to admit her smile has a smidge of evil in it.

"I like the way you think." I smile back with a devilish curl to my eyes.

"So what is going on with your capability?" Nat changes our chat back to me.

"I told you I don't know. The way it works is I think about doing something and then will it to happen. But now, flexing my will or even just thinking about something without meaning to put will behind it, it's as if my will gets the muscles of Governor Schwarzenegger—before politics, you know like during the Conan years. It moves like that, without actual intent."

"So, you can't control it?"

"I can most of the time, just not all of the time, and I don't know why. I feel awful about throwing Drake." I look down at my cooling coffee.

"Eh, I don't see anything wrong with that except the teachers might find out." Nat is completely fine with me "bowling with boys."

"Nat, someone could have gotten hurt."

"They'll be fine." She's still unfazed.

"You are a hot mess. This is serious. What happens on Monday if, in front of the whole school, something goes wrong, like I think 'gosh I'd like to crawl into a hole right now,' and a sink hole opens up under rows five through twenty-one in the auditorium?" I am truly worried.

"Can you do that?"

"I've never actually tried that particular thing, but I do believe I could," I say with confidence.

"Then shame on them for making you apologize on stage." Nat's teasing me now.

I notice the time. "Hey, this is great, but I need to head home. I need to get a couple hours in on my science project."

Nat calls her mom and, after a bit, we head to the front of the coffee shop. As we come to the front room where people order their drinks, Adam stands up from a chair by the door.

"Hey, Adam, I didn't know you were here," I say.

His face grows serious and half-asks the question without words. "Where else would I be?"

"Oh, you hang out here a lot?" I ask.

Again, he turns his head to the side and looks at me funny. It's a gesture that seems familiar somehow.

Nat says hello as well then adds, "My mom should be here soon to take us back. See you later, Adam." She gives my arm a tug.

"Are you going to be at the match tomorrow?" he asks quickly.

"What match?" I'm not up on extracurricular events.

"There's a home wrestling match against the Lewis and Clark Tigers. It would be great if you were there," he says with a hopeful look in his eyes.

"I have a lot of work to do on my project. I'm not sure I have the time." I am thinking about that and wanting to get back outside.

"It's going to rain tomorrow. I can take you. I was going to help Gus with some props," Nat says, ruining my excuse.

Testing my newfound mental connection, I think really sarcastically, "Thanks a whole bunch," to see if she can pick it up.

She smiles in faux sweetness. So, I am sure she gets the message. Let's see if I try to run any Drake interference for her again.

"When is it?" I ask Adam.

"It starts at 1:30, and it takes usually an hour to an hour and a half to get through all the weight classes."

"I haven't seen a high school wrestling match. I've seen all kinds of wrestling. I mean, I am from the south, but this will be a different experience for me. Thank you, Adam. I look forward to learning something new."

"That's a relief," Adam responds, and his face lights up in a beautiful smile.

Nat drags me out to catch our ride home, and we make plans to meet up tomorrow around one o'clock.

Night comes and I hear the wolf sound off with a few of his friends. That is the first time I realize, down to my toes, my wolf isn't out there alone. Wolves run in packs. Why is he the only one I have ever seen?

Chapter Five

I wake up early. I have a ton of energy, and it's hard to focus on research. Like Nat said 'it's raining cats and dogs'. The hill in the backyard has so much water running down it I swear it looks like you might catch a trout. With no jaunt in the woods to relieve my excess energy, I have never felt so cooped up. Nat's mom honks to let me know they're here, and I blow through the door like a starting gate.

I'm prickling with get-up-and-go, and Nat looks at me worriedly. "You all right?"

"I'm a little more than all right. I am jazzed today," I say, adding a quick hello to Nat's mom.

"Have you put any consideration into decaf? Maybe herbal tea?" Nat asks, looking at me with concern.

"I haven't had any coffee today. My heart is racing already. I couldn't go out today, so maybe this is just cabin fever?" I talk like my next word is racing the last out of my mouth.

"You up for this today?" Nat is just as sure as I am this energy burst is a recipe for disaster.

"We'll see." I continue to fidget all the way to school.

We get there at a quarter after one, and Nat comes with me to the gym for a bit before she is supposed to meet Gus. Pulled out from the walls are the bleachers, and there's a huge mat in the middle of the floor. The mat is about two and a half inches thick with one large circle surrounding a smaller circle. The small one is about five or six feet across. Inside the smaller circle is a long rectangle. Off the mat, chairs are set up in a line on either side. There are various water bottles and towels at the foot of each of the chairs, and gym bags sit on the floor behind the row. You can tell the team sides by the school colors represented on the items strewn around.

The Lakeside cheerleaders sit on the floor in front of the bleachers that bracket the mat on the adjacent side to the chairs and square off the space. Across the mat from the cheer squad is a table with three more chairs. A box with electrical cords coming out the back sits on the table along with a flip score tally, what looks like a few notebooks, and several pencils.

We find seats next to the table and situate ourselves a couple rows up on the bleachers. Nat sits on the end so she can go when she needs. I notice all the chairs have tennis balls covering the leg ends so as not to damage the basketball court. My thoughts ramble, thinking how tennis balls are useful. You can play with your dog, use them on old people's walkers, and now another thing they are good for—how versatile. Nat just shakes her head. So I tell her, "Look here, if you don't like what floats through my head, get out of it."

She's laughing as someone sits down on my other side.

"Good afternoon, ladies," Drake greets as Nat's laugh dies unfinished.

"Oh, Drake." I'm surprised and unsettled. Nat says nothing, just looks out over the mat. I start with my motor-mouthed apology. "Listen here, Drake, I really did not mean to send you into those boys yesterday. I was just gonna slide you down, and remember how I said I was a bit off? Well... I went off... Then you went flying. Anyhow, I am truly sorry. Are you all right?"

"No harm done. I understand." He puts his arm around my shoulders and gives me a side hug.

At that moment, the teams enter from the hall where the boy's locker room is located. That weird vibration noise shakes the room. Drake looks over as he lowers his arm from around me. The noise peters out. The wrestlers enter in a line from smallest to largest. All of them are in sweat suits representing the school colors. They look like two sets of Matryoshka Dolls— those Russian nesting dolls. Two of the last three of the Lakeside team I recognize. Adam is followed by Hamilton, once again looking at me as though he would like to see if my head comes off as easily as his kid sister's Barbie's if he applies enough pressure.

Nat says, "It's not you, it's him," with a sullen attitude.

I switch my gaze to Adam, give a smile, and a wave.

Drake asks Nat, "Would you like me to sit by you?"

This snaps me back to my group versus the young men in sweat suits, my head swinging from Nat to Drake and back again.

Nat, a bit flustered, says, "No. I gotta go." She shoots from the bench seat like a spooked jackrabbit and heads out.

I start to get up, but Drake put his hand on my knee to keep me in place. "She'll be back. You should stay here."

I turn to him, and we're practically nose-to-nose. "All right I'll stay, but she's my friend, Drake, and I won't have you taunting her, so cut it out."

"Ha. Taunting her? Is that what you think I am doing?" he asks.

A ruckus starts over behind the chairs on the Lakeside side of the mat. Adam and Hamilton are in an argument. "Do they test for steroids at this school, 'cause that boy has some serious anger issues?" I put the question to Drake.

"That's just Hamilton; aggression is part of his nature," Drake says.

I look away from the confrontation and notice for the first time one of the cheerleaders is Sara Ackers, and she's shooting her laser death stare again. Aside from her raccoon-bruise eye mask, she looks exhausted. I would feel sorry for her, but she's Sara, so I can't muster up any pity. In fact, the whole cheer squad looks like they haven't slept in a week. I figure they must have had a sleepover, and if the rest of the team is like Sara, I wouldn't so much as blink in case another one of them had a secret sharpie collection in their overnight bag.

"They look like hell," I say to Drake in observation, not cattiness. Really.

"They do look drained."

All of a sudden, Adam is right in front of me. "Oh." I say in surprise, "Hey, Adam."

"Hey, G.J., glad you came. Would you like to sit down front with some of my friends?" He gestures to what looks like the JV squad, shoving and roughhousing with one another like a tin tub full of puppies.

I look from the squirming group to Adam and back again.

"G.J. and I have a lot to discuss, Adam. Don't you need to be down with your team?" Drake says like the matter is settled and places his hand on my knee to keep me in place again.

Adam looks at me with worry.

"I'm all right here for now, Adam. Thank you, though." I remove Drake's hand from my leg.

Adam looks over his shoulder, and we all clearly see Hamilton point at him and point to the chairs in an undeniable order to return post haste.

"You sure, G.J.? You could sit with us down by the mat," Adam says.

I look over at the furious face of Hamilton Calhoun and think there is *not* a thing on this earth that will get me near that boy on purpose. "Adam, honey, I don't think the fans are supposed to be over there. I'm fine just where I am. Don't you worry about a thing. You just go wrestle your little heart out." Drake begins to move his hand back to my leg and I say, "Drake my leg is not a hand rest; please keep any parts you want returned to yourself."

That makes Adam smile. Then he leans over and gives me a sniff. I squint at Adam unpleased. "Okay, G.J., if you're sure you are okay here." He has his hands up as if he were balancing a house of cards as he slowly moves away.

"I'm fine, Adam." I give him a bright smile.

Adam stares, then gives his head a little shake and goes back to his team. As soon as he makes it there Hamilton is at him again, gesturing at me and making it plain as day he has plenty of opinions about me—none of which seem good. Somehow, I am sure he's not telling Adam he likes my outfit.

The match starts shortly thereafter with the one hundred and six pound weight class. The smallest boy on each team takes off his warm-up suit. They're shirtless and have on what looks like boxer briefs without a hole in the front but with a bunch of extra cloth at the top. Now, I don't usually put much thought into boys who would have to climb me for a kiss, but the little man on the Lakeside team is top to bottom muscle. While he was in clothes he'd looked like a small boy, but when he took off that jacket, I swear my brain went to that primal place of sheer appreciation for a perfectly put together human form. It takes me a second to switch my conscious mind back on. I am so very glad Nat isn't here, because some thoughts you really need to keep to yourself.

The two young men pull at the extra cloth on their suits, and it stretches up to somewhat cover their torsos as well. On their feet they wear thin-soled shoes that come up like Converse high tops with a little more cushion than the normal canvas.

The two boys meet the referee in the center of the small circle at opposite sides of the small rectangle. The clock is set and the ref brings the two boys into position with a V motion of his hands. The wrestlers crouch a little with their hands up in the classic wrestling stance. Then the ref gives a sharp whistle as he slashes one hand down to indicate the match has begun.

The two competitors start to circle the ring facing each other, bobbing and weaving as if they're about to do something. From the crowd and the teams on the side you can hear the teams yelling directions to the young athletes. "Shoot the single, Mikey."

"Now, now, now."

"There it is. You got it."

"All day," which I take to mean they think he is taking too long to do something, although I don't know what.

With a dart of movement, the Lakeside wrestler dodges in and grabs the leg of the Tiger's one hundred and six pounder. The resulting twisting movement somehow has the Tiger lunging backward and trying to make it to the outside of the bigger circle. The Lakeside wrestler wraps his legs and arms around the other boy and ends up on the Tiger's back as they hit the ground. The ref makes a hand gesture, and the Lakeside boy very quickly hops up and backs away from the boy below him.

The Tiger stands up, and they start circling again. The instructional cheers continue. Adam and Hamilton along with the other team members focus wholly on the two small men on the mat, calling out their advice. The Tiger shoots in and tries to grab the Lakeside wrestler's leg. Missing, the Tiger takes a moment to get back to his circling stance, and the Lakeside wrestler shoots in for a counter attack. Down they go, the Tiger desperately trying to turn his body over, so his back isn't to the mat. Once he gets his belly down, I see what wrestling is really about. Slowly the Lakeside wrestler works the other boy's arms behind him, overpowering each of the muscles of the Tiger. Have you ever arm-wrestled? There is that feeling of when you are pushing with all your might but the other person still breaks your strength and your hand goes slamming back? That moment of struggle happens in every sinewy tissue of these boys' bodies.

The Lakeside wrestler's whole body is in play, all the way down to his toes. It's not like he is only working with his top half. Mikey, the Lakeside team member, entwines his legs through the Tiger's legs, and he is trying to flatten the Tiger out by arching his own back. As he stops that, he works the arm of the Tiger down toward his groin. The shout things like "navy," "arm bar," and "cross face," which sound like pure gibberish to me, but every once in a while they say, "That's it, Mikey."

The Lakeside wrestler somehow takes the Tiger's one arm and holds it between his opponent's legs by the wrist. Mikey has his other hand, locking the Tiger's other arm in place and bracing it behind the Tiger's back with the first elbow, immobilizing it between the Tiger's legs. The two boys roll, the shoulders of the Tiger are on the mat, and Mikey is sideways, locking his arms in place behind him and holding the Tiger upside down. The ref drops, lying flat next to the boys, his focus on the Tiger's shoulders. The ref swings his arm in a precise motion of a count. After several swings, he toots his whistle, and Mikey releases the sweaty, purple-faced boy from the Tiger's team.

They all stand up, and the three meet in the middle of the ring. The ref encircles both their wrists in each hand and abruptly raises Mikey's, declaring him the winner. The two athletes shake hands and return to their teams. I am completely fascinated. This has nothing to do with the wrestling where you throw someone over the ropes and hit him with a folding chair. This takes an insane amount of skill and athleticism. What is even more impressive is the lack of chest beating and trash talk about a 'smack down'. The two young men just went out, compared muscle to muscle, move to move, and when it was over, they went back to their teams to receive praise, condolences, or advice for the next time from their peers and coaches. Although it did not take too long, both young men are slick with sweat and want their water bottles while listening to comments, receiving slaps on the backs, or getting advice from their coaches. The loudest ruckus comes from the cheerleaders slapping and clapping to the rhythm of Queen's *We Will Rock You.*

Now don't get me wrong. I believe cheerleading is the most disrespected sport around. They are athletes in their own right, and a football game would not be the same without their support and enthusiasm. But, there is a time and a place for everything. This moment is *not* the time or the place for the pep of the squad. What just happened on that mat was amazing, beautiful, motivating, and so pure in its simplicity of a true mano-a-mano competition. It seems sullied by the arrogance of that cheer. It is as if you just ate a lush rich chocolate and before you even swallow, you pop a pickle into your mouth. I like pickles but not with chocolate and certainly not before I've ridden the rush of the chocolate bliss. Maybe I am a bit more into chocolate than most.

The ref goes to the table and chats with the people there. The next weight class, one hundred and thirteen pounds, arrives at the center circle. These boys go at it in a different way. They seem to be trying for takedowns and reversals, adding up the points on the board. Two points here for a takedown, one for an escape. I wish I had a rulebook, so I'd know what is what. I'm so curious about how things work, and I'm a bit frustrated I can't interpret all that's going on. But I'm glad I came. It isn't simply the ability to openly gawk at some of the finest specimens of the male form since Mr. da Vinci's Vitruvian Man. I see this as an art, something to appreciate like pointillism. You can stand back and see the overall artistry or get up close and marvel at the minute details. Hooked like a squirming fish, I itch to know more.

Drake seems aware that I'm interested in the sport and doesn't say much unless it's time for the cheerleaders to motivate a crowd that is waiting on the next weight class. At one such moment he says, "How did you make me move?"

My head isn't in the moment, so I turn and look at him in question. "Pardon?"

"You said you don't perform any rituals, so where does your power come from?" He leans close to my ear, so I can hear him without him having to speak up.

"I don't know. I just do it," I reply.

"It takes energy to do things of that nature. Most people have to perform a ritual in order to draw it. You don't?" he asks as if we're sitting there discussing something as normal as what we had for lunch.

"What do you mean, 'most people'? I am the only 'people' I know of that can do things like that at all, with the exception of your step up from smoke signals," I tease.

"Step up..." he starts indignantly. "G.J., you really have no idea, do you?"

"I have loads of ideas, but like I said, if you think I know anything about some crazy rituals, you would be mistaken. If it takes energy, as you say, to do what I can do, well I have no idea where it comes from. I just know it's there when I want it." I explain it the way the old men in the front porch rockers at the general store off Rt. 10 would talk about the weather. As if it were some sort of news flash it was hot and humid in Louisiana in the summer.

Drake watches me for a minute like I'm going to change my mind about how my ability works. But that boy can stare for two or three lifetimes if he wants because I'm not changing this tune.

The whistle blows again, and we are now up to the mid-range weight classes. The weight class is one hundred and fifty-two pounds. We're getting to the point where these are no longer pint-sized perfections. At one hundred and fifty-two pounds of pure muscle, you're into full-sized man. Sure, neither of these athletes are my height, but I'm not planning on picking a fight with them. When the sweat suit comes off this young man, his shoulders look like a biology class's display of how muscles are supposed to be assembled. You can see the straining lines in his tissue as if it's all the skin can do to hold back the bulge of this still-developing man's power. I'm a touch embarrassed as Drake pushes my lower jaw up to meet my upper teeth from my unintentional gape.

"G.J., were you raised in a convent or somewhere without Calvin Klein ads?" Drake smirks.

I blush so hard I get an actual head rush. "Don't give me any guff, or I will start to harass you about your Nat obsession," I shoot back in pure defense.

He looks startled. "What? What do you mean?"

I grin at his hyper defensiveness. "Me thinks he doth…"
"Don't be trite," Drake grumbles.

"Don't openly mock the unbridled burgeoning hormones I may display from time to time."

He laughs softly. "Done and done."

There's a slamming sound from the mat. The Tiger is desperately trying to reach the outside of the larger ring. The Lakeside one hundred and fifty-two pounder is dragging him back in. The two boys are slick with sweat, and the Tiger gets what he wants as he literally slips away. The whistle blows, and the two young men come back to the middle. From what I can tell, this isn't considered an escape because they start with the Lakeside wrestler slightly to the side and behind the Tiger who is on his knees and palms. One of the Lakeside wrestler's hands is on the lower wrestler's arm and the other on his abdomen. The whistle blows, and the Lakeside wrestler tries to shoot the hand on his abdomen up to the Tiger's neck, while the Tiger tries to pop up to a squatting position, putting both hands on the Lakeside guy's arm at his waist to stop the neck-grab effort. This move doesn't work out so well for this Tiger, and before I can even focus on what is happening, the Tiger is in a classic move that even the WWE people use sometimes. I only watch professional wrestling for the soap opera. There's no way I could grow up in the south and not know the drama that brought John Cena out of the ashes of the likes of The Rock and Hulk Hogan. Don't judge.

The half nelson is perfectly executed and has the Tiger's neck at such an awkward angle I'm sure it's going to break. The Lakeside wrestler's fingers turn white as he holds firm to the base of the skull of the other young man. Our team's man pushes and pushes his body taut down to his toes, which he braces on the floor. This explains the flexible sole shoes. His legs spread wide to give him the leverage he needs to tip the other wrestler, so once again the ref falls to the floor and begins the count that will end it. The count restarts twice as the Tiger struggles, and his shoulders lose the position needed to keep the count going forward, but in the end, Lakeside prevails again.

"Is our team as good as they look or are the Lewis and Clark fellows not up to snuff?" I ask Drake.

"Our team is pretty badass. Most teams don't look forward to the matches with us."

"Do you play any sports?" I ask.

"No, I'm busy with other clubs and the student council."

"You're on the student council?"

Laughing he says, "Just call me Mr. President."

"What?" I gawk. "You are only now mentioning this? You should have a jacket or at the very least, a nametag warning people you are so important? What in the name of all that is holy are you doing talkin' to me?"

"Slumming it," he teases and nudges my shoulder.

"Turtle butt."

"What kind of person says that?" He laughs.

"This kind. What are you gonna do about it?" I fake challenge.

"Wait patiently for your next poetic remark." His laugh lowers to a smile.

"How many weight classes are there?"

"There are six left. Each guy has to weigh in at or below their weight class until you get to heavyweight, which is everything from two hundred and twenty pounds all the way to two hundred and eighty-five pounds. Few guys actually weigh in at two eighty-five. It's just kind of a catchall for anyone over two twenty. They just changed the classes a while ago."

"We have someone in that weight class?" I'm surprised.

"Yeah Stanzi, the guy on the end." He indicates with a jut of his chin toward the chairs.

"THAT GUY IS A STUDENT?" I say in the too loud voice that happens whenever shock takes over my vocal chords.

Drake shushes me. "He's a senior. This is his last year."

Lowering my voice I say, "I thought he was a coach."

"No, the coaches are the two bald, buff, short guys that never take a chair."

I had noticed the little men pacing and squatting but had not paid that much attention to them. After a few seconds, my brain does some behind the scenes calculations that find Hamilton somewhere in the vicinity of two hundred and twenty pounds. This makes me extra uncomfortable that he has sworn himself my enemy.

There is a break in the action during the one hundred and eighty-two weight class; one of the wrestlers gets blood on the mat from a bloody nose. I can't tell if it is spontaneous or due to a move from the other wrestler. While the mat is being cleaned and re-swept even the cheerleaders run out of steam. It seems as though when not making sure the crowd has spirit, Sara Ackers does all she can to squash me with her death stare. She leans over, whispering to her friends on her squad, and they all focus on me. It's hard to ignore people so blatantly talking about you. The cheerleaders are warming up for something big because they all start working on the same movements, but they aren't yelling out what they're saying, just kind of mumbling under their breath.

The referee calls the match for that weight class because the one wrestler's nose won't stop bleeding. Adam quickly removes his jacket and pants. Holy moly. I am going to melt. It's just not right for there to be a body like that on anyone. I am actually sweating. I catch my hand just before I fan myself in open admiration. This vision ends all chances at coherent speech with this boy in the future. He wraps himself up in the rubber bands that make the shoulder straps of the uniform. Drake leans over and asks if I need a tissue for my drool.

"Shut it, Nat man," I retort.

The match begins. This time it looks like Adam gives the opposing Tiger his leg. I don't understand. The Tiger takes the advantage, and I worry about Adam. What happens if he gets hurt? I wish the other wrestler would just lie down, so I don't have to watch this particular match. And then the Tiger lies down on the mat.

Nobody understands what's happening; Adam just looks down at the guy for a second, while his coaches yell for him to get on top of the guy. Adam is reluctant to take advantage of the moment. I worry more. I lean over to Drake. "Um, you know that issue I seem to be having. I think it might be best if I go now."

"You're doing that?"

"Not really sure but I think maybe so." I start to leave.

"G.J.." He grabs my arm. "If you aren't sure, just stay here and let's see what happens."

Trying to pull free of his grasp I answer, "I am not staying here to find out and getting someone hurt. Let go."

His hand flies away from me. Drake is shocked at my control over him. "Okay, go."

I shuffle out of the bleachers and try to make it out of the gym. There's a crowd around the door that I wish would get out of my way. They all float over about ten feet so quickly some of them lose their footing and they fall to the floor.

Drake is on my heels as I race out of the room saying softly, "Control it, G.J.. Just calm down."

Again, the loud rumbling noise starts, and I will the ceiling not to come down on everyone's head. I run out the door with Drake giving chase. I wish he would stop following me. I hear his feet stop. He calls out, "G.J.." But all I can do is run away as fast as my feet will carry me.

Chapter Six

I burst outside into the cold. The buckets of rain have slowed to an icy drizzle. The pinprick bite of the chilly water striking my hot face seems to be what I need. I move around the side of the building, so I'm not in line of sight from the gym doors. Once again, my will went wacky. I feel like a danger to the world. Why is this happening? I'm getting cold and really want to go home and crawl in or under my bed. I try the building doors as I come across them. The Budweiser Clydesdales could not pull me back to the gym. On my fourth or fifth try, I find some success and work my way through the halls to the back of the auditorium where Nat is supposed to be helping Gus.

I hear Nat's laugh and smell the fumes from paint as I enter the workspace. As soon as Nat catches sight of me, she knows there was trouble. She comes over and hugs me. "What the heck happened?"

"I blew up again." I flash through the outbursts of power in my head.

"Whoa. You okay now?" She holds me away from her, looking at me cautiously.

"Since I am never sure when I am not okay, I can't speak to that."

Gus puts down his paintbrush and asks, "Is everything all right?"

I smile weakly at him. "I just would like to head home if that's all right with you, Nat."

"Gus, do you mind if I head out?" Nat asks.

"No, not at all. I can finish this up later. I take it that it's still raining outside?" he asks, looking at my drowned-rat condition.

"Not as bad as before, but the water is still coming down," I answer.

"Why don't I take you both home? Let me clean up real quick," Gus offers.

"Do you drive?" I ask, trying to pinpoint his age.

Gus smiles. "Yes."

His car is more than a high-school student should be allowed—an Audi RS-7. The inside reminds me of the console Scottie tinkered at to beam up Kirk. The car looks like it should get a speeding ticket while it's in park. I'm not sure I should get in all drippy like I am. The leather is so pretty, and I'd hate to ruin it. Saying so, Gus laughs and tells me not to worry.

"You take the front G.J.. You're taller," Nat offers.

The watery scene blurs more by the speed in which Gus handles the car. While he seems in control the whole time, I know far too much about the physics of hydroplaning to be anything but scared witless. We arrive at my house in mere moments, and I thank Gus for the ride.

"No kiss goodbye?" he asks.

Nat smacks the back of his head from the back seat of the car.

"Have a good night, guys," I say, shaking my head, and I walk into the house.

I do a fair amount of moping this afternoon. I put on my softest yoga pants that have bleach stains and my coziest sweatshirt. I play all the thought-provoking, heart-rending songs I can find. I let Carrie Smith and Adele release my hurt and confusion with their passionate vocals. Bored with my pity party, I decide to work on my science project to get my mind off my crazy life.

I hear the barking toward evening. Looking out my back window, I see the wolf standing in the rain on the hill behind my house. If that creature thinks I'm heading out in the rain for a walk, he's crazy. Or I am for thinking the animal would have any such thoughts at all. There's a whole lot of wild happening today. I go back to work and ignore the yapping. Or I try to until I start to hear a scratching at my aunt's back door. I am so happy Aunt Celia is at one of her events. Heaven only knows what she would say. She probably would call animal control. Too bad I like this dumb beast 'cause that would probably have been the right decision rather than what I do. Yes, I know when one of Mother Nature's feral creatures comes knocking at your back door, you probably would not make the decision to go shake hands, but I throw on a coat, open the door, and slide out. I'm at least careful to keep the muddy creature off Aunt Celia's kitchen floor.

As soon as I'm out, the animal jumps up and puts its paws on my shoulders, lapping greedily at my face. "Get down," I complain as I shove him away. "Ugh, now I am all spit sloppy. And look, you got mud all over my jacket. How am I supposed to get that off?" I look at the wolf with my very best shaming face. To his credit, he does look a little chagrin. He tentatively sniffs my hand and licks my fingers. I slide down the back door and sit under the awning that covers the back step of the house. It's relatively dry. "Miss me?" I ask him, and he starts the slobber attack again. I giggle. "Ticklish, remember?"

He stops licking but sticks his nose in the collar of my jacket and sniffs around my neck.

"Not helping the whole ticklish thing," I try admonishing him again.

He gives a few more huffs to satisfy whatever thing that animals satisfy by taking in scents and then sits next to me expectantly. I put my hand in his fur, and he leans in to my touch. He licks my wrist, encouraging me to continue. "I'm glad you came." His fur is wet on the outside, but as my fingers burrow in, the under pelt is thick and dry. He shivers as I scratch. "I lost it again today. I was having a good time watching this wrestling match, but then something happened and *poof*, I am out of control again. I wish I knew what was going on." My mind wanders through the events of the day. "And Drake... ugh..." I end exasperated with myself at having controlled him again. He's going to hate me.

The wolf puts his muzzle on my cheek. I rest there for a few minutes just enjoying the closeness of this beautiful creature. His head comes up quickly, looking at the back door of the house. He licks me once right on my startled mouth and runs off toward the woods. I feel the loss of his warmth. Standing up, I go inside and take off my coat. I stare at the mud stains, trying to figure out how to undo the damage as Aunt Celia about scares me out of my skin.

"Hey, G.J.," is all she says. Even something as innocuous as that can frighten a body if you don't know who the person saying "hey" is there.

Dropping my coat, I swirl around to face her. "Oh hey, Aunt Celia," I reply in that nervous you-just-caught-me-doing-something voice that always seems to give a person away.

"What are you up to?" She looks at me with curiosity. It's almost like parental figures can sense when they should know something. They may not know what they need to know, but they get that look on their face like they are a split second from putting on their sleuthing hat and pulling out their magnifying glass.

"Just needed some air. I've been working on my project for a while, and my head was getting bored of doing the same thing." My babble seems to raise her suspicion.

"Really? That's not like you. How was the game?" she asks.

"Fine," I answer, trying to not prattle on.

"Uh-huh." She narrows her eyes at me. "The *game* was good then." She stresses the noun in that sentence.

"Yep."

"Okay, what is up? No way would you let me get away with calling a wrestling match a game. That was a test. Only time you have nothing to say is when you have too much to say."

I hate people knowing your habits so well that they can use them against you. "Aunt Celia, you just used parental judo. No fair."

"All is fair in love and parenting. Don't make me force you to keep a journal, so I can read it or make up a phony Facebook account so I can friend you to know what you are doing. Spill."

Aunt Celia knows about my unusual gifts, and she has never seemed concerned. She and Mama just acted like I was normal, and the fact that I could do these things was not something that should concern anyone because I was a good girl. She is so angry that Mr. Decker punished me to such an extreme without even a phone call to her. I have a feeling Mr. Decker is about to meet Aunt Celia's temper. She listens to everything that has gone wacky with my gifts, and it takes her four or five minutes to stop laughing about what happened to Sara's underwear. She roots for the bowling of the boys and is only concerned about today's match because I'm so upset by it.

"Aren't you worried I'm gonna hurt someone?" I ask.

"Not really. Listen, sweetie, you are not a violent person. You won't hurt anyone. Trust yourself. I happen to know a few folks. Let me make contact with some people, and I will see if we can track down what is going on. Maybe it might be good if you get some of it out of your system. We both have a lot on our hearts right now. Your mom is the first loss you have ever had to deal with. Your troubles might be as simple as grief. Or not. We will try to figure it out, but remember something for me, will you?" She stops until I look at her.

"What?"

"I am on team G.J. whatever might happen, I am here, and I am never too busy to help. I love you kiddo. You are all I have left of your mom. You mean the world to me." She pulls me close and kisses the top of my head.

"I love you too, Aunt Celia," I say as the corner of my eyes dampen.

****

Sunday, the sky is clear by the time service is over, and I reward a few hours of school and project work with a packed lunch and a walk in the woods. I explore even further this time, cresting the hill behind our house and working my way down the opposite face. It's really steep on this side, and I lose my footing a few times. As the ground starts to level and the trees grow sparser, my stomach begins to growl. Finding a log not far ahead, I sit next to it, so I can lean against it for a backrest and start to unpack the food I've brought. About two bites in, I hear people. Sandwich in hand, I rise up to look around. In the backyard of the house

I have accidentally wandered up on are Adam and Hamilton, shooting hoops with a whole group of boys.

Come on, really? Could this be happening to me? I am half-up and half-down. I can't decide if I should duck and crawl away like the coward I am or just calmly walk away. I am not proud of what I do next. The wind blows and several of the boys turn their faces to catch the breeze; I guess it feels good after their playing. In doing so they spot me. I grab my bag and run.

There is no graceful way to scurry. And being a five foot and eleven inch young girl running in sheer mortification uphill, I do believe I deserve the howls of laughter I hear behind me. I cannot say that if I was faced with a video of the moment, I would resist being doubled over in laughter at the Big Bird sized chicken I am making out of myself. But I prefer to die of embarrassment on my own turf. As difficult as that hill was to get down, it is extra hard to climb. I'm doing my best billy goat impression, but it's not an easy row to hoe. I wrench my ankle something awful and actually cry out, but I keep going. The worst thing that can happen happens. As I hobble over the top of the hill, tears falling from pain, frustration, and shame, Hamilton Calhoun catches up to me. Why can't this guy leave me alone?

"Stop walking," he yells.

With my head down, I keep moving, pain shrieking like a banshee up my leg with each step.

"What are you, stupid? Stop walking," he hollers again, closer this time.

I will drop before I quit trying to reach the safety of my back door and get away from him; I keep going.

He makes a frustrated sound, and I can hear him close behind me so I turn. There is no getting away. Swiping at my tears, I ready for battle.

"What the hell is wrong with you?" he snarls.

"I didn't know anyone was there. I saw you, right before you saw me," I blurt at him like a machine gun.

"So you ran the second we saw you?" His voice is full of skepticism. "What a dumb thing to do."

I put my head down, hiding my discomfort at my moronic reaction.

"What did you do to your foot?" The question is more of an accusation than out of concern.

I will *not* look up at him or respond.

Huffing out a sigh, he asks again in a slightly less hostile tone. "Your foot, did you hurt it?"

"I'll be fine. Just please go away." I still have my head down.

He puts his fingers under my chin and brings my eyes up to his angry ones. I just can't meet them. I am so horribly ashamed. I close my eyes as tears leak from their corners. My face is hot with the crimson color I must have turned by this point. I shift my weight and wince at the twinge my ankle gives. "What was that?" Hamilton demands.

"Nothing." I try to deny and move away, but the swelling, which has settled a bit, causes me to inhale sharply and grab Hamilton in reflex. Realizing what I'm doing the second after I do it, I let go and am on my way to the ground.

Surprised, Hamilton grabs me just enough to ease me the rest of the way to the forest floor. I'm down with my back on the cold ground. Hamilton moves to my feet. He grabs my sore ankle. I release a cry of pain, and he lets go quickly. "Fine, huh?" he says in condescension. "Take off your shoe."

"What?" I'm nonplused.

"Take off your shoe; let's see what you did to it," he demands like the bully he is.

"Look, Hamilton, I'll be fine in a minute. Go on back to your little friends and I'll make it home on my own."

"Take off your damn shoe," he says, completely ignoring my request.

I look away in that way people do, thinking by looking somewhere else they might *be* somewhere else.

He sits with his back to me, holding my leg by the knee under his arm. With his hands, he works at the strings on my boots. I try to wiggle free, but this boy is strong. His back is so big, and I can't see around him.

"Stop." I can feel the relief of pressure on my ankle as he works the laces down. "I am never going to get my shoe back on." My foot slides free of the boot. Dear Mama that hurt and I grab Hamilton's back in pain.

"Your foot is huge," he says. Now I might be overly sensitive, but given the historical evidence of what he has said in the past, I just know he is criticizing the size of my feet.

"You can't get to five eleven and not have a foot to balance it, but thank you, Hamilton, for the observation. Now if you wouldn't mind…"

He cuts me off by turning and dropping my removed boot in my lap. This huge boy proceeds to scoop me up as if I am a three year old with a skinned knee and takes off toward Aunt Celia's house. It takes me a minute to gather my ability to speak. I honestly cannot remember anyone picking me up past the age of six. He is just moving through the trees like he doesn't have the tallest girl in school in his arms.

"Hamilton, you can't carry me home," I object.

"I am the only one in our class who *could* carry you," he rebuffs.

Every time he opens his mouth, he reminds me why I can't stand him. Adding annoyed to my raging emotions I explain, "I'm not saying it's impossible—although I do have my doubts. I am saying you don't have to do this. I will get home just fine."

"Don't be dumb," he snaps.

I do so hate it when someone calls me dumb. I am cradled by and seething at this boy. It feels so strange being carried. Hamilton's arms are solid. I'd have thought they would shake with the strain, but nope. He holds firm like a forklift. Not the best comparison for my personal image, but it's accurate. The only show of strain is that he's breathing heavily through his nose.

"You're sweaty," he states.

Honestly, who says that to a person they are insisting on holding? I lower my shoe from my lap so it isn't right in his face. "Sorry, I was walking around for a while before I stopped to have lunch. That was when I heard all you all."

He huffs again in what I can only assume is disgust.

"If you are going to insist on doing this, then why don't you just put me on your back?" If he gave me a piggyback ride, I wouldn't have to watch him glower at me and my sweaty self wouldn't be so intrusive on his breathing.

"I'm fine."

My mama's manners slap me upside the head, and to fill the awkwardness, I say, "While I don't think this is necessary, I do thank you for being kind enough to see me home." The words actually hurt as they come out of my mouth, but I try to sound sweet.

"Not necessary?" Again, he comes at me with angry. "You think I would just leave you out there with an injury?" He stops talking for a few moments. "Why would you run in fear like that? You know there are wolves."

I flinch at his response. "I wasn't saying that. I was recognizing that you were doing a nice thing for me." I'm finally annoyed enough to meet his eyes in defiance. "So I will try it again. Thank you, Hamilton."

"You don't have to thank me." He's looking at me with such intensity I squirm. He looks down at my foot and picks up his pace. "We need to get ice on that."

We reach the woods behind my house, and Hamilton goes straight for the back door. He has to set me down, so I can get my key out of my backpack. While I'm rummaging for it, he puts his hand on the scratches the wolf had made. "It's no big deal." I dismiss the damage, not wanting to share my wolf with him. I unlock the door, and he lifts me up and moves me into the house.

"Where?" he asks, and I guess he wants to know which way to go to put me down.

I point toward the living room. He sets me on the sofa and finds every pillow he can to prop up my foot. Then he wanders off to our kitchen, and I hear him banging around. After a bit he returns with a plastic bag of ice wrapped in a kitchen towel.

"Thank you. I should be just dandy now." I'm working on the laces to my other boot as he walks back to me.

"Dandy? Who says that?"

Freeing my foot, I take a moment to enjoy the sensation you get whenever you get out of the tight article of clothing that has bound you for hours. You may not really notice it while it is on, but boy does it feel awful nice coming off. I look up to take the ice pack from Hamilton. He is staring down at me like I've just licked a squirrel's tail. "*I* do."

"Huh?" He seems surprised I have said something, and it obviously doesn't correlate with whatever is running through his head.

"I do. I say dandy, peachy keen, right as rain, happy as a clam, hunky dory, and many other things I learned growing up around my mama and her friends, and I would appreciate it if you would not make your snarky comments about it."

Would you believe he has the nerve to look hurt? "What do you mean?"

Is this guy kidding me? "Thank you for the ice pack and for carrying me all that way. That was really nice of you. I do appreciate it, but I am fine now. You can get back to your friends." I pull out and dust off the manners Mama instilled in me, after I notice I've dropped them like a hot potato just because I'm dealing with Hamilton. *"I should not sink to his level"* is on repeat in my mind.

"Where is your aunt?" his asks.

"She should be back any time now," I lie.

"What does that mean?"

"You do seem to be having trouble understanding me." I try to joke at his second question in as many minutes about what I mean. He doesn't find it funny.

"What time will she be back?" he says it slowly, almost like he has a bad phone connection.

"I don't rightly know," I respond just as slowly.

Hamilton searches the room for a moment then sits at the end of the sofa on the other side of my foot.

"What are you doing?" Panic takes over my face.

"You can't be alone." He of many words grumps.

"I most certainly can. I'm alone all the time. Me and alone are great friends." I'm babbling, I know, but that happens when I get flustered.

We sit starring at one another for… I'm not really sure how long. He breaks the moment by saying in a quiet growl, "I'm not leaving you."

"Why? I can handle it from here. My aunt will come home, and she'll take me to the doc in a box or the hospital if we decide it is necessary." I try reason. I should know better.

"Ha. How is your aunt going to get you to the car? She can't move a girl your size." He laughs like I channeled George Carlin.

I have nothing to say to that. I sit, blinking at this rude boy or man or whatever he is. Is he truly going to sit in my house insulting me until my aunt decides to come home? I look away from him, trying to figure out how to make him leave, short of throwing the table lamp at his head. It's too nice a lamp to waste on him.

I hear him making sniffing noises, and I look up sharply. This lunatic boy is leaning over slightly, smelling my foot—the same foot that has been in a hiking boot for hours. I defy any of you to be confident in what your foot smells like after a day of romping around in the woods. I jerk my foot away. In the hasty movement, I bump it on the back of the sofa, making me holler in pain. I close my eyes and shut my mouth to hold in all the swear words that are flashing through my mind.

"Why did you do that?" he asks, leaning back from me as if I'm the nut.

I have to take a couple deep breaths to get through the pain. Then a couple more to gather my thoughts enough to do anything but scream those obscenities, I've just choked back. "Why did I pull my sweaty foot away from someone who already tells people I—and I believe I am quoting here—'smell strange' end quote?" I put my finger to my chin in mock thought. "Let's see. Why would anyone do such a thing? Maybe so that same person can't run back to his friends and discuss the finer points of my need for odor eaters with my new classmates." My voice has somehow remained in a conversational tone.

"I didn't say that..."

"You most certainly did. The very first day I started at that school, in fact the very first minute I was a student, better yet, the very first words you ever said to me were that I stank." My voice has now lost its conversational tone. I'm firing off my words faster than bullets in a Wild West shoot out and just about as loud too.

"Stop yelling," he says calmly.

Dear heavens, I cannot stand when a person acts like they win simply because they are not as passionate about a subject. I think passion means you care, and I do care about this, so I think I'm in the right yelling and all.

"G.J.?" Aunt Celia calls from the front door as I hear the telltale slam that she is home.

Hamilton stands up quickly and acts like nothing's happening.

"The TV is really loud. I could hear it all the way outside." Distracted by digging in her purse, she doesn't see Hamilton until she is almost in the room. "Oh, hello." Aunt Celia sweeps her eyes from me to Hamilton. Focusing back on him, she narrows her eyes. "You're a Calhoun, aren't you?"

"Hamilton Calhoun. G.J. was hurt in the woods, so I brought her back here, and we were waiting for you." He pauses then adds, "Ma'am."

"G.J., are you all right?" Aunt Celia drops her purse and comes over to me.

"I think she should see a doctor. It looks like a bad sprain, but you should check for a break." Hamilton is being extra helpful.

"G.J., is it so bad you can't handle it?" Aunt Celia asks. She knows and I know I can normally heal my injuries. "Or do you not want to risk it?" Now she's asking if I'm not sure if I can do it with my abilities out of whack.

"I stayed to help get G.J. to the car," Hamilton explains.

"Aunt Celia, I will be fine. If you could take Hamilton home, I will take it easy and should heal up right quick." I'm letting her know, if he will leave, I will take care of it.

"Oh, of course. Hamilton, are you ready? I can run you home now. I just forgot the book, which won't take me but a second to grab. Thank you so much for seeing G.J. home."

"It was my pleasure," he says with all the sincerity of Eddie Haskle. I wish he were closer, so I could sock him, and I'm not normally a violent person.

"Great, I'll run and grab it. I am already late for book club, but I called and let them know I would be delayed." And, with that, Aunt Celia hurries off to grab what she needs.

"Book club? She wasn't going to be back 'any time now.' You need a doctor. What is wrong with you two?" he says in a hushed tone.

"Hamilton, I appreciate your concern, but I will be fine if you just leave me to handle it." I'm speaking quietly but vehemently right back as if we were arguing in a library.

He looks at my foot and then at me. "You will?" He sounds like I'm a pointy stick loose in his shoe. "Stay off that side of the hill." His eyes hold clear warning.

Aunt Celia comes back and they head off. I set to healing my foot. It is a handy trick being able to focus and fix things. With what a klutz I can be, it saved Mama and me loads on doctor's bills over the years. It does hurt like the dickens though, and I am not ashamed to say I let loose those curse words that I had been holding back so valiantly earlier.

Chapter Seven

Sadly, Monday actually arrives. I was hoping the world could just flash forward to Tuesday, but the space-time continuum isn't big on skipping steps without something Steven Hawking and friends are busy dreaming up or debunking. So, off I go to face the student body. I think it will be good to pretend I'm saying sorry to someone I like. As long as I won't have to speak directly to Sara I will be smooth as glass. Like I am ever smooth. Who am I kidding?

Classes are abbreviated for the assembly this afternoon, so it seems as if we just finish attendance as the bell rings sending us off to the next class. Sara spends the time in P.E. looking so superior that if classes weren't short, I might get dizzy from all the eye rolling that is required of me. Before it's a decent time for lunch, that's where I head.

I meet up with Nat at our table. I skip the lunch line entirely. There's a good chance my stomach will try its "throwing arm" out if I attempt to get anything into it. Nat looks at me with concern. "Are you going to make it?"

"Who me? I'll be fine once I hyperventilate in front of all my peers," I deadpan back.

Drake sits down across from us. "Ladies."

Nat glares at him.

"Drake, about Saturday…" I start.

"G.J., don't worry about it. You were upset. I'm glad you made it home all right. I was worried," Drake says. "No one noticed a thing."

"The people I sent flying didn't notice?" I ask skeptically.

"They thought a person had pushed into someone at the edge of the group and they all went tumbling. People believe what is easy," Drake explains.

"What are you doing here?" says a voice from behind me.

I close my eyes. Not Hamilton again. A tray slams down next to my arm. Opening my eyes, I see the world's most persistent persecutor taking the seat next to me.

Looking at me he asks, "Did you go to the doctor? I didn't get a chance to ask in P.E."

"Why do you need a doctor?" Drake and Nat ask at the same time. They look at each other, but Nat looks away.

"I don't need a doctor. It was nothing I could not handle." I'm doing my best to evade the subject, but Hamilton bulldozes forward like he's clearing way for a new super mall.

"Your foot was repulsive. I saw it, remember?"

"Why yes, I do remember. I also recall telling you I would be fine. And lookie here, I am as I said yesterday, dandy." I turn my profile to him.

"Don't give me that. I am the one who had to haul you out of the trees." He actually sounds angry with me.

"I didn't ask you to. In fact, I believe I asked you not to." It's a wonder the words make it past the locking of my jaw.

Drake asks, "What happened?"

"I twisted my ankle while walking in the woods. Hamilton was kind enough to come help me out. But it really wasn't necessary." I really want this to end.

"You were running away from me and sprained your ankle or worse on the steep hill behind my house, which you should not have been on in the first place." Hamilton is glowering.

"Hamilton?" Drake seems to ask Hamilton some unspoken question.

"It wasn't like that. I wasn't chasing her. I was just trying to catch up with her." Hamilton is now on the defensive.

"I didn't know it was your house. I didn't even know you were there. I told you." I'm repeating myself like a bad country song.

"Why, when we saw you, did you run?" Hamilton Calhoun is actually trying to sound reasonable.

Nat bursts out laughing, and Drake smiles. I have a feeling it's due to the spluttering noises I'm making trying to free up some retort that will just *not* shake free.

"G.J.," Nat's breathing hard, trying to catch her breath or put the brakes on her laughter. "Do you think running from Hamilton was a good plan?"

"This was not a planned moment at all. I was caught off guard when I saw them there. So I just wanted to leave as quickly as possible. Running was my best option available for as fast as possible."

"Them?" Drake looks at me with a more serious demeanor.

"Yes, Hamilton and all his friends," I answer.

Drake's face is as angry as I have ever seen him. I have no idea what's going on. "What happened to your leg?"

"It was cool. I caught up to her by myself and carried her home." Hamilton sounds as if he is convincing Drake about something, but I have no clue what. From the corner of my eye, I think I see Hamilton shake his head.

Drake's voice fills with skepticism as he says, "Really? By yourself?"

"Maybe you couldn't handle it, and I'm not saying it was easy, but yeah by *myself*." Hamilton answers.

At this discussion of how hard it was to carry me without the aid of a crane or tamed elephant, I decide I've had enough. "I am off. Here's hoping the whole student body gets sick, so no one is there for my public humiliation."

Hamilton starts to stand too. Looking at him in challenge, he says, "Your ankle can't take all your weight. It'd be too much for anyone." And once again he has found the sweet spot in the seven-minute conversation lull of the cafeteria so everyone hears him.

I glare, and Nat narrates my sentiment by saying, "Hamilton, you are such an idiot."

I leave without another word.

Science class seems a little empty. Adam is there at the table and waives me over excitedly. "Hey, G.J.. Thanks for coming to the match. I'm sorry I missed you after."

"Oh." The match was the last thing on my mind. "Thank you for inviting me. It's an amazing sport. I really don't know too much about it, but I would love to learn," I say in all sincerity.

"You liked it?" he asks in open anticipation.

I smile. "Yes, indeed I do. I'm not a person who feels comfortable when they don't understand the lingo though."

"I can explain whatever you like," he eagerly adds.

"Sounds great," I slip in before Mr. Alberts begins class.

Drake isn't in science. I wonder where he's gone. When class is over, Adam walks me to my next classroom. He's so sweet not to mention my little romp in the woods. I know he had seen me plain as day. He, at least, is a gentleman.

My last class is almost completely empty. And it's down to me and three other students when one of my classmates asks for a pass to go to the nurse. On the way to the auditorium there are crowds trying to get in the bathrooms. That's my first indication something is wrong.

Walking in to meet my fate Mr. Decker, a woman I have never seen and Gus are all standing on stage. Mr. Decker waives me over. "Ah good, G.J.."

I hesitantly walk up to the stage. Gus is fiddling with the sound system but stops and gives me a wink and a smile. I smile back. The woman is standing up from drawing a circle on the ground in front of the podium. "You'll stand right where I marked," she says, imperiously to me indicating the circle.

I nod. "I'm sorry, I don't believe we've met. I'm G.J. Gardener." I hold out my hand in introduction.

"I know exactly who you are, young lady," the woman snaps at me. "I am Mrs. Ackers, Sara's mother. You should be ashamed of yourself."

I should have known. In keeping with my strict "respect your elders" upbringing, I choose to keep my mouth shut. I mean how does one approach the subject of her being the parent of one of the most hateful people I have ever met? She is a well-dressed, petite woman. Sara favors her mother in more ways than just in bitchiness. They both might get a few more compliments on how pretty they are if they didn't look like they just pounded a movie theater sized box of Sour Patch Kids. You can tell appearance is as important to them as are brand names. For me, high end is the Isaac Mizrahi I have from Target. God bless that man for his fashion for the masses. It would be nice though if his sizings weren't for young men's bodies. Most ladies have a curve somewhere on them. I personally have more than my share. Mrs. Ackers is sporting a designer suit and Louis Vuitton shoes. I am not too big to admit I'm jealous of those shoes. I am certain there will not be a need for high heels for me in my lifetime, but I do love the look of cute shoes.

Mr. Decker peeks up as a teacher waddles in the way adults do when they feel like they are too old to run or their slip-on shoes might go flying if they try. She reaches Mr. Decker, whispering and wildly gestures. Reminding me of a humming bird feeding, she buzzes up to his ear, sticking her mouth close , quickly pulls back, and flutters till it's time to buzz up again. Mr. Decker appears concerned and asks for our forgiveness while he checks on something.

Mrs. Ackers is fidgeting and mumbling to herself. I start to feel bad now that I know Sara's mama is the loose bulb in the chandelier. She looks hard at me then fidgets even more and mumbles faster. Gus takes the moment to sidle up and say hello.

"Do you think we should find out if she's missed a dose of medication?" I ask him.

"You don't seem bothered by what she is doing," he says with some curiosity.

"Who me? People like that don't trouble me. There was a guy who hung out in front of our dollar store back home. He would always have a shopping cart full of recyclable cans. Only when I say always, I mean it. He never did turn one can in to be recycled. He just liked to have all the cans. Now I don't know about up here, but canned beer is big down where I used to live, and most people drink at least one Coca Cola every day. Ernie, that was the can man's name, he got so many cans he had to tie them onto his grocery cart, and when he was behind it, you could not even see the top of his head. Well, he had a lot to say to himself, too. But when he spoke to Mama and me, he was as nice as can be. As long as you did not mention the cans, he tended to be a little jealous and protective. He was just sure everyone coveted his cans." My nervous babble is on the loose again.

Gus laughs. "You really can't tell what she's doing? She's been in here since lunch."

Not clear on what he is talking about, I ignore him and move on. "Do I need to do a sound check for you or something?"

"No, I've got it covered," he says.

I start looking around nervously at the empty room. "Where is everyone?"

Gus shrugs. "I have no idea, but this is odd. Do me a favor. On your way to the podium, drag your feet."

"I don't want this to take any longer than necessary," I reply.

"No, I mean make sure you break that circle on the ground with your feet. It's important, G.J.. Just do it." He's very serious, and I decide to honor the request, because if someone gives you an ominous warning, I have seen enough movies to know you follow the appeal. Or else. I never have liked the "or elses" in plots. That's always where the people you were rooting for have the worst things happen to them.

"All right, I will."

Mr. Decker comes back in just then. "Well, it looks like the assembly is off."

Mrs. Ackers is on her feet, declaring her outrage. "Why on earth would you do such a thing?"

"Unfortunately every pupil in this school is going home sick." Mr. Decker's face shows concern. "We have called the local authorities, and the CDC has been contacted."

I grab Gus's arm for support. "Dear mercy."

"G.J., are you ill too?" Mr. Decker is torn between wanting to show care and not wanting to get anywhere near the plague that must be in this building.

"I got her, Mr. Decker." Gus takes me over to a seat behind the stage.

"Where is Sara?" Mrs. Ackers asks almost frantic.

"Either in line for a restroom or at the nurse's office. There is a line there as well," Mr. Decker informs her.

As she hustles herself out of the auditorium, she turns to say, "This is not finished. You, young lady, will pay for what you have done to Sara."

"Do Sara and she subscribe to *Bad Villain Quote* magazine?" I wonder aloud once the door closes behind her.

"I need to go meet the authorities when they arrive." Mr. Decker excuses himself, ignoring my comment. I have a feeling he's hoping the CDC will give him one of their full-body hazmat suits if he's really nice to them when they get here.

Gus is rubbing my back in slow circles. "You okay?"

"Yeah, but I think this may be my fault," I confess dismally.

"Why would you think that?"

"At lunch I wished this would happen and now it has. I didn't mean it. I mean, I guess I did, but heavens." I shake my head in disbelief that I've infected a whole school with the hurls by making an off-handed remark.

"G.J., what are you talking about?" Gus asks.

I can't believe I'm responsible for this epidemic. Who wants to be the start of a mass illness? I bet you could take a poll and, with the exception of a few dictators, there would not be one person who said, "Ooh ooh, me, me, me." I'm just staring off in my mental woes.

"G.J.?" Gus is so concerned it's sweet.

"Gus." I take a deep breath. "I can do things. With my mind. Big scary things and, well, I think I just did."

"Okay? Show me what you mean," he says not seeming at all curious about the part of that confession; I think a body should be.

"I really don't want to cause any more trouble." I'll admit I'm whining like Luke Skywalker in episode IV.

"You won't. Try something small," he urges me.

In need of a confidant that is not painting a bathroom Technicolor, I try to push Gus back. Nothing happens. Not wanting to overdo it, I try to move the podium. It slams into the back wall of the stage, splintering. "Whoops."

Gus looks at it stunned and horrified. "How? What did you do?"

"Well, the good news is I tried to do that to you, but it wasn't working, so I switched to the podium." I'm relived I hadn't done that to Gus.

Gus looks at me for a long moment. "What did you do to make that happen?"

"Willed it."

"Did you say a charm or do you have a circle somewhere nearby that you are channeling?" he asks in a desperate need to figure it out.

"No, I just make things like that happen. What am I supposed to tell the CDC? 'Hey y'all, I just made several hundred people sick. You can pack it up and head on home.' They'll take me in, and I will end up in some government program like those movies Drew Barrymore made at the beginning of her career." Here comes that yammering I tend to do.

"But it won't work on me?" Gus asks now fascinated.

"It didn't. I'm afraid to try again."

"Don't be. Give it your best shot."

"Gus, honey, I like you too much to want to turn you into matchsticks," I protest.

He pats my knee. "I like you too, G.J., but I know you won't hurt me."

It is the knee pat that convinces me. I fling my will at Gus, but not a thing happens. It is like an opera singer on mute. I can tell something is leaving me, but there's no production of what I'm trying to do.

"See," Gus says confidently and puts his arm around my shoulders. "I didn't think anyone like you existed anymore."

"Pardon?" I am so befuddled.

"You are a Witch. A true Witch. I'm surprised there are any of you around any longer. I thought between the Crusades, the Trials, and poor bloodlines your kind dwindled down to nothing, but I guess there were some latent men who have carried on. Hmm…" He eyes me speculatively.

"I'm not a Witch. I do not have a cat, I don't ride a broom, and I swear I have never believed the woo-woo about crystals. I do not even own one peasant skirt."

Gus smiles. "Those may be the marks of the Wiccans but not a true Witch. That explains Mrs. Ackers," he says like he's figured something out. "Who is your father?"

"I don't rightly know," I say a bit sheepish. "My mama never told me."

"Interesting." Gus is deep in thought.

"Gus, what in the name of Uncle Sam are you saying?"

"Do you love nature?" he asks.

"What does that have—?"

"Answer the question," he overrides my objection.

"Yes." I huff at him.

"Are you good with animals?"

I think of my wolf in particular and nod.

"Do you need to perform any kind of ritual to produce magic?"

"I don't do magic," I protest. The look on his face makes that statement seem a bit silly I qualify. "I just am able to do stuff." Yes, I know that sounds lame.

"Don't be embarrassed. Be proud of what you can do. There has not been a true Witch around in a very long time. Like over one hundred years. Remember the Trials were back in 1692-93. While they got rid of several Wiccans and some women who were not at all of power, there were not many Witches left after the Crusades, so the trials about ended them. The hardest part was that the Wiccans who were killed were the good ones, the ones who thought of

Wicca as a way to be part of the earth and the power of nature. They used the energy they could collect to move the environment to a better spiritual plain. The ones who escaped and carried on were the ones who could lie and play to the nastier side of politics. This really hurt the religion. Many feared openly believing in Wicca, which made them hide and keep the knowledge private. In the Americas, the Puritan faith rejected the mere idea of Wicca, and in the battle between the two powers, the male-dominated world obliterated the female-driven Wicca.

"Wicca did originate from Witches. The power of the Witch is in the woman. Witches wanted to share their connectivity with nature, and the knowledge that comes with that with every woman. There are male Witches, but they never have the strength of the female. Women are the embodiment of nature. They have cycles, they nurture, they give bounty or food, and shelter. Isn't that what nature itself does for us? The female body is nature's most powerful creation. It is the mirror of nature itself. It only makes sense that females carry the strongest gifts they have to bestow." He is on a roll.

Thinking of Hamilton carrying me out of the woods, and the wrestling meet, I'm not fully signed on to the strongest part, but I haven't heard most of this and want to hear him out before I form any conclusions. That is just the way I work. So, I encourage him to continue.

Almost as if he has read my thoughts, he goes on. "Men have physical strength, but they thirst for what a woman has to offer. This can manifest itself in many ways. Some men acknowledge their mothers, sisters, spouses, or other influential females have given them some inestimable thing that has made them better. When there is a disconnect between the main female influences in their lives, many psychologists suggest this is where some lifelong troubles begin. Men are

genetically coded to crave the female form. It can be a bit
obsessive. The coveting can turn into a need to dominate
or control, but this does not come from superiority; it
comes from the feelings of inferiority for which they have
to overcompensate. Some men desire to be women and offer
to the world the gifts traditionally thought of as female. It
is all very interesting. If you view history from all sides of
the prism, not just the best-propagated version, you can
see how much PR has controlled how women are viewed.
Some women who knew 'healing' were no more than early
physicians, but they were called evil because they understood
more and questioned the established male-dominated field.
To keep their customers, so to speak, the physicians of the
time discredited anyone who would challenge their profession,
as did priests who chose prayer as the only form of healing.
Medicine would be much further along had they chosen a
different path. Some of those healers were actual Witches
though, and that is why the myth prevailed. Religion played
a key role in suppressing all women, not just the Wiccans."

"Um, Gus, darling', how do you know all this? I mean
is your TV limited to the History Channel and the local
ERA movement's cable show?" What he is saying is a touch
too much like the theories of those people who are waiting
to catch a ride on a comet's tail. And I am too tall to wear
tinfoil on my head. I might end up the local cell tower if I
do. Besides, you can say what you want. I know Jesus walked
this earth, suffered, and died to save my soul. If you don't
believe, don't. I don't think the measure of your humanity
is how big your Bible is. Living in the south and growing
up the only child of a single mom, I have heard the most
pious of folks use the gift of the word to bludgeon. I don't
think those people really believe either. If you choose to be
a good person and do what you can to help the world out,

then you get the message. You just don't care to give credit. I'd take the non-believer saint over the constantly-begging-for-forgiveness faithful sinner any day. At some point you really do have to wonder if God is thinking, "You again? What is it this time?" I am sure those folks are going to max out their "get out of hell free" cards. But I am not supposed to judge, so I will let whoever handles that worry after them.

"I've picked a few things up over the years." Gus's smile is spectacular. "But getting back to you. Witches draw energy that comes from everything: emotions, movement, wind, sun, rain, earth, animals, plants, people, and whatever. Wiccans try to call on the elements by drawing circles, but usually the earth gives them their power. The rest of the elements can be controlled somewhat, but they have to direct the energy of whatever element they are working with. They can make the wind a strong breeze or have a fire grow large. They can influence water to move or not. Witches, true Witches, can pull the power in them in order to conduct magic. G.J., if trained, you could do almost anything. If you were to combine ritual with your natural ability, you could be one of the most incredible beings to inhabit the planet in quite some time."

"Is this your version of a pickup line?" If my face is reflecting the full force of my skepticism, Gus will never need it defined for him again in his life.

"You are amazing." Gus tries to continue to praise me, but I tend to handle compliments like hot potatoes.

"So do you think I could make everyone healthy? I mean, I did just change the altar everyone in this school prays to the holy porcelain one. Before there is a run on candles and a full-out shrine is built, I'd like to set that right." I feel so bad that I have made everyone sick.

"Give it a shot." Gus encourages with a "why not?" shrug.

I think about the kids in the school and send my will out to undo the illness in them. I close my eyes and push out with my mind. Vaguely, I hear Gus mumble something like "I thought so." After a few seconds, I open my eyes.

"Now what?" I ask.

"Let's go see." Gus stands and offers me a hand up. He continues to hold my hand as we move toward the auditorium doors.

"How come you weren't sick?" I ask.

"Witches have no effect on me." Gus is being somewhat evasive; I can tell.

"If there hasn't been anyone like me in over one hundred years, how do you know?" See, logic is often a frequent guest in my head.

The doors open and Adam comes in looking flustered. He spots me, and his face registers relief, and then annoyance as fast as flipping channels on the TV. "Hey, G.J., are you all right?" He walks up and reaches out for my hand still joined to Gus.

Gus pulls back on our hands so fast the change in inertia shocks my arm, and I slightly stumble behind him. I let out a shocked squeak, or maybe it's a chirp. Whatever it is, it leaves an embarrassing echo rolling around the room. Gus answers for me. "She is fine." His voice doesn't hold the same kind of fun quality I usually hear in its tone.

"I didn't get sick, Adam. Are you all right?" I ask from over Gus's shoulder. He does look a bit disheveled. I don't care if you are the most practiced of bulimics, you can always tell if someone has wretched. They just have this look like they did all they could to keep their eyes in their sockets.

"I'm fine now. Thanks for asking. I came to get you. My dad came to pick me up and school is being closed early because of everyone getting sick. I'd like to take you home, if it's okay with your aunt." He's looking at Gus with caution.

"Wow, um, that is awful nice of you, Adam. Did you happen to notice if anyone besides you is doing better?" I'm still worried.

Gus is still holding my hand behind his back. "Have you seen Mrs. Ackers?" Gus asks Adam.

Answering me first Adam says, "It seemed like everyone just stopped. The nurse said it was probably food poisoning. Mr. Decker is going to have the CDC check the cafeteria when they arrive." He looks at Gus. "She was signing Sara out down in the front office last I saw her. Why?"

"She threatened G.J.." Although I'm behind Gus, whatever silent communication is happening between the two of them registers a response on Adam's face.

His eyebrows rise. Adam asks me again, "Are you okay?"

"I'm fine. I think 'threaten' is a strong word. She is just defensive of her baby. I understand. I mean, I did give Sara the black-eye equivalent of a Zorro mask. And then that other mess. So I don't blame her for being a little spiteful," I say. "Shoot, if somebody did that to anybody I love, I might do a pretty good impression of Loki from the Marvel comics."

At that, Gus turns and both he and Adam look at me. Gus takes a second, shakes his head, and says, "If you go with Adam, will you be okay? I need to clean up the stage and build another podium before anyone notices."

"Oh, gosh, I'm sorry." I really hadn't meant to create smithereens out of school property.

"Don't worry. It won't take long," Gus says. Then he places my hand in Adam's. "I'm trusting you to watch her."

"I still need to call my aunt and go by my locker." I fish my cell phone out of my back pocket. Gus takes it and, faster than those kids who win texting championships, dials something. I hear a buzzing from his pants.

"I'll call you later," Gus says.

"Not smart, dude," Adam says.

"I'm not worried," Gus replies dryly.

I slide my phone from his hands while trying to figure out what all the posturing is about. Pulling my hand from Adam's, I take a few steps away and call Aunt Celia. The two boys behind me move closer together in a huddled private chat.

I tell Aunt Celia I'm fine, and I will get a ride home with Adam. She tells me to say "hello" to his father. Then she says, "Guess now is as good of a time as any for you two to meet." I think that is awful nice, and it makes me feel better that she knows who these people are and wants to introduce me to her friends. As I hang up, I turn back and say, "All set."

I catch the tail end of Adam saying coolly, "…one on one no, maybe not, but there isn't just one…" He stops realizing my attention is back on them.

Gus catches my hand and actually kisses the back of it, which just makes Adam grab it away from him. "Later, G.J.," Gus says as Adam leads me away.

I look over my shoulder and glance at the stage. I had not noticed until now that right about where the podium had been there is a scorch mark on the stage floor itself. Did I do that?

Chapter Eight

The boy Chris, who had been with Adam and Hamilton at lunch the day I sent Drake flying into them, is sitting in the front seat. Adam takes my backpack and walks to the trunk as I slide into the back seat. I'm halfway in as I realize Hamilton is sitting behind a man I assume is Adam's Dad. Before I can back out and find another way home, Adam gives me a nudge, and I end up between the two broad-shouldered boys in the back of this mid-sized car. Why? Please tell me what I did to deserve this. Actually, I think this one is my fault. Why had I not realized they would all ride together?

"You must be G.J.. I have heard a lot about you. I'm Jack Wyfle, Adam's dad. How are you feeling? The boys seem to be fine now, but when I got the call, I was very worried. These guys never get sick." He has a rich warm voice and looks like Adam will once his features settle into manhood. He heads the car out onto the main road.

My shoulders cannot find a comfortable position, so I am at an awkward angle. The shoulder near Hamilton forced forward and the one toward Adam forced behind, so my torso is facing Adam. I turn my head to reply. "Thank you so much for the ride, Mr. Wyfle. I am sorrier than I can say that everyone got so sick. But I am just fine. I did not get ill at all. My Aunt Celia asked me to say 'hello' to you. We hope we aren't putting you out by the favor." This is just how you address adult folks back home, but silence reigns in the car like they aren't sure I'll stop talking.

"Please tell her it is no trouble, and 'hello' back. How is she doing today?" Mr. Wyfle looks at me in the rearview mirror with a smile in his eyes.

I am still in my contorted position, trying not to settle in to touching the boys I am pressed against. That is almost impossible, but I tell myself to give it my best effort, so I do. "Well, she is just fine. Thank you for asking. It is new for both of us, me living with her, but Aunt Celia's great, and we are getting along."

"I was sorry to hear about your mother. Please accept our condolences," Mr. Wyfle says with genuine sincerity.

A little taken aback, I think Mr. Wyfle is the first person to offer condolences since I've been here. My voice breaks slightly. "Um, thank you. That is right nice of you to say." There is nowhere to look away with Adam one way, Hamilton the other, and Mr. Wyfle flicking his glance in the rearview mirror while driving. I decide looking down is as good an option as I have at the moment.

All of a sudden, Hamilton lurches his arm from where it is wedged behind me. In doing so, he slams me forward into Adam, or rather my forehead into Adam's teeth. "Ow," Adam and I cry out at once. I slap the spot that the pain is radiating from. I'm trying to find the path of least humiliation for me to check for damage. Opening one eye, I see Adam, and he has blood all over his teeth and chin. His eyes are squeezed shut, and in a warning voice, he calls out, "Dad."

That rumbling earthquake sound returns. Mr. Wyfle calls out, "Hamilton?" in a stern questioning voice as he pulls the car over.

Hamilton lifts me back over his lap, laying me across him. I have no intention of staying in such an awkward position, and my head feels concussed and wet. Mr. Wyfle turns from the driver's seat surveying in the back of the car. "Whose is it?" he barks at his son.

Adam looks sick. "It's hers."

Hamilton tugs on the hand I'm using to cover my head, and I see the blood. Now I have never been the subject of one of those "When Animals Attack" videos, but all four of the men in the car look like wild creatures about to charge. "I'm all right, if you would just let me up." I'm still struggling against Hamilton's hold.

Adam flings himself out of the car. Mr. Wyfle looks at Hamilton. "Can you keep it together?"

"I won't hurt her," is his response. Mr. Wyfle might buy that, but I sure don't.

"Chris, get out. Now." Mr. Wyfle orders fire at the boy. "I'll take care of them." And he too leaves the vehicle, slamming the driver's door as cars whiz past us.

"Will you get off me now?" I struggle against Hamilton's hold harder now that we are alone.

"You're bleeding," is his reply, and he doesn't let me go.

"Hamilton," I say in a calm voice. "I will be fine. Just let me up."

"Adam bit you." It's almost like he's become a primordial man with short bursts of words based on immediate thoughts.

"Be reasonable. Adam did not bite me. You shoved me at him, and my head hit his teeth. It was what normal people call an accident." I'll admit my condescension is not pretty.

"He has your blood in his mouth. He could have swallowed it." He looks out the window toward the passing traffic.

"Well, now that is an unsettling thought. Especially given that it might be the only thing in his stomach after today's, um, group sick events." I screw my face up in disgust, but then my forehead hurts so I stop.

"You are going to have a mark from his teeth on your forehead. Everyone will see it. Doesn't that bother you?" He has the strangest look of disbelief and hurt on his face, but maybe it's the odd angle I'm seeing him from.

"Hamilton, I won't have a scar. Why does this bother you? This is the most awkward way to hold a discussion. Would you please let me up?" I ask really nice or as nicely as I can drum up at the moment.

"You're bleeding." He still refuses to let me up. "How can this do anything but drive me crazy?" He looks down at me with regret.

"It was an accident." I'm somehow in the role of consoler. How did that happen?

"Oh man, Adam." Hamilton's hand shoots forward over my head and smashes into the headrest in front of us.

Needless to say, having been raised by a single woman, large displays of testosterone tend to make me jumpy. "Hamilton, could you please define 'accident' for me to the best of your ability?" I'm still trying to rationalize with him.

"You don't understand." He looks out the window again.

"No, I think I do grasp the meaning of the word 'accident'. I'm not sure *you* do. Look, this is no big deal. Don't let this freak you out, okay."

He looks at me, and his eyes scream *how can it not*, but he doesn't say a word.

"Look, you know… you were right… yesterday my ankle… it was bad." I have to do this delicately.

His eyes take on a moment of victory.

"But obviously, I'm fine now. Right?" I wait for his concession before I go on.

He nods slowly, a little unsure.

"Watch." I close my eyes and focus on healing my forehead. It doesn't take long.

Hamilton stares at me. He takes his thumb and wipes my forehead. But that isn't good enough, so he licks his thumb and wipes again. That does it for me. "Ew, get off. You are not my mama. You don't spit-clean a person you aren't related to. Ugh, who does that?" This time he lets me fight my way upright.

"That is amazing." Finally comes free from his thoughts.

"It is a good trick." I smile. "So I am not sure what to tell the others, but I am okay. If Adam is okay, we have what you call a little deal, not a big one. Everybody can relax."

Hamilton sits there so long doing some sort of mental ping-pong that he is not letting me in on. I think he has a whole debate team in his head. Finally moving, he reaches out carefully and smoothes his fingers against my forehead. "You don't have a mark at all," he says in wonder.

"Nope, not a scratch on me," I say cheerfully.

"How?"

"Please don't ask. I won't tell you. Then, you'll get huffy and start finding ways to say unpleasant things about me that I've never even considered. I feel like we've had a moment here, Hamilton. Let's not spoil it." I turn and start to look around the car for where the others have gone.

"G.J., what…" Hamilton begins, but luckily Mr. Wyfle hops back in the driver's seat.

Turning he looks at me then Hamilton. "Everything okay in here?"

"Yes sir. I'm fine. Not sure what happened, but I am just fine," I say.

"There's no mark on you." Mr. Wyfle looks to Hamilton then back to me. "You don't have a mark." He seems a bit stunned.

"No, sir, not a mark on me," I say and shoot Hamilton a sideways glance to confirm he won't spill the beans.

Mr. Wyfle hoots a great-relieved laugh. "Thank God. I would never have had a chance with your aunt if that had happened." He turns forward, still laughing. Hamilton seems to ease back in the seat a bit. Maybe the older man makes him calmer. Mr. Wyfle focuses his attention on pulling out into traffic.

Good thing he does or he would have had to catch the eyeballs that I am sure are popping out of my head. Mr. Wyfle is hitting on Aunt Celia? No wonder Adam has been so nice to me. My head is doing its best impression of the teacup amusement park ride. I honestly can't pick a thought and actually think on it. I finally realize we are moving again with less than the number we started with on this wild ride.

"Mr. Wyfle, where are Adam and Chris?" I ask in alarm, turning back to see if they are still on the side of the road.

"The boys decided to run home," he says as if that makes any sense at all.

"They'll be fine, G.J.." Hamilton spreads his legs and lays his arm across the back of the seat.

I try to take up as little room as possible, pressing my body up against the back passenger door. My hair keeps catching on something behind me, and I run my hand down to smooth it several times, but every time I do, it feels like nothing is there—although, I do bump Hamilton's hand once. I'm so relieved to get home that I think I know how happy the Pilgrims were to see Plymouth Rock. I say my thank you's as the car is pulling up. As it comes to a complete stop, I hop out like grease from a griddle.

From his rolled-down window, Mr. Wyfle says, "G.J., we're all so relieved you were not marked. Please tell your aunt I will call her tonight."

I wave and scoot in the house as fast as I can. The car sits outside for a minute. I really don't care what they do. I just need to go out to the woods. Now. I have to clear my head. I go straight to the back door. I'm almost to the tree line when Hamilton calls out, "Where are you going?"

I let a swear word own prime real estate on the tip of my tongue. I take a deep breath and turn. "I just need some air," I call down the hill to him. "Was there something else?"

Hamilton is standing at the side of the house like he had come around back. He holds up my book bag that I'd left in the trunk.

That swear word is right at home on the verge of spilling out of my mouth. I hold back with all those lessons of Mama's. "Thank you. I plain forgot." I walk back down the hill in defeat.

He stands, holding it out and making me walk all the way to him. A normal person would meet me halfway. But I think we have established Hamilton is not normal. After reaching him, he pulls back at the last second, making me look him in the face. "You should clean up before you go in the woods. You have blood on you. You should never go in the woods with blood on you."

He has a point, so I nod and reach for my bag again.

Again, he pulls it away so I will look him in the eye. "Stay off the steep side of the hill."

I grab my bag and start to walk away. Over my shoulder, in a growl of frustration, I call out, "Hamilton, I am not stalking you." I hear him laughing as I slam the back door behind me.

Chapter Nine

After putting away my book bag, I decide to call Nat and make sure she's all right. What a bad friend I am. She's probably worried. When I do finally reach her, I make several layers of apologies. Nat is sure I had made her, as she puts it, an "Olympic medalist of vomiting." I tell her I'm not sure that is an actual sport and she tells me of course it is; Ancient Greece is where vomitoriums are from. I feel pointing out that it's Ancient *Rome,* and that they were actually corridors in the Coliseum not rooms where you puked, would add insult to injury, so I let her roll with it. She makes me swear that if I make any more offhanded comments, I have to say the phrase, "Except Nat." I'm not sure how helpful this will be, but I agree in order to mend the fence.

Hanging up, I decide the coast must be clear and head back to the woods. It's only been about fifteen minutes, when I catch a quick movement from the corner of my eye. Scanning the woods to see what it is, I see the pelt of a wolf behind a tree. It takes a three count in my head to realize this is not my wolf. It is as big but has different brown markings on its coat. That swear word from earlier is back in position. I look at the wolf, and it looks at me. Its head lowers. Not in submission though. Is it curious?

"Hey, big guy," I say softly. Then I see the smaller second wolf. Nervously I amend, "Guys?"

The second wolf isn't my wolf either. So far, these two aren't growling or aggressive. The first wolf looks me right in the face. Wolves have these amazing golden eyes that are true breath stealers. I'm entranced. The smaller wolf moves closer. I'm not afraid. Both slowly edge closer, sniffing the air as they come. I wish I had some ability to tell what's happening with their emotions before they get too close. They can smell fear, so I'm glad I'm in the insane state of not being afraid of them. Why am I unafraid? Well, I think that goes along the lines of why I like hot sauce on my eggs; it's just the way it is.

"Hey there, handsome fellas. Are you out for a walk, too?" I ask.

The brown wolf is close enough for me to reach out my hand. He doesn't lick or sniff it. He rubs his head under it so my hand caresses him. He repeats the move until I pick up my own rhythm of petting. He sits down next to me. The smaller wolf lays down a short ways away, panting and lazily watching us.

"You just looking for some love? We all need some snuggling now and again." I pet him for a while, then feel like this is going on too long. "I really came out for a walk. So as nice as this is, I'd like to get moving."

I stop petting and begin to move away. The smaller wolf that has been lying down gets to his feet and growls. The brown wolf turns his head lightning fast and nips my arm. Luckily, all he gets is my sleeve. This produces that fear reaction I had previously escaped. From behind me, I hear a low rumbling growl that is far louder than the one from the second wolf. Dear heavens, I'm in the middle of a pack of wolves. Pulling my sleeve hard out of the brown wolf's mouth, it catches on his tooth as I yank, and he and I yip in pain and surprise as the cloth breaks free. I turn just in time to see my wolf charge.

The smaller wolf knocks my wolf to the side in mid lunge. The brown wolf races in to join the fray. They seem to tumble and roll snapping and biting. I'd thought these three were packing up on me, but I realize my wolf is trying to defend me. There are squeals of pain and I can tell that at least one is bleeding. It is violence in its raw state. My heart feels like it will explode the beats are so hard and close together. I'm panting right along with the wolves as they tear and lunge at each other. I know I have said before that I am rather a smart cookie, but that is only when my brain is working. It isn't at the moment. Horror has frozen every cell I use to form thoughts. My wolf keeps turning to me,—barking— but I'm not picking up his message whatever it is. Two against one is not a fair fight, but my wolf is holding his own and then some. He is unstoppable.

I hear the crack as his jaws snap the rear leg of the smaller wolf, who made an echoing shriek of agony. He folds over on himself and starts licking the injury stemming the flow of blood. The brown wolf uses the moment to bite into the shoulder of my wolf, barely missing his neck. The miss cost him. My wolf turns and gets hold of the other one under the chin, pinning him to the ground by his throat.

Blood pours from a shoulder wound on my wolf. This is what brings my brain cells out of their cryo state. I use my will to separate all three wolves. My wolf growls in disapproval and gives me his most menacing stare. "Hush up. You're bleeding," I admonish him.

He tries to come toward me, but I have him held in place. Growling, he shows me how much he likes this tether.

"I need you three to cool it. My heart can't take this. Seriously. I will not watch you kill each other. I am not one of those wildlife photographers who film the whole life of an animal then blithely keep filming as the animal gets slaughtered. I never have abided them sitting back and watching it happen once they are emotionally invested. So hush. Now, I'm gonna heal you. But when I am done, I won't have you tear at each other again. So don't do it. Just calm down." I say, trying to get a hold of the situation and my emotions.

My wolf makes some strange sound, almost of protest, but I go forward with the healing. It takes a bit, but after a minute or two, I'm pretty sure they are all patched up. "I'm going to let you go now. If you have at each other again, I will separate you again. Got it?" I'm using my stern voice.

My wolf pads over to my side and sits down in what I guess is a sign of protection. I shake my head. The other two have their heads lowered and turned to the side with their necks exposed in submission. I look down at my very-proud-of-himself wolf. "Okay, hot stuff, no need to gloat."

He turns his head under my hand and licks my fingers. The brown wolf whimpers. My wolf turns his head and gives him a look of warning. Noticing his smug state, I want to go console the other wolf but am afraid if I do, I will start another fight. I do, however, say, "Look, tough guy. I'm not sure what you think you just proved, but I am not a bone to be fought over. You may have these two cowed, but I am not so easily impressed."

I'm not sure if his next action is in response to what I said or if he's just trying to shut me up, but he jumps up, putting his large paws on my shoulders and knocking me to the ground. I yelp, and the other two wolves charge forward again. My wolf stands over me with his head lowered, growling a warning to the other two to stay back. I use the moment to push him off me with my will, suspending him in midair. He barks at me in protest and whimpers. The other two wolves skid back, staring in disbelief.

I stand and dust myself off. Then I look up into the face of my wolf as he hangs there annoyed and uncertain. "Listen up. You will not do that again. You hear me. You are not the boss of me. I will hang out with you as long as you don't try to be my Alpha."

Would you believe that crazy animal, while in the defenseless position of literally twisting in the wind, tries to intimidate me? We have a world-class staring match. He won't back down. Floating and all, this animal still thinks he is in charge. The other two wolves stand beside me, looking between the two of us. "Have you had enough?"

My wolf still sends me his defiant stare.

"I have homework to do. I will let you down, but I mean it. People will call you the Tinkerbell wolf if you try that again." The other two wolves chuff.

Letting him down, he lowers his head in annoyance and won't look at me. Well, that makes me feel bad. I don't like that I've hurt his feelings. The other two wolves watch us. I put my hand out in peace. My wolf just looks at it and then turns away. "Okay, I'm sorry," I say, my hand still outstretched. He looks again then away again. I don't want to leave it like this, but how exactly do you make up with a wolf? I go to him and get down on my knees, petting his neck gently. Still he turns away. I put my arms around his neck and hug him as my last-ditch effort to make amends. It takes him a second, but he turns his head into the embrace, snuffling my neck. He starts to lick me and goes a little hog wild pushing his nose across my jaw and taking a dominant stance over me.

"You just can't help yourself, can you?" I laugh as the licks tickle me. "Okay, okay, I am glad we made peace, but I do have to go now."

He turns and chuffs at the other two wolves. They pad forward, heads low. They sniff carefully as they come closer.

Finally, with my wolf standing sentinel, their sniffing becomes nuzzling and both of the new animals are filling their lungs with my scent. Now if you think about how sometimes your neighbor's dog can get a bit aggressive in his sniffing, these guys take that to a whole new level.

I am rolling on the cold ground, laughing and squirming. My wolf joins the other two, and we all wrestle and play for a few minutes more. I finally squeeze out, "Stop, I can't breathe," in between bursts of laughter. My wolf nips at the other two and stands over me protectively until I catch my breath. Heaving and trying to slow down my need to fill my lungs, one last giggle bursts from me as I look up at my wolf. Smiling, I reach up and stroke his face. He turns his head into my hand. "Okay, handsome, now I really do have to go."

I'm sure I have all manner of woodsy litter in my hair, and I am double sure there will be the need for some pretreating this load of laundry. But these three have lifted my mood. I feel lighthearted even, riding the euphoria of a really good laugh. He licks me again, and I get up dusting off as best I can.

As I start back, I feel a vibration in my butt. Realizing it's my phone, I answer. "Hello?"

"G.J., how are you, my lovely girl?"

"Hey, Gus. I am actually really good right now." I smile at my wolf walking beside me.

"I hope all the better now that I called," Gus flirts.

"Don't get me all caught up in your charms," I tease him back, smiling still from my romp with the wolves.

Then my phone is gone. My wolf jumps up and snatches it, without touching my hand, and is busily crunching it to small pieces of, what only worked when whole, bits of technology.

"No." I try to get my phone away from him, but it is far beyond too late. And while I can heal a living being, I cannot fix inanimate objects. "Ahhhh." I sound off in frustration.

The wolf looks up at me like he's the one who should be offended.

"Why?" I ask the beast, as if he'll answer.

The other two wolves come over and help in the kill of my vicious cell phone. I sigh in defeat. "I need to talk to him, you toothy maulers." I grump like a kid who didn't get a toy in her happy meal. "He thinks he knows what I am."

At that, all three tilt their heads at me.

"Forget it." I go over to the pile of what used to be my phone. The wolves stopped their destruction. I sift through it to see if the SIM card is still intact. I find it with a tooth bite right in the center. "All my numbers," I complain, but really I don't have that many in there. Then I think about what else is lost. I suck in a quick burst of air, horror on my face. "My pictures of Mama."

I collapse on myself in despair; tears own my eyes. My wolf tries to get near me to lick at them, but I stand quickly and storm away. He follows, and I spin on him and yell, "Stay away." I put up a wall of energy, like a barrier he can't cross. He howls, frustrated he is impeded. Blindly, I make my way home alone.

Chapter Ten

On the bus the next morning Nat jumps on me. "G.J., what happened to you? Gus called me, trying to reach you. He said you guys were disconnected and then you weren't picking up your phone."

"It's broken." In my head, I show her the image of the wolf munching it like Big League Chew.

"What an idiot," she says under her breath.

"Thanks. I did not have the slightest inkling the animal would react like that to my harmless cell phone. What's worse is there were a few pictures of my mom on there that can never be replaced."

Rubbing my shoulder Nat says, "I didn't mean *you*. I am sorry. That is awful."

"Nothing to be done about it now. I won't have a phone for a few days though. Let me give you the house number." I rattle it off while her zippy thumbs record it in her phone.

"You missed the commotion. The CDC found fecal matter in the lunchroom, so that was blamed for the whole mess yesterday. Maybe it wasn't you. Mr. Decker had the whole food prep area cleaned by the CDC's recommended people. Everyone is trying to figure out how it got there. There is talk about DNA samples." She laughs. "The last thing this town needs is DNA samples."

****

The morning goes by in a blur, and soon it's time for lunch. There are far more packed lunches today; after Nat's informational on the bus, I'm not in the mood to tempt fate by eating anything provided by the lovely hair-netted ladies. So, I'm first at the table. I ran into Drake at our lockers earlier in the day and made my apologies—again. I'm going to have to buy a pack of "I'm sorry" cards like you would "thank you" cards if this keeps up. He was as gracious as always about it. Drake is a good guy. I'm alone as Hamilton walks up to the table. I roll my eyes; I can't help it. The interaction between us to this point demands it of me.

Sitting down across from me he asks, "Are you all right?"

It takes me a second, but then I touch my head where Adam's teeth had cut me. "Right as rain, don't worry. I don't have a scratch on me."

He looks at me funny. "I'm sorry." His voice is so low I can barely hear him.

"Come again?"

A little louder he says, "I'm sorry."

"For which thing?" I ask.

"What do you mean?" He screws up his face in utter confusion.

"I am all for letting bygones be bygones, so don't get me wrong, but I don't think someone can accept an apology unless they know what you are apologizing for. So now, for which thing that you have done are you sorry? Or is this supposed to encompass them all?" I ask in honest curiosity.

"What have I done?"

"Are you kidding?" My eyes must be blazing in disbelief, because he sits back bewildered.

At this point Nat and Adam come to sit down. Adam is the only one who doesn't notice the staring contest between Hamilton and me. "Hey, G.J.," he greets. "You all right today?"

"What do you think I have to apologize for?" Hamilton ignores the newcomers.

"I'm fine, Adam. How are you?" I motion for him to sit next to me.

Adam puts his tray down and begins to sit. Hamilton shoots him a look, and Adam moves down a little, so he isn't right next to me. Focusing back on me, Hamilton fumes and asks again, "What is it you think I have done?"

I look at Nat. "Is he serious?"

"Other than yesterday, I don't know what I have to be sorry for," Hamilton says.

Adam says, "Does she know?" Surprise is evident in his tone.

"Um, Hamilton, I would not go there if I were you," Nat warns him.

Hamilton looks sharply at Nat, who is shaking her head. Then he looks at Adam, whose eyes are so wide in fear you can see white all around his pupils. Drake has made his way to our table and is sitting across from Nat. Chris is the final member of our luncheon group and sits next to Hamilton across from Adam. Hamilton uses the distraction of the others joining us to gather his thoughts.

Drake senses something is up and questions Nat with his eyes. This of course frustrates her since she is used to mining people's minds for understanding, and Drake is forcing her to read his expressions. I bring him up to speed. "Hamilton was just apologizing, but can't seem to explain what he is apologizing for. I am not sure if it is for him marking me as the smelly girl…"

"I haven't marked you—"

I continue as if he isn't speaking. "Calling me big at every turn…"

Hamilton looks surprised. "You *are* big."

I narrow my eyes. "Shoving my face into Adam's teeth…"

"I was trying to put my arm around you to console…"

Drake interrupts, although there's concern all over Nat's face. "Did he break the skin?" Drake looks at Adam, who looks away.

I keep going. "Or making sure that everyone in this school knows he cannot stand me in any way, shape, or form." I finish with a flourish I'm rather proud of, almost like a magician when they get to "ta-da."

Adam and Chris look at Hamilton, whose face is bright red. I think he is going to lunge across the table and attack me. Then Adam starts to laugh. Chris echoes him. Drake is still trying to find out about the teeth; he gets up and circles the table turning my face in his hands. "Did you get marked?" He rubs his fingers across my face.

"Drake, I'm fine. Stop touching me." I try to pull my face out of his hands, but he pulls it sharply back to continue his examination.

The table shakes, and my head hits the floor. The last thing I remember is being hit by a heavy weight and falling backward off the seat. My leg wrenches something awful, and the pain explodes like a Fourth of July professional pyrotechnics display as my skull meets up with the industrial tile floor.

****

Shadows cross my eyelids as someone moves between the light source and my still form. I hear a murmur of discussion, but my head hurts too bad to make actual language form from the words. It feels as though I have to push up my eyelids instead of the natural lift that served to open them in the past. I moan with the effort.

Someone hurriedly grabs my hand. "G.J.? Sweetie, are you okay?"

Aunt Celia has tearstains down her face. I realize I'm in a hospital room. Why are the lights always so bright in hospitals? I bet if the environmentalists wanted to really save some energy they could curb consumption a ton if they lowered the wattage of the average hospital light bulbs. "Hey," I croak. My throat feels like one of those home decorators from HGTV has gotten loose in there with their texture wall-covering faux finishes.

As she smooths her hand gently over my head, I realize I have some sort of covering on it. I reach my hand up. "Don't worry about that right now, G.J.." She lifts a remote from the bed and presses a button.

From behind her a low, familiar voice says, "We are so glad you're awake. Your aunt has been half-crazed worried about you." Mr. Wyfle's face appears over Aunt Celia's shoulder. He puts his hands on it in support, and she clutches it with her free hand. As strange as that seems, I can't register shock. My skills are fully taxed by keeping my eyes open and remembering who I am.

"G.J., I know it hurts, but you can't fix it. They took you to the hospital. The doctors have taken x-rays and have seen the damage to your skull and your leg. If you try to take care of it, they will know. You can do a little at a time, but not all of it. Do you understand?" Aunt Celia is concerned, and she is rushing to get all her words in, making me take a few seconds to put them in order in my head as to comprehend her.

I try to nod, but decide that's a really bad idea. It feels like I'm sloshing a bowl of Jell-O with nails in it inside my head. So I say, "Yes, ma'am."

She smiles at me. A third figure appears now and comes to the other side of the bed. As slowly as I can manage, I turn and see a woman with a white coat. "So, you are back among the conscious?" the tired-looking older woman says.

I smile weakly.

"Let's get her a cup of ice chips," she says to someone out of my line of vision. She looks down at a computer tablet in her hand and pokes at it a few times. "My name is Dr. Pauls. Can you tell me your name?"

I try to clear my throat. "G.J.. It's short for Glory Juniper."

"Excellent." Dr. Pauls beams. "Do you know where you are?"

"In the hospital?" I'm fairly secure in my guess.

"Good. Do you recognize anyone in this room?"

"Aunt Celia and Mr. Wyfle. I'm sorry, but I don't recall meeting you before." Mama would be so proud that I keep my manners rolling even when injured.

"That's quite all right." She continues through the basic series of questions that prove my vision and hearing are okay. She tests my reflexes and pulls up one of those spinning stools that make doctors look like short figure skaters when they roll around on them. "Here is where we stand, G.J. You suffered a serious blow to the head as well as a fractured femur. We had to drill your skull in order to relieve the pressure that was building up. Your vitals are good. And we seem to have avoided the worst-case scenario. We are going to keep you for observation for a few days, and then we will send you on home. You will need to keep all weight off the leg for at least a month. In a week, I will send you to an orthopedist for another x-ray, and they will go from there. There is a very long recovery time for the leg injury, four to six months for the bone itself. It will be at least a year before you get full function back, and that will be with extensive PT—sorry, physical therapy. Everyone is different of course, but we will need to keep a close watch on you." She looks at me to make sure I'm following, which surprisingly I am. "I think we are out of the woods on the head injury, but like I said, I want to keep you here a couple more days just to be sure." She pats my good leg as she rises.

As an afterthought as she leaves says, "Don't worry. Your hair will grow back soon enough and is the least of your worries."

I blink then look at Aunt Celia. My eyes wide in terrified question. Aunt Celia has a watery smile and says, "Honey, I will buy you the cutest hats you have ever seen. I do not give one fig about your hair, and neither should you."

I raise my free hand to my head.

Mr. Wyfle adds, "You are so pretty, you don't need hair."

I know he is being sweet, but I also know better. I rest my head back and close my eyes. Sometimes a person can be handed one too many things to deal with. In my whole life, does a bad haircut really matter? No. Does it matter to me at this very moment? Yes, it sure does.

Aunt Celia squeezes my hand. "You get your rest, sweetheart. We'll have you home in a few days."

I try to nod but, once again, have to stop. I squeeze my eyes shut even tighter.

****

I wake up later, and it's dark outside. I have no idea how long I've been asleep. My head feels a little less cloudy. I'm not perfect by a long shot, but I'm better than I have been, so I take that as a good sign. It's so tempting to fix it, but Aunt Celia is right. If we were still down south, there would be a revival somewhere. I could say I attended and am miraculously cured, but I'm not sure how that will play in the upper northwest. A light is on behind my head somewhere, but it is dimmer than when I was awake before. I turn my head to look around. Pulling away from the shadows, Gus moves toward me. "Hey." I smile at him. My voice is still rough and my throat gluey.

"Hey." He looks mad and concerned. "When do you get out of here?"

I shrug gently. "Not really sure. Is there some water around?"

He looks around and pours me a cup from an ugly yellow pitcher. "Why did he do it?"

"Why did who do what?" I ask after I finish my first swallow. I almost have to force my throat to operate properly. It's out of practice, and there's a huge glob of something I would rather not consider that needs to be washed away.

"Hamilton, he did this to you." Gus waits for me to fill in the blanks.

My brain runs through the events leading up to hitting my head. "I guess I made him mad when I told him off. Lordy, I knew he was angry with me, but I never thought he would physically attack me." I'm stunned. Boys didn't do stuff like that back home. I'm not prepared for feminism to smack me, quite literally, so hard. I guess Hamilton is a liberated man.

"What I don't get is why you didn't defend yourself?" Gus looks at me in worried question.

"I honestly did not even see it coming. One minute I was looking at Drake, and the next I was in a hospital. If I had known to expect such a thing, it would not have happened."

"It looks like it hurts," Gus says.

"I wouldn't recommend it over ice cream on a sunny day." I smile at him.

"Can you make it better?" he asks, darting a look to the open hospital door.

"Not for a while, there are too many checkups. When they spread out, I can heal it to the next expected level immediately after I am seen and heal from there naturally until the next appointment. That is the best way I can think of to avoid any unwanted interest in my recovery." It's tiring to talk, so I sip my water again, letting the coolness refresh my brittle throat.

"This is unacceptable." Gus's beautiful blue eyes flash like someone is holding a flashlight inside his head and shining it out through his pupils.

"Here, here. Just for the hair loss alone," I joke, hoping to lighten the mood.

Gus looks like he is going to storm the castle. "That beast is going to learn a lesson." He's slightly calmer, but I'm pretty sure he's itching to play punching bag with Hamilton's head.

"Leave it be," I say tiredly. "You are sweet to be mad on my account, but nothing good will come of more people getting between Hamilton and me." I would continue but as if the words "speak of the devil" are a method of conjure instead of an overused phrase; Hamilton is in the door of my room. I look at him, stunned he has the nerve to show up. I wonder if he's here to apologize or finish the job. I'm so focused on him, I don't see Gus move, but he is right in Hamilton's face. It doesn't matter that Hamilton has him by a few inches. Gus is not the least bit intimidated by his size.

"Gus, please. I need to talk to her." Hamilton sounds as tired as I am.

"Never... again." Gus's voice is low and so angry. I think it alone could've skinned Hamilton.

"She just said you shouldn't get in the middle of this," Hamilton calmly challenges.

"She has a head injury and she can't fix it thanks to you," Gus spits at him.

"You can't fix it? Why can't you fix it? I thought you could fix it." Hamilton's voice goes from question, to concern, to despondence.

I just look away. I'll be damned before I explain myself to him.

"She doesn't want to see you right now. Leave," Gus commands.

"Please, Gus. I wouldn't let me near her either if I were you. Adam is ready to kill me as it is." His pause draws my attention back to him. "But please."

Gus looks at me. The "pleases" make me feel like this is an apology not an assassination, so I let Gus know it's okay with a flick of my eyes. Gus lets Hamilton into the room. Once past him Hamilton turns to Gus and says, "I need to talk to her alone."

Gus looks at me again, and I shrug as if to say "whatever" in order to not be responsible for the decision. He shakes his head, comes over, and kisses my forehead. "You are remarkable." He whispers low in my ear. I smile at him and watch him give Hamilton a warning look before he leaves.

Hamilton looks everywhere around the room, trying to avoid me. Finally, his eyes settle on me. "God, you look awful."

I close one eye and look at him as if I have not heard him right.

"Are you bald now?" is his next utterance.

I shake my head and wince at the action.

"Your face looks all puffy. Why is your face puffy?" he asks in what sounds like disgust.

At that, I close my other eye. This atrocious boy put me in the hospital and came to say these things to me. As he tries to speak again, I put my hand up to stop him. "Hamilton, did you come here to literally add insult to injury?" I open my eyes and meet his.

"What? No. I...I just don't know what to say."

"I can't really help you out there. I have never done something like this to anyone. So I am not exactly sure what you would say either. I can think of a few things not to say, but I think you have hit those already, so let's move on, shall we?" I say as close to my usual tone as possible.

He looks sick. I mean, he honestly looks like I need to call the nurse to get him a bucket. He takes a deep breath and exhales in a clean-the-slate kind of gesture. He tries again to start a conversation. "I heard you broke your leg, too."

"Actually, the way I hear it, *you* broke my leg. But what are semantics in a case like this." My tone is light, but I hear the spite in my voice and am not proud of myself.

"God," he curses and looks up at the ceiling.

"Please stop that. I never am comfortable when people take the Lord's name in vain." I wiggle my shoulders, unsettled.

"Really? That kind of stuff bugs you?" He seems caught off guard by my statement.

"Hamilton, I'm tired. Can you just state your business and head on home?"

"Yeah, you look tired," he says.

I glare at him.

"God. I mean, gosh. I mean… Oh hell, what is it with you?" He seems angry with me.

"Are you really going to act mad at me?" I'm incredulous.

"Yes." Realizing he's said that out loud he corrects, "No." Then he flops back in the chair, taking another cleansing breath, and repeats, "No."

We sit there, me waiting for his apology and him seemingly without a functioning vocabulary.

"I don't know why I can't talk to you," he says it slowly as if each word has to clear some sort of litmus test to make it out of his mouth. When he's done, he kind of nods to himself like it meets with his approval.

This statement, however, makes no sense to me, so I wait for some sort of clarification.

He looks at me for my approval. I look back at him with skepticism and confusion.

"Nothing I say works," he clarifies.

I feel my cheeks rise and forehead pucker in my very confused face.

"I don't think you smell bad."

I cover my eyes, clearing the corners with my thumb and first finger, then pinching my nose. "Thank you?"

He pulls my hand away from my face, holding it as it reaches the bed.

"I like that you're big," he continues.

I pull my hand away and turn my head from him. This guy needs to enroll in a boot camp for apologies. He has zero idea how it is supposed to be done. "Hamilton, I think you may need to leave now."

"This is the first time I have been here when you have been awake." He smiles. "You snore a little."

"Yeah, I'm sure. Now, it's time for you to go." I find the remote and push the call button for the nurse.

"G.J., please, I don't have to say I'm sorry to anyone. Ever."

Maybe it's the brain injury, but that makes about as much sense as putting ants in your piggy bank. I guess my face lets him know how I feel, because he goes on.

"All that seems appropriate is to say I'm sorry to you all the time." He sounds exasperated. "I hate it."

"Hamilton, I hate to point this out, but so far in this visit, you haven't." I pray the nurse will come get him out of here soon.

"What?"

"You have not yet said you are sorry for attacking me and putting me in the hospital. I thought that was what you had intended to do, but so far you have said everything you can to offend me and skipped the apology. I guess you've missed your favorite pastime while I've been in here. What did you do before I moved to Washington?" My sarcasm is an ugly thing. I can only imagine what it looks like on my puffy, bald face.

"I didn't attack you. You think I attacked you?" He has this look of abject horror on his face. "God... gosh ... Christ," he splutters as the nurse comes in.

"Young man, I am sorry but visiting hours are over," she says in that way nurses speak that make you think they are packing heat.

"Wait," he objects, but the nurse comes over and takes him by the arm. "G.J., tell her I can stay."

"I think it's best you didn't." I won't look at him as I sense they are moving out of the room.

"Please, G.J.." It's the note of true pleading that makes me look at him as the small woman in scrubs pushes him out the door. "I am sorry." The nurse closes the door, leaving me alone in the empty hospital room. My mind revisits the expression on Hamilton's face long after the sound of his voice has dissipated.

Chapter Eleven

All in all, I spend eight days in the hospital—four of them were before I first woke up, and the other four I spend trying to get comfortable in a hospital bed. That has to be an impossible feat. Who can get cozy on a plastic-wrapped foam mattress? I'm not talking memory foam either. I'm talking dining-room-chair foam. I think it's like restaurants with uncomfortable seating so that people never get too comfy and naturally feel the need to move on. There is no wondering about how people get bedsores.

Nat comes by with my schoolwork, which keeps me somewhat busy, but I feel like I am falling behind anyway. I know people think you can learn things by telecommuting, but I like being in a classroom and the give-and-take with the class and teacher. I think it helps my brain feel fuller somehow. Hamilton never makes it past the nurses' station, if he ever tries to return. They are better than a barbed-wire fence at keeping out the riff-raff.

The biggest shock is when we go home—because we don't go home. We go to Adam's house. It isn't until we are pulling up that Aunt Celia breaks the news. "Jack and I decided this would be a good time to do a trial run. You know I'm not big on getting married again, but Jack is sure we can make it last. So, since you are going to need someone around all the time, this will help split up the duties. Jack and I will trade off working from home, and Adam has agreed to help out when we need him in the afternoons. They have a room on the first floor all set up for you. It is really for the best. When you get better, we will see how things stand. I think he really loves me, G.J.. I know you are going through a hard time, but I could use the help, and I do care for him." Aunt Celia has so much hope in her eyes, so what am I supposed to say? She is careening toward the altar with my best interest at heart.

"This is a great plan." My voice is fake, so I clear my throat and try again. "I'm sure everything will work out." That attempt is better, but I'm sure you can find the same amount of sincerity if you called for the weather.

The door behind my back opens unexpectedly. I am turned sideways in the back seat to accommodate my straight bound leg. I find myself in Mr. Wyfle's arms. "Here are my girls," he says as if we are already the newest incarnation of *The Brady Bunch*. "Adam, hold the chair still so I can get G.J. in it." He slides my body backward into the seat he has hauled up to the car door. It takes all my self-control to not holler out a giggle. His arms are right on my sides, and I am ticklish. But thank heavens I hold it together.

I look up and see Adam staring down at me. His face is, well what can you say about an expression that holds as much confusion as it does fear and caution? "Welcome, G.J.." His father slaps him on the back as if he has done just what they have rehearsed.

"Oh, Jack, you shouldn't have," Aunt Celia says, and I wonder if she has just gotten a piece of jewelry that includes what used to be coal about a million years ago. Thankfully, she is only thrilled over the ramp Mr. Wyfle has built for my arrival. Now I know he is wooing Aunt Celia, but I have to admit it is a lovely gesture.

"Wow. Thank you, Mr. Wyfle," I say truly grateful and hating that he had to go through all the trouble.

"G.J., please just call me Jack. With any luck you'll be able to throw an 'uncle' in front of that pretty soon." He smiles and winks at Aunt Celia, who shakes her finger at him in mock scolding. It is odd to watch your caregivers flirt. I'm not sure I'm going to survive this courtship. Mama never dated or flirted, and I guess I need to get over this uneasy feeling about Aunt Celia and her love life. She isn't dead, and it isn't fair for me to begrudge her happiness.

"Thank you, Jack," I say, coming to grips with my new situation.

"Well, it is easy when you have free labor." Jack slaps Adam on the back, harder this time. Why is that the sign of affection between men? *Hey, I think you are swell...* whack.

"Dad." Adam looks like he wishes he were anywhere but here.

"Thank you, Adam. That was right nice of you." I look up into his face. Adam gives me a shy sideways smile.

"It's cold out here. Let's get you settled in." Jack hustles us all toward the door.

My room turns out to be a study on the first floor. Adam's house is big. I'm talking the kind of enormous you would think to see on *Real Housewives*. I wonder what Jack does for a living. I am across from a family room area, and the kitchen is right next door. The windows from my new quarters face the woods; it is the same hill I was on the day Hamilton carried me home. Aunt Celia fusses until she thinks I'm settled. The room has all my stuff. My project is on a desk up against the wall. There is a huge bed with about a million pillows. Arranged are my computer and books so that I can get to them. On the table next to the bed is the picture of Mama and me making those mud pies. They could not have done a better job trying to make me feel at home.

"This is really nice. Thank you."

"It's not too much?" Jack asks worriedly.

I shake my head. I'm speechless.

"You and the boys did great," Aunt Celia says, rubbing Jack's back in a sideways hug.

"It was the boys mainly. I just told them to get her stuff, and they worked until they had it all done. I did pick out the bed and furnishings. I hope they suit you, G.J.. I have never had to shop for a young girl before. This family has been mostly male until you girls." Jack gives Aunt Celia a shy, hopeful look. My head is spinning, and I don't think it is from the injury. How did I miss that Aunt Celia is serious with anyone, much less Adam's dad? She's never said a word. I thought she was on the all-male tour of Spokane. So lost in thought, I only catch the fact that someone has asked me a question because the room grows silent, and everyone is watching me as if I should have an answer.

"Pardon?" I ask the group, not sure who has spoken.

"I'd like to invite the boys over to thank them. Are you up for that tonight, or should we give it a few days?" Aunt Celia asks me.

"Boys?" I ask, buying time and trying to figure out if that means another run-in with young Mr. Calhoun.

"The boys that helped move your things. We can do something easy like pizza." Aunt Celia is not being helpful.

"I guess that would be fine. If I get worn out, I'll let you know," I say, trying to be sure I have an out should the need arise.

Jack wraps an arm around Aunt Celia and says, "Let me show you how I have you set up." He is so happy I think he is going to split. It's like the last ten Christmases exploded on him today as he ushers her from my room.

Adam starts to follow, but I call after him. "Hey, Adam, can you show me where we are in science?"

He seems surprised but goes over to my desk and grabs the book. Turning back, I motion for him to close the door. It takes him a second, but he gets the message. He comes toward me when I do the upside down inchworm with my finger, motioning him over. "What?" he whispers.

"I won't bite," I whisper back, which makes him give a huge smile. That boy can definitely grin. "I am a bit out of my comfort zone here. How long have they been dating? I mean, did you know? Is this as blind-siding to you as it is to me?"

"Celia and Dad?" he asks in surprise. "Man, Dad's loved her since she moved here. He's done everything he can to keep her living here. When she married the last guy, I thought he was going to go mad. It tore him up something awful. Dad has been after her since the day he laid eyes on her. I don't know why he didn't do anything about it until about six months ago," Adam says with earnestness to his face.

"Really? Did Aunt Celia know?" I'm stunned.

Adam shrugs. "I guess she must not have, since she married that last guy, but since then Dad has not been subtle. I didn't think he was before, but what do I know? When she went down to get you, he was half out of his mind." Adam laughs at some memory he doesn't share. Shaking his head, he continues, "He was sure something would happen to her or she would not come back. When you came back, he started to seriously try to put the pressure on to get married. Celia has been kind of anti-marriage from what I can tell."

I nod my agreement. "I never did hear what happened with the last husband, but she's had a string of bad luck in the spouse department."

Adam laughs, and under his breath, he says something about luck. As I look at him in question, he says, "Dad will never hurt her. I'm serious about that. And while you complicate things, Dad will take on anything to make sure you are okay, too. You guys are safe here."

I smile. "I always complicate things. It's a life skill."

"I don't mean that."

"I know, I know. Don't worry. I was joking around." My smile grows more encouraging. "Is this going to be weird for you—having me here, I mean?"

Adam tilts his head as if that will make his words fall out in the right order. "I'm happy you are here, G.J.. You know I like you." He stops, and I think he's done.

"Thanks, Adam. I like you, too. If things don't work between your dad and Aunt Celia, I hope we can still be friends." I mean every word.

Adam sits back and blows out a long breath. "Things have to work out with Celia and Dad. He won't survive if he loses her now." Adam sits forward again, studying me as if he can figure out some puzzle, and the pieces are on my face. He reaches forward and touches my forehead where he bumped it with his teeth. "I'm so sorry about that mark. More sorry than you know." His fingers are gentle, and I close my eyes.

"Adam, there is no mark. See, not a scratch." I open my eyes and smile at him.

Before his open mouth can form words, a dog barks outside the window. This startles Adam, and he jerks his hand away like he's been caught thieving the crown jewels and looks about as guilty. He hops up awkwardly, but I grab his hand.

"Hey, I'll be okay soon. Thanks for setting up my room. You did a really nice job. That picture by my bed means more to me than you can know. That was so sweet of you to put it there. That makes this more comfortable to me. You're a sweetheart." I push the sincerity in my voice. I mean it, but being housemates with this crew is… well, odd.

Adam eyes me as he moves. He backs out of the room, smiling in the saddest, sweetest way. "I'm glad you like it, G.J.. I always want you to feel at home here." Then he leaves and closes the door.

I look after him for a few moments. I feel like somebody just put me in a blender and hit puree. In a month's time, I have lost my mama, moved to what I consider a different world, started at a new school, found an arch enemy or two, made a few friends, and have been trying really hard to not want to crawl up and stay buried with the one person who was my world—my whole life.

A few minutes after Adam leaves, Aunt Celia walks back in. "G.J., how are you doing with all this?" The door closes behind her, so I feel free to speak.

"Well, I can't say I am prepared for everything, but it wasn't like I had really settled at your house yet, so I'm fine. Is this what you want?" I ask, trying to see if this is Jack or Aunt Celia who wants this to happen.

She takes a deep breath and looks me in the eye. "I have had so many bad romances. I have always been in love with love. I'm not sure I have ever been truly in the big L. But I have known Jack for years. I had a huge crush on him when we first met, but I thought he wasn't interested in me in that way, and we settled into a truly great friendship. He's been incredibly loyal to me as a person. He helped me with my career, he's been my shoulder through so many of my romantic mistakes, and I really care about him. I was sure I needed a creative soul as a life partner. I wanted a touch of the wild side of life. But all that ended up getting me were partners that found some other whim more important than our relationship. Jack is solid. And I have to admit it is very nice being adored. Even though he has been around and been there through my whole time up here, I am gun-shy right now. I was so hurt when David left." She takes another deep breath. "I still don't know what happened. But Jack is so sure this is right, and I have always cherished him. I really thought all his flirting was just his nature, but he says it is only with me." She lets out a laugh and shakes her head. "Nothing is settled, but this will be a good test run. I hope it is okay with you."

"This whole place is new. I have never lived with men before. This might help me get along out in the world." I smile at Aunt Celia.

"You are such a cool kid." Her smile changes, and I know we are both missing my mom. Before we get too sappy she says, "Hey, I've got an email for you. Remember I said I was going to check into a few things? Well, I got a response. Are you up for it?"

"Actually, can you tell me what level I can heal to? I'm a bit sore and want to move this whole 'on the mend' thing along. I am not a good patient." I smile at her.

"Oh, sweetie, of course. I should have let you work on that earlier." She reads the release documents from the hospital on what we should expect. And, I bring my body to that new level. That is intensely painful. I have never had an injury that is this bad and am kind of glad I'm going to do this in steps. Yowee. I am pretty sure avoiding this kind of damage in the future would be the best course. Regardless of my ability to heal, it is still no fun and the process hurts. "G.J., are you all right?" Aunt Celia is worried.

"I'm better than I was, but I can't say that was a bowl of cherries." I wipe the sweat that has formed on my head.

"Can I trouble you for a glass of water?" I'm shaky with the aftereffects of the healing and need something to cool me down.

Aunt Celia hops up. Before she whisks out to get me a drink, she slides the email she has gotten on my desk. I take a moment to look out the window. There in the tree line sits my wolf, watching this house. How in the world did he find me? That is a silly first thought. The woods back there are his home. He probably wanders all over. He is most likely wondering what I am doing in this place instead of where he usually finds me. Who am I kidding? He doubtless has no idea this bald chick staring at him from this new place is me. I put my hand up and waive to him like a little kid excited to see someone they knew.

"Who are you waving to?" asks a low voice behind me.

I swing my head around and find Adam holding a glass of water. I'm so surprised I just blink at him. He leans down to see what I can see and curses. Water sloshes over the side of the cup and lands in my lap. I make that "ahhh." exclamation you make when cold water drops on you. Adam curses again, and I wonder if there are sailors in his family tree. Then he grabs a folded towel that is laying out for my arrival and starts trying to soak up the water in my lap by heartily dabbing at it. I scream in pain this time. Adam drops the towel in horror that he has just hurt me.

"G.J., I am so sorry. I forgot…" If he is going to say more two things interrupt him: Jack and Aunt Celia running into the room and the wolf slamming up against the window.

Adam falls back, and I turn to the window, trying to see if the wolf has been hurt. I wonder if these are your average double panes, because, if they are, that needs to be their next ad campaign. The wolf pops up in the window and starts raging at the glass like Cujo's crazy cousin. Aunt Celia screams, and Jack pulls her to him and curses. I can now see how Adam became a proficient. Jack glares between Adam and over the snarling barks beyond the panes says, "Get out there and get rid of him."

"No." I yell over the din.

"Jack, you can't send Adam out after a wolf by himself. He is just a boy." Aunt Celia is horrified.

"Hush up," I yell at the canine. His nails scrape at the sill as he tries to keep his head up to see in. He drops down to a low growl. I have my hands on my head. The loud noise and confusion feel like the wolf's claws are using my brain to keep purchase to see rather than the abused windowsill. "Ow." My eyes squint.

"G.J., move away from the window." A growling Jack holds Aunt Celia, and he seems to be growling right back at the wolf.

I try to turn my wheelchair and bang my leg into the wall, yelping again as agony moves though my body once more. The wolf appears stunned, wildly eyeing the room to see what has happened. Adam lunges forward trying to help. The wolf goes bonkers again. Adam gets behind my chair and moves me toward the door. My leg and head hurt so bad I can't wait to get out of the chaos. Jack sends Aunt Celia out of the room with us and closes the door behind her.

Adam wheels me to the family room area, which is beautiful but very manly. The lack of the cacophony that my new room has bouncing around in it is bliss. Adam sits on the arm of the sofa he has parked me near. Aunt Celia shakes and keeps looking at the door to my room in terrified concern, hugging herself with her own arms. "It's all right, Aunt Celia. The wolf is harmless."

Both Adam and Aunt Celia say at the same time, "Harmless?"

My head is killing me, and I do another quick mending. So what if I'm a *miracle* healing? I can't take this much longer.

Rubbing away the remnants of the headache I say, "He can't get in the window obviously, and something he saw bothered him. He'll go away now that we aren't there. There is nothing to worry about, and there is no need to get rid of him." I plead to Adam to leave the wolf alone.

Adam's jaw tightens, and he glances away before he speaks. "Dad is going to handle it."

I whip my head back to peek at my bedroom door. *Handle it how?* Worried for the wolf, I try to wheel myself back to my new room. In the process of turning around, Adam catches my chair.

"G.J., don't," Adam warns, but I'm not going to have it.

I send Adam flying backward, landing on the couch with a huff. I continue to roll toward the door.

"G.J., why would you do such a thing?" Aunt Celia shouts.

I reach my goal and fling the door open with my power. Jack is sitting in the now open window. He turns and says something in a low voice, and soon I see the wolf dart back up into the woods. Jack turns back and smiles at me. I know something is off. Jack just had an actual chat with my wolf. I tilt my head sideways. His smile fades a little. The wind behind me foretells the arrival of one or both of the other two people in the house.

"Ceily, are you all right?" Concern for Aunt Celia is first on Jack's mind, but not mine.

"I need a word with G.J.. Jack if you… Why is the window open?" Aunt Celia is a sharp cookie. I do love that woman. So, whatever she wanted to say to me can wait.

"I needed to make sure the animal was gone." Jack hedges the truth, and I narrow my eyes at him. He closes the window and crosses over to Aunt Celia. "Whatever you need to say to G.J. we should handle it together."

"No, this is something we need to deal with privately." She tries to push him off.

Jack sighs. "Celia we need to really give this a try. If we are going to be a family, then we all need to work things out together. Please don't shut me out." Jack is so earnest it makes me want to have him join us, like it's Christmas dinner and not a scolding I'm headed for.

"Jack, this is so new for G.J., and she has done something I need to address. Please let me handle this alone." She's sticking to her guns in order to protect me.

"Jack, she doesn't want you to know I'm a Witch," I say.

"G.J.." Aunt Celia's eyes are huge.

"Young lady, neither your aunt nor I will let you say things of that nature about yourself." Jack has the stern parental voice I have only seen on Nick at Nite.

Aunt Celia looks at me and shakes her head slightly, warning me off saying anything more. But it doesn't stop my motor mouth.

"Jack, I do not want to scare you, but I am an actual Witch, or so I have been told."

Aunt Celia looks at me sharply. "You have?" She seems surprised.

"G.J.," Jack says, "adjusting to any school can be hard, but we will help you with the disruptions that have been haunting you. Don't believe what the kids in school call you."

"Aunt Celia, are you sure this is the direction we are moving?" The penetrating stare I give Aunt Celia lets her know I want to support her new life by being honest, and I won't hide who I am.

"I am not sure this won't end it. Are you comfortable?" she asks and glances at Jack.

"Eh, I will never be comfortable being the odd man out, but if we are going to live here, I would prefer they expected my abilities. Mama never made me ashamed I could do these things."

Aunt Celia's eyes grow a little misty, "Do I make you feel that way?"

"Young lady, your aunt is so proud of you, and she certainly does not think you are a Witch." Jack is trying so hard to charge forward while trying to navigate this unknown scenario.

"Thank you, Aunt Celia and Jack. You are so kind. I am, however, a Witch. I just found out recently. It really is the only thing that makes any kind of sense, if you add everything up. So I guess I am fine with it for the most part. I do have a bunch more questions, though. I will say it's nice to have something that puts a kind of order to what I am able to do. You know me. I like it when things are explained." My babble reflex has kicked in again.

Jack looks stern as he tries again to make me not say bad things about myself, probably thinking it's a self-esteem issue. He tries to lecture it out of me. Aunt Celia seems more concerned with who it is that told me. They are talking over top each other, and my poor head is not going to take much more of their attempts to create the perfect form of white noise.

So I pick them both up with my will. Aunt Celia is shocked that I would do it, and Jack is shocked that I *can* do it. Just then, Adam walks in—I guess to see what all the fuss is about—and yells, "Put them down." I'm fairly proud of his ability to grasp the situation so quickly. I put them down. Jack is harder to keep upright since he tries to get himself down on his own, which kind of spins him this way and that.

Chapter Twelve

Aunt Celia is first to speak. "Couldn't you have started with a lamp or a book?" She puts her hand on Jack's arm. Jack's gaze jumps from Aunt Celia to me. Adam edges his way between his father and my wheelchair.

"You… you know she does this kind of thing?" Directing his question to my aunt, Jack is doing his best to sound calm, but you can tell he is bouncing like a ping-pong ball between incredulity and anger.

"Of course, I know. She's my niece. I told you G.J. is special. I just didn't explain *how* she is special. I want this to work between us, Jack, but G.J. is right. I will not have her hide who she is in her own home, particularly since she is being forced not to heal herself due to so many medical records after the accident. If this is really her home, *our* home, then you and Adam need to know about G.J.'s abilities." Aunt Celia doesn't raise her voice, but Jack seems like she has sucked the wind from his sails.

"Dad, she's a nice girl. She's not someone who will abuse it. Not like the others. It will be all right. Don't ruin everything you have built with Celia over this. You will regret it." Adam carries the wisdom of the ages in his simple words.

"Thank you, Adam. That is right nice of you to say. Jack, I do apologize for picking you up out of the blue like that.

I'm just tired, and you two were so upset and concerned that I could not get you to understand what I was talking about unless I did something a touch drastic. I promise, my mama raised me better than to pick people up all the time, and I won't do it again without your permission." I peer around Adam at Jack.

"Without my permission?" Jack is completely at a loss. He looks at Aunt Celia, and it grounds him somehow. He reaches out and pulls her into his arms. "Give me a little time to come to grips with this. This is unexpected and amazing. You have to admit this is not something you come across every day."

Aunt Celia smiles at him and nods. "I adore you. Take whatever time you need." She goes up on her toes and kisses the big man.

The doorbell rings, forcing the little clutch of us to look from one to another in a silent promise to keep this within our newly-formed family. Jack nods and walks out with Aunt Celia to answer the door.

Adam turns on me after they leave. "Why would you do that?"

I'm not sure which part of what just happened Adam objects to, so I stay quiet while he explains what is upsetting him.

"You shouldn't show people you can do those kinds of things. It could be dangerous for you." Adam sounds concerned and a touch hostile.

"Adam, I am not running around showing people willy-nilly. I showed all you all because this is supposed to be my home. If I do show people, what can they do about it? People would think they were crazy before believe there are Witches. You said Aunt Celia and Jack were hopefully going to be in it for the long haul. I don't want to be a distraction for them. I think letting you in on my dirty little secret now rather than later will be better in the long term. Don't you? What if they do work out, and your dad found out we kept this from him? That just seems like the start of a bad soap opera to me." I smile in that way you do when you want someone to understand and know that you aren't trying to stir up a fight.

Adam reaches out and touches my cheek. "I just worry about you." He smiles back, letting me know he gets my point.

"Isn't this precious?" a voice sounds from behind Adam.

I close my eyes. What is Hamilton doing here? I think he has done enough at this point. Adam pulls his hand back fast, like I'm a striking rattlesnake. I'm stunned he is so cowed by Hamilton. Since both of these boys know I can do things, I pick them up, put them on the other side of the door, and slam it in their faces. I will be iced like a cupcake before I will deal with that nonsense today. My indignant moment doesn't take long to come to an end.

Knock, knock, knock. The force of the banging makes me flinch. "G.J.?"

I'm unhappy to discover it is Jack making the racket.

"Yes, sir?" Somehow, I'm sure my questioning voice though the door isn't going to deter Jack from wanting to speak face-to-face.

"Open the door." Jack is trying to remain calm, bless his heart.

I swing the door open, and Jack comes in closing it behind him. I give him my sad-puppy-who-peed-on-the-floor face and say, "I'm sorry."

"Would you like to explain what that was all about?" Jack asks, sitting down to see me at eye level. "Did you not just tell me you don't do things like that?"

"If given a choice, no I would not like to explain it. But since I really don't think I am going to get away with it," I sigh, "I'll do my best." I take a moment to map out what I want to say. "Both of them know I can do stuff, so I wasn't exposing them to anything they were not already aware of. But honestly, Jack, I have no interest in having Hamilton insult me one more time. Adam seems to be intimidated by Hamilton, and that just bugs me to no end. And I don't want to have to deal with that nonsense at the moment."

"Hamilton insults you?" Jack looks like I've told him there is an iceberg on the equator.

"With every word he utters around me. The boy has made it clear he hates me, and I know he and Adam are friends. Oh my goodness." I put my head in my hands. "He is going to be here all the time, isn't he?" I peek through my fingers at Jack for confirmation.

"G.J., he lives next door," Jack says with an apologetic smile.

The groan I utter must have been loud because I hear the door handle jiggle like someone is trying to get in. I'm rather impressed Jack has had the forethought to lock it behind him.

"I am quite sure this is some sort of miscommunication. Hamilton is a good kid. He has been part of the pack of boys in this neighborhood since he was born. He is a natural leader. I think the two of you need to sort this out." Jack acts like he is going to continue, but I hold up my hand.

"Please don't make me deal with him today. I haven't recovered from the last time I saw him." I must seem pathetic, because Jack takes pity on me.

"Okay, kiddo, you do not have to see him for long, but you should at least thank him for moving over your things." Jack's concession is more alarming than he can know.

"*He* moved my things?" I ask, dumbfounded that this awful boy has been alone with my belongings. I feel so violated. It had not bothered me when it was nameless, faceless people or Adam who had gone through my stuff, but to know someone who has been so hateful toward me has been alone with my belongings makes me cringe and scan the room wondering if he has booby trapped something or did something gross like lick all my book spines. I shiver.

"He actually arranged the whole room for you. He made sure we got everything and sat in a chair to see if you would be able to reach what you needed."

"That was good of him since I am in the chair due to his attack," I say begrudgingly.

Jack gives an admonishing smile. "That was an accident, G.J.. Just say thank you, and I will get him out of your hair."

Has Jack lost his mind? How is jumping over a table and slamming someone's head into the floor an accident? And I'm supposed to be thankful? I currently don't have any hair for him to get out of since Hamilton squashed my skull. I can be a bigger person. I can be polite. I will eat this crow with proper etiquette for the sake of Aunt Celia and her relationship with Jack. And I will have a place saved in Heaven for all the sacrifices I'm making. All I can do is nod.

"Good." Jack is supremely proud of himself for his parenting moment. It's sweet. Too bad I want to check his sanity at the local inpatient hospital for making me do this. Jack unlocks the door. Hamilton walks in with Adam following.

"Why did you do that?" Hamilton towers over me, looking menacing. Adam leans against the wall with his hands behind his back.

I clear my throat. "I understand I am to thank you for helping with my move over here. I do so very much appreciate your assistance. My room looks wonderful, and I really could not be more pleased. So… thank you." My somber gaze moves from Hamilton, and I smile genuinely at Adam who looks like he grows an inch. Then I look at Jack in a "is that good enough?" face.

"I have something I need to say to you," Hamilton says.

"I am all ears." The corners of my mouth tilt in what could be mistaken for a smile, if you don't notice the dangerous glare in my eyes. Everyone here knows I can end the conversation in the blink of an eye. But I am curious if he will finally say something, anything that can be considered remotely nice.

Hamilton shares a look with Jack and Adam. Jack starts moving toward the door, and while Adam seems more reluctant, he follows his father's lead. Although I'm annoyed with Adam's desertion, he does leave the door open. Hamilton moves to close it, but I say, "Please, leave it open. I would feel safer."

Anger flashes in his eyes like a lighthouse beam when he turns back to me. Dear me this guy is intense. "Safer?"

I take my hands and do a Vanna White impression, starting at my bald, bandaged head and finishing with a flourish at my straight-bound leg and toes. "Safer."

Hamilton blows out a breath and looks to the ceiling as if his thoughts have escaped in one of those bubbles you see in the funny papers attached to the characters' heads. That's the sad thing about getting news on the Internet; you lose out on the comic section. Maybe that is why people seem so grumpy these days. Their news is delivered with none of the lighthearted relief, unless they watch the Daily Show. But satire is not always the best way to be informed. Getting hold of his words, he finally starts to speak. "I…" He stops. It's odd how he seemed so determined to talk to me, yet he has nothing to say. I wait already forced to thank this boy. He can kiss my patooty if he thinks I'm going to help him out beyond that. "Man, you really look like hell. It's hard to even look at you."

My eyeballs are getting such a workout, rolling every time this guy opens his mouth. As my gaze settles back on his, I slightly shake my head in annoyance. "Well, thank you for this delightful exchange. I do appreciate your part in making me so hard to look at. Now, I would appreciate it if you left me alone."

I begin to push him out. He starts sliding backward and grabs hold of my chair with Mr. Miyagi speed, so I start to roll with him.

"Let go."

"Stop pushing me away," he shoots back.

"Stop saying the world's rudest things to me."

"Stop taking things the wrong way on purpose." His voice is straining because I'm trying my best to mentally pry his fingers off my chair.

"Quit being so mean." My voice rises, and I push hard, which only manages to slide us both toward the door.

"I am not trying to be mean. You just make it so hard," he growls in my face.

"Hamilton, you are truly a moron," comes the dulcet tones of my hero BFF, Nat.

I stop pushing, and Hamilton spins to face her. "I am trying to talk to G.J.."

"I can tell, because she is annoyed and frustrated. Which is exactly how someone who should be recovering should feel. Only wait, no, they should be calm and resting." Nat's words dance up and down the octave until they land on the perfect sarcastic note at the end. I do admire her ability to do that.

"Nat, you know I don't mean it to be like this," Hamilton says in defeat.

"I have known you a long time. I know you are not a bad guy. I also know you were going after Drake, which I can appreciate. But right now, you are way over the top on the overbearing. G.J. is injured thanks to you. No matter the motive. It is made even more difficult that you hurt her so badly she was seen by doctors and cannot heal herself. Whatever it is you want right now doesn't matter. This is about G.J. and her recovery. Back off." Nat is a fierce little thing when she wants to be. It doesn't hurt that she is backed up by yet another visitor, who has walked in during her diatribe. Gus looks about as menacing as I have ever seen a person—except Hamilton, who is doing his best to maintain that title.

Gus turns his gaze to me, and his face softens. "How are you, doll?" he asks me, making Hamilton force this strangled growl from his chest.

"Peachy keen, my head seems a bit cold, but I guess I now know what Mr. Clean feels like." I smile back.

"Why…" Hamilton starts.

"Not now," Nat roars at him.

"We came by to see your new digs," Gus says looking around. "Nice." His voice takes on a tone of appreciation.

"Thank you. I really like it. I don't know how permanent it is, but it is really cozy and convenient."

"You really do like it? You aren't just saying that?" Hamilton asks.

I ignore Hamilton.

Nat says, "Hey, Gus and I need to talk to you." She looks at Hamilton as if he should take the hint and leave. He doesn't.

Gus goes with the more forward approach. "Leave." He stares hard at Hamilton who is now doing his best ignoring pose.

Gus moves up into Hamilton's space. I could have told Gus trying to intimidate Hamilton is like staring down a rock, but he feels the need to attempt it anyhow. Hamilton puts on his bored face, which lets everyone know he does not intend to go away.

Nat surprises the whole lot of us by saying, "Gus, it might be helpful if he knows, too."

Gus swings his head back to her and gapes in disbelief. "Why?"

"G.J. is in danger. If Hamilton is willing to help, we should take it. Be smart. He can be an asset. Cut the posturing and think about it," Nat explains impatiently.

"Danger?" Hamilton does that thing where he just repeats what people say as a question.

"Keep your mouth shut and listen, or I will get Mr. Wyfle in here to pull you out by your ears." Nat is not messing around.

"Why would I be in danger from anybody but the obvious?" I shift my eyes and point to Hamilton, who begins to speak, but Nat puts up her hand in warning.

"Not one word." Nat glares at Hamilton before continuing. "Gus, why don't you start since you are the one who noticed?"

Gus walks over and squats down in front of my chair so he is eye to eye with me. He really has the most beautiful blue eyes. It always takes me a minute to focus on what we are talking about. But whenever he does that weird sniffing thing, he breaks the spell, and I'm able to move my attention back to the discussion. "Do you remember when you came in to the stage area that Monday?"

Hamilton makes one of his many strange noises.

"I have a crushed skull, not a mashed brain. How could I forget?" I ask.

"Good. Do you remember the circle Mrs. Ackers asked you to stand in at the podium?" he asks.

Hamilton seems to get even more alert, if that's possible.

"When you pushed the podium, the power you drew from was a Wiccan circle. I think that was why it was more than you were expecting. Mrs. Ackers had drawn a circle, intending for something to happen to you. What I'm not sure of is whether it was the presence of that energy that caused you to get too much juice or if that spell was directed at you." Gus thinks he is making sense, but I'm pretty sure I am missing large pieces of the foundation of this story.

"Sara's mom is a Witch?" I ask Gus.

"No, I told you Witches are rare. You are the only one I know of. Mrs. Ackers and several of her friends are Wiccan, as is Sara. They practice the art of ritual to affect the earth and elements and cast spells. Mrs. Ackers' coven is not particularly spiritual either. They tend to use the faith as a way to get what they want and to intimidate. They are much practiced, but they don't have anywhere near the power you do. I told you how rare you are." Gus touches my cheek and smiles sweetly.

Wow, is this guy breathtaking. I shake my head to bring my brain back to what he's saying. "So you think I go to pull power, and if there is a circle going, I get too much juice. All that extra power makes me over cast somehow. Like I plug in a different current level in Ohm's law?" Nat, Gus, and Hamilton look at me with blank faces. "V=IR?" I prompt them to see if that helps.

"Which one is current again?" Gus is the first one to get with my program.

"I is current. Voltage equals Current Intensity by Resistance. That is the basic circuit." Sometimes I forget other people don't read nearly as many science books as I do for fun.

"Okay," Hamilton starts slowly. "So you think it is the intensity that is making the change and not the resistance, or lack thereof, which is the variable causing the variation?"

Huh, who would have thought he would be able to catch up so quickly? I wouldn't think a boy who can't figure out how to avoid insulting me after several conversation attempts would have picked up this theory like he is. I think it just proves he isn't trying to keep a civil tongue in his mouth.

"No, I am not sure which part of the equation is what is being fussed with, but since we are talking about power, I thought the law was apropos."

"If we use that theory…" Hamilton starts to debate, but Nat speaks over him again.

"Hello, people. We have a bigger picture here. Have your geek club meeting later. Mrs. Ackers is trying to use magic on G.J.. And from what I can tell, it is not to make her prom queen, unless it is to recreate the pigs-blood moment in *Carrie*. We know Sara is out to get G.J.. Now she is siccing her Palinesque, lipstick-wearing, pit-bull coven after our girl. They are dangerous. G.J. is the target of a crazy group of pissed-off chicks in peasant skirts." Nat seems out of breath due to her venting moment.

"No one will touch her," Hamilton says, his voice rumbling.

"Right, only you get to abuse me?" I question him.

"So far they have not done anything to G.J.. They have only tried. And from how her abilities have been going off the wall all the time, I have the feeling this was not the first time they have attempted it," Gus says. "I am not sure G.J. can be affected by what they are trying to do."

"You think every time my abilities have gone wrong it was an attack on me?" I ask. "What if it's just when they attempt to do anything, and I attempt something at the same time?"

"These women have ongoing circles. They go out in the woods and leave a ritual going to continue to hold its power for long periods of time. Right now, I am sure there is at least one circle active in the woods as we speak. Have you tried to do anything lately?" Gus asks.

I look at Hamilton. "Nothing much." Nat must be in my head again and see me putting the boys outside my room because she laughs. I wonder if it's easier for her to get to my thoughts now that I have no hair to get between her brain and mine.

Nat's laugh dies, and she says, "It will grow back, and it does not change how beautiful you are."

I give her a sideways "yeah right" look that you tend to master by the time you are thirteen at the latest. My thoughts change back to what Gus just said. "Circles in the woods?" My eyes grow distant, remembering the circles I have come across.

"You mean the dead spots?" Hamilton asks and inspects me.

"You've seen them too?" I ask.

Hamilton gets the strangest expression on his face. Nat jumps in with, "Now is not the time. We have enough going on." I'm not clear who she is talking to.

"I've seen these circles. They are not right. Everything in them is missing. I mean every kind of life and energy. They should not leave open such a draw on the world. It's… it's… well… it's just plain greedy; that's all." I shiver, remembering the vacancy left in the once vital space. When I was down south, a boy in my school was missing for a few days. We didn't think much of it until someone went to visit his mama. Turns out, he had advanced-stage childhood leukemia. He never came back to school. The memorial was about a month later. That was the kind of vacant that circle was—the "absent kid desk" kind of vacant.

Nat grabs my hand and squeezes. It is an odd thing having a friend that truly can follow your thoughts.

"Those circles in the woods are because of Sara's mom?" Hamilton acts surprised.

Gus looks at him in disgust. "You think because Sara is a pretty little blonde she is not dangerous? You need to meet the women I know." Gus dismisses Hamilton as if he is an impudent three year old.

So, Hamilton thinks Sara is pretty. Boys do tend to like the smaller girls. "You've seen the circles too?" I ask my same question to get us back on track.

Hamilton shakes his head again to dismiss something. "The circles in the woods?" He looks at me in a hard way that says, *"You must be stupid,"* adding verbally to the sentiment by the tone in his, "Of course."

Nat shakes her head as if answering some unspoken question. My head is spinning. Gus asks, "What do the circles look like?" His question is directed at me.

"I've seen two of them so far. They are dead spaces in the woods. Completely unnatural," I explain, trying to regain some semblance of intelligence after Hamilton's dismissive attitude.

Gus probes, "Could they be burn-out spots or lightning strikes?"

"No, even my wolf knew there was something wrong. I had to draw the energy back in order to fix them. It was stolen. The ground was raped almost."

"Your wolf?" Nat and Gus exclaim in horror. Hamilton says the same thing, but his face is pleased. It almost looks like—but I'm not sure—there is humor or joy in his expression.

"G.J., you can't claim a wolf. Don't get comfortable with wild things. You have no idea when they will turn..." Gus starts.

"No, no, no, I'd like to hear more about 'her wolf'." Hamilton can mock me all he wants. I won't feel bad about my wolf friends.

"Guys, cool it. G.J. is just explaining the wolf that has been around her," Nat's manner is bizarrely sarcastic, "or was with her when she saw the circles. I already told you not now. Stop or I will out you."

Hamilton crosses his arms in a challenge. "In Jack's house?"

Gus flicks his gaze away like an annoyed big cat who knows prey is there but chooses not to attack at that exact moment.

It is clear to me I'm still under the effects of my head injury. I obviously am missing something, but I really don't care at the moment what. "Nat, I have always been good with wild animals. I have spent most of my life in the woods.

I don't know how to be indoors, and I think the idea of spending the next few weeks unable to crawl around in the forest is going to kill me." In the middle of my diatribe, Adam comes in and stands near the door. "Never in all my days have I had to spend more than half a day indoors, and now it seems I am destined to be housebound. I have met a few beautiful wolves in the woods. I'm not afraid of any of them. But there is one that I have seen that I consider *my* wolf. I don't know why. None of this is the point though. The circles that these women are drawing from are killing the earth. They can't do it. It's almost like they are robbing every essence from the ground. I have to get out there and return all that energy to where the good Lord intended it to be." I stare out the window as if I can see a circle if I try hard enough.

"G.J., calm down." Gus grabs my hand and tries to soothe me.

"She is nuts," comes Hamilton's indignant tone. "She can't go traipsing about in the woods with other wolves and Wiccan circles. She can't even stand up."

"And whose fault is that?" Adam is in Hamilton's face. Adam is taking this whole big brother thing seriously.

Gus is up and stands behind Adam in some odd show of solidarity. "Right, Hamilton, who did this to G.J.?"

If it's at all possible, Hamilton gets an inch taller. His arms go back and his head cocks as if he's looking for weakness in the two shorter boy-men. "You know it was Aldrich…"

"Speak of the devil," a voice sounds from the door.

Adam and Hamilton form a wall between the door and me so fast I can't see who is there. "Out, now." Hamilton's voice has a rumble that shakes the room. I try to find a balance in my head, but it feels like my brain is on one of those boards people put a can under in order to learn how to get sea legs.

Nat moves behind my chair. She leans down and whispers, "Don't get into this now. You aren't up for it. And after everything, they won't have it."

"I came to see how the beautiful G.J. is faring." It's Drake who's come to see me. "I wasn't sure she would feel comfortable in this new den."

"It is where her aunt thought she would be…" Adam's head shifts as if to recognize I am here, "safe."

Something unspoken is obviously passing between these three, so I do what I do best and start talking. "Drake, thank you for coming to see me. That was so sweet of you. Please do come in."

The heads of my human wall spin toward me so fast I think their noses will smack each other. "You're inviting that guy in here?" Hamilton is outraged.

"You are so right, Hamilton. It is getting a bit crowded. If you are uncomfortable with my invited guests, please feel free to take your leave." I am as sweet as pecan pie.

His response is an inaudible grumble. He and Adam still block Drake's entrance to the room. Gus says, "Hey, man, I'm glad you're here. We were just talking about something G.J. saw in the woods on the hill."

"Do tell." Drake advances and is unfazed as the wall of muscle crowds him.

"Drake, why don't you come sit by me?" I bid him.

"You want this guy, who has been bugging you, to sit by you?" Hamilton asks as if I want a pickle and marshmallow sandwich.

Well, now it's my turn to look at Hamilton like he has been hit by the dumb stick one too many times. "Drake has been nothing but a friend to me since I have been here. As I told you before, *you* are the one who has been nothing but plain ol' despicable since the moment we met. Let my *friend* Drake through, please." I emphasize friend to make my point.

Adam looks at Hamilton's astonished face and starts to laugh. The poor boy has to find a chair he is howling so hard. Hamilton's face goes from flushed-with-embarrassment red to livid puce in short order. I hope his ears will act as a whistle on a teapot and let out that steam like you see in cartoons. Or I'm afraid of the awful mess the explosion of his noggin will cause in my lovely new room. Hamilton's furious eyes fall on me, and the oddest thing happens. His anger moves in his eyes through a series of unnamed emotions, and I swear the boy ends up on hurt. I tilt my head to see if by watching at him at a different angle the real feeling will show, but I am surprised it doesn't change.

Drake pushes past the still-heaving-with-laughter Adam and the unmovable statue Hamilton has become to see me for the first time. He stops for a second and finds a way to gently let me know my appearance is awful. "Well, this is a new look."

"I have always liked the clean-shaven style." I give him my brightest smile. "How are you doing?"

"I've been a bit worried. Why are you still like this?" Drake references my state of being with a gesture of his hands.

"There are too many doctors involved, which was probably best, since I was unconscious and had a doosey of a concussion." I slip the conversation toward the easy banter we have always had. "But now, with so many eyes on my recovery, I can't just 'I Dream of Jeannie' blink and make it all go away." I shrug. "So you get the gimpy version of me for a while. I will say that I had to heal my head a bit more than I should have because it felt like I was the bell in a prize fight, but I hope the doctors chalk it up to a miracle and don't look too closely."

Drake turns to Hamilton. "You are an idiot."

Hamilton looks like he'll object, but Adam says, "I second that. Drake, I am glad to hear you weren't harassing G.J.. That would have been uncomfortable."

Drake nods. "The fact that you thought that explains a few things that were not making sense. Next time, talk to me. I know our… families aren't always on the same page…"

Gus coughs a laugh.

Drake continues. "But at least have the decency to give a guy a heads-up."

"If you are done talking in man-code, can we get back to G.J.?" Nat asks from behind me. She has been so uncharacteristically quiet I thought she'd left.

"Of course, Natalia. Please bring me up to speed on your thoughts," Drake prompts her, which makes Nat get so still it seems like she is hunting crickets.

Gus brings the topic back around to the circles and explains what we have seen.

"That sneaky little…" Drake interrupts. "I bet she had the cheer squad try something at the wrestling match. I thought it felt off. No wonder G.J. stopped Adam's match with her thoughts."

"You're why my match stopped?" Adam asks. "Why?"

"I just didn't want you to get hurt," I say rather sheepishly.

"You were trying to protect me?" Adam is kind of awestruck. He smiles and says, "G.J., you don't have to do that."

Hamilton lets out a deep noise of frustration. "She obviously thinks you're weak."

"I did not have control at the time, remember? I just did not want someone I like getting hurt. It was a passing thought that went poof." By the time I get to the word "like," Adam's grin and Hamilton's scowl have equal and opposite growth. Realizing what I have implied, the temperature of my cheeks feels like they appear somewhere between fuchsia and rosy red.

Drake brings us all back to what is important. "The point being, Sara has it out for G.J. and has started a coven in the cheer squad. That means they are able to do these things in school. Wow, no wonder nobody wants to mess with them. What power hungry—"

"Look," Gus jumps in, "I really don't think with G.J. around they will be able to do anything using power. G.J., I think you are a magnet for energy. Essentially, every time you get near that kind of power, it draws to you, so you inadvertently suck it away from the person or people who have called it. Drake, you said Sara was trying to do something at the match the other day?" Drake nods and Gus continues. "Instead of them being able to do anything to her, G.J. somehow pulled it into herself, so when she just thought about something it whipped out of her with the force of the energy those girls had called." Gus laughs. "I wish I had seen their faces when they failed doing something they thought would work."

"What about Mrs. Ackers? You said she was after G.J. too? Can she hurt her?" Adam asks. "Should I let my dad know?"

"Listen here. First thing I'm gonna do when I can get all patched up is head up in those hills and end every one of those circles I can find." I'm so furious about those people robbing the land. It's plain as day what they are doing is hurting nature.

"You can end it?" Gus asks. "You really are amazing." I have to look away from his pretty blue eyes. They can get too distracting, particularly when they are eyeing me in that way that just makes a person feel special.

"What is so amazing about her?" Leave it to Hamilton to bring me right on back to modest.

Gus sighs. "Most of the time it takes knowing the workings involved in order to undo what has been done. And it goes without saying that a person would have to have more power than the original caster. It can be seriously dangerous to anyone who tries. How did you do it?"

"I just called the energy back. It wasn't hard." I dismiss the attention Gus is putting on my ability. I mean, really, how does one accept a compliment for doing something that is so easy for you to do and your conscious won't let you leave that way anyhow?

"Why do you think the only way they are going to come at G.J. will be in a way that doesn't work? These ladies are determined. If they find out what G.J. can do and that she is shutting down their circles, they are not going to leave it at that." Nat's concern is sweet.

"Let's cross that bridge when we come to it," Gus says, dismissing her theory.

Aunt Celia sticks her head in and calls, "Pizza's here."

With a look, we all decide to work on this problem later.

Chapter Thirteen

The rest of the evening moves on to jokes and laughter among this group of people who are becoming my friends and family. More of the letter jacket crew shows up, and they're actually nice guys, once you understand half of the jostling and roughhousing is their testosterone relief. It's strange to think I might be happy in this very different world from where I grew up. Hamilton actually fits into the conversations and jokes in a far easier manner whenever Mr. Wyfle and the other boys are around. He is less intense somehow and manages to make it through the balance of the night without an insult. Well, maybe he has one or two, but I let those slide.

Finally exhausted, I have to beg off any more activity for the evening. I say goodnight and start to roll toward my door. Someone grabs the back of my chair and pushes me. I lean my tired head back and look up into Hamilton's upside-down face. I sigh. I would prefer to keep the semi-good mood toward this boy, but I'm sure he is about to ruin it.

"I'll go scout out the woods over the next few days and try to find all the circles. When you get better, I'll take you to where they are, and you can fix them. I can tell how important that is to you," Hamilton says to the back of my bandaged head.

It's a good thing I'm sitting down and facing forward because anyone looking at my face might think I've gone into shock. "You don't have to do that."

"I want to," he says as he rolls me into my room. We stop, and the most peculiar thing ever happens. I feel Hamilton's large hand on the back of the bandages on my head. His touch is so hesitant and gentle I kind of freeze like a water molecule at negative one hundred degrees Celsius. "I swear, G.J., I never wanted to hurt you. I am more sorry than you will ever know. I really thought it was Drake that you hated." His voice is so soft that I'm not sure I would have heard him if things weren't so quiet in my empty room.

By the time, my stunned psyche allows me to move again, Hamilton is gone. I wouldn't have guessed he could have given such a sincere apology, but I decide to accept it. Maybe since we are now officially neighbors and he defers to Jack in some manner, he is trying to play nice. I feel unsettled that Hamilton realizes if it isn't Drake I hate, by implication it must be him.

I roll to my desk to work on my science project for a bit and find the email Aunt Celia has left there. She cut off the top part of the paper, which I think is odd. The part that is left reads:

> Her abilities should not be affected by what has happened. She does draw energy from those who practice around her. Her natural draw was what almost killed her mother when she was carrying G.J.. Beth's body just could not take the power G.J. can channel. That is why I had to leave.
>
> Something else is going on. I would look into local covens. Have G.J. try sensing energies. She should be old enough to begin learning the different sensations

each line of energy has. Once she does that, she may be able to find the source. I appreciate this more than you know, Ceily. Take care of our girl.

P

Who in the world is P? Whoever it is, they pretty much confirmed what Gus, Nat, and the rest of us were pondering earlier. Is P my dad? I thought he left long before Mama even knew I was on the way. What did P stand for? If Aunt Celia knows how to reach him, why can't I? I roll to the door and call her in.

Holding the email out to her I ask, "Who is P?" before she even makes it into the room.

"G.J., I have been asked to keep that from you. I would tell you if I could, but it is not safe for you to know." She is just as unhappy to keep the secret as I am that she is keeping it.

"What does that mean?" I ask. "Is P in the CIA or the witness protection program?"

"That is more on target than I think you intend. Really, honey, it is for your own good that you need to leave this alone. I am just trying to help. I do not want to upset you." She moves to put her arm around me, but I lean away.

"Is P my father?" I try to keep my eyes on her to gage her reaction, but she walks behind me.

"G.J., I don't doubt you are intelligent enough to factor things out. But you will not leave it with any answer I can give, so don't ask."

"How is knowing if my father is in contact with you going to harm anyone?" I am getting angry.

Aunt Celia lets out a deep sigh. "I really hate this, Beth," Aunt Celia says to my dead mother.

"Did Mom know you kept in touch with him?" I ask.

"G.J., I can't. I swore I wouldn't. Please, honey, don't push. Let me get back in touch and see what I can tell you." She holds the word "can," letting me know I will never get the whole story—if I am given any at all.

"Can you tell me what P stands for?" I push.

She comes back around so I can see her and gives me a look that says "nice try." Kissing me on the head, she bids me goodnight.

Right, like I won't be tossing and turning as I wrestle with thoughts of my father that I had so far in my almost sixteen years been able to ignore. I get online, shoot Nat an email with the newest events, and struggle into my nightclothes. I read. I research. I listen to music. Every time I try to focus on something, my thoughts go back to that dumb old email. What I really want to do is hack Aunt Celia's email and get P's info from there. It is never a good sign if you begin to justify illegal behavior. The term "slippery slope" runs through my brain, and I have visions of my new home being the women's correctional facility. My thoughts remind me, after my stay at the hospital and the not-so-cozy mattress there, that I'm just not cut out for life behind bars. And if a school suspension will prevent me from getting into a good college, I am fairly certain a stay in juvie would pretty much hamper all my future plans.

At about midnight, I hear a knock on my door. "Come in."

Adam stands in the door with only jammie pants on. I can tell you that gets my mind off dear old dad right quick. It is better than rebooting a computer. Actually, I think the sight of him with no shirt on just shuts down all my mental processes at once, and I don't think they are going to come back online as long as he is like that. "I saw your light on under the door. Are you having trouble sleeping? Is the bed okay?"

He said, "Bed." He said, "Sleeping." He said, "Light," and, "door." He is talking. Put the words in the right order and find a response. I imagine I am working at the processing speed of a 386 computer. I close my eyes. Maybe if I am not looking at him I can respond. "The bed is good."

I hear him walk in the room. I think I might be sweating. I open one eye and peek at him. "Mistake" is what category that choice falls under. He is within arm's reach. Mercy help me. I must be the biggest pervert in the world. This guy is potentially a brother figure. *Get a grip, G.J.* I try to go clinical. It is just skin. Everyone has skin. *Everyone has skin.* Everyone... I'm doing my darndest to convince myself this is no big deal until I feel the mattress next to my hand sink. My eyes fly open. I'm sure my eyeballs are making for an escape.

"You can't sleep?"

I shake my head.

"Me either." He lowers his head and glances up at me with a shy smile. "This is strange, isn't it?"

I nod.

"I'm happy for Dad and Celia—don't get me wrong, but I had no idea when she talked about you, you would be... you."

At that something, maybe just the subliminal part of my brain begins to function, and I tilt my head to see if by doing so, I can move the working part of my thought processes to the forefront.

Before I can reattach my ability for speech, Adam continues, "Wow and now you live here. What am I supposed to do with that?" He lets out a laugh.

I just stare at this beautiful boy on my bed. Is he saying...? No. Is he? No. I am so involved in my mental debate I don't hear the beginning of what he says next.

"...is about to burst. Especially after the other day, like this isn't more awkward. It's great but... man... I don't know."

He runs his hands though his hair, which makes the baseball under his skin of bicep bunch. And now I'm wholly focused on his arm muscles. Jiminy Cricket, I am unprepared for all these amazing looking young men to surround me. "I can't tell if I am the luckiest guy alive or totally screwed."

A giggle bursts out of my chest from nowhere. I use my will to grab any shirt out of my drawer and fling it in his face. "Put it on," I instruct with all of the authority of Louis Gossett Jr. in *An Officer and a Gentleman.*

"Huh?" He eyes me, startled.

"Put. It. On." I am fairly certain I am being clear, but for all I know it might be gibberish.

Adam holds up the shirt. It reads in large lettering "G.R.I.T.S." and underneath that it says, *"Girls raised in the south."*

"Why?" he asks as his beautiful muscles stretch and flex in order to wriggle into my t-shirt. I have to close my eyes until I feel it's safe for me to open them.

After an appropriate amount of time passes, I open only one eye to be sure he is appropriately covered. Seeing the coast is clear for my other eye, I stare Adam right in the face. "Dear Lord, please don't do that to me again. I don't think I can take it. I think I can now accurately explain why women used to faint all the time. When you are not exposed to such things and then confronted with them, I think all oxygen vacates the space between your ears."

"What?" Adam asks in all innocence.

I squint at him. "Adam, there is no way in this world or the next that you do not have a clue how you affect people with the way you look. Sweet heavens, you are lethal. If we are going to hold a conversation, you cannot do that to my mental processes. I think I might just curl up and die if I had to spend all my time at home worried about if you were gonna show up half-naked. Please, for the sake of my sanity, keep all those muscles contained." I realize my mouth has sprung that awkward leak it tends to whenever my mind is just kicking back into gear.

Adam smiles that smug smile a boy can get when he knows you find him attractive.

I take my pillow and put it over my face. Through it I muffle, "Kill me now."

"G.J.," Adam coaxes as he tugs on the pillow. I refuse to come out. "It's all right. I'm glad you said something. It was weird sitting here with you, and I was the only one talking."

"Smart aleck," I call through the cushion.

He finally gets the pillow free. "Is that why you can't sleep? Too much manly goodness around?"

I cannot hold back my smile as I roll my eyes to dismiss him and my embarrassment all at once. "No. I wish that were my issue."

"What is it?" Adam settles back on the post at the foot of my new bed, using the pillow he has just taken from me to cushion his back.

I scowl at his thievery. He just smirks in response. I sigh in resignation. "Do you know I don't know who my dad is?"

Adam's sweet face takes on concern. "No, I didn't know. Do you mean you've never met him or you don't even know his name?"

"Not even his initials. Mama kind of never talked about him. I only knew that when she moved into the house where I grew up, she was already pregnant with me, and none of my neighbors ever saw anyone who could have been my daddy. And trust me, Mrs. Clem was better than the FBI or a stalker when it came to surveillance. I would swear that woman was not above going through our neighbor's garbage just to get the scoop, but I never saw her doing it."

"So now that your mom is gone, you're wondering about him? That seems natural."

"No, that's not it. Today Aunt Celia gave me this." I float the email from my desk over to Adam.

"That is so cool." Adam smiles at me then takes the sheet and reads it. Once he's done he asks, "What happened to the header?"

"She didn't give it to me. She even cut off the bottom." I point to the fraying.

"You think this is him? Did you ask her?"

"Yep, and she told me it was too dangerous for me to know who wrote the email. She wouldn't even confirm it was my father. I mean, unless he turns out to be Darth Vader, I'm not sure why that answer might have ominous repercussions."

"Did you just make a Star Wars reference?" Adam asks.

"Honey, I have mad sci-fi skills. Don't make me open up a can of Star Trek knowledge on your butt, too."

"You are truly awesome." he jokes, and then he brings the subject back to my paternal gene possibilities. "How does Celia know how to reach him?"

"Hence my inability to catch the elusive Z's," I say.

"Ah, Super Brain is working the problem," Adam concludes. "And here I thought it was something mundane like all the crap that has happened to you so far and all these dudes you just moved in with."

"Those are the back burner thoughts. The dad thing is what I am stirring right now."

"Well, I am not sure I can help with the dad thing, but if I can do anything about the rest of the load on your mind, let me know, and I will." He gives me the half-smile you would expect to see out of a genuine offer of support.

"Thanks. Maybe it won't be so bad having a brother." I smile back.

Adam closes his eyes and hits his head on the post. "That has got to be worse than the friend zone."

"What?" I am sure I have misheard him.

Adam sighs, and this time he looks at me with one eye shut. "Nothing, just something I have to work on." He heaves himself up to a standing position. "I am going to let you wrestle with this yourself for tonight. Call me if you need me." He leans over and I think he is going to kiss my cheek, but he takes a huge inhale right at my neck as he tucks my pillow behind my head. "Goodnight," he says on the exhale.

"Really? Why do you people do that?" You'd think at this point the sniffing wouldn't take me aback, but you have all these people sniff you and see how easy it is to get used to.

"We'll get into that another time." He heads for the door.

"You can return my shirt now. I'll close my eyes." I do as promised.

"Wouldn't dream of it. This is mine now."

I open my eyes to see him rubbing his hands over his chest through the fabric. "Adam, why in the name of all that is holy would you want to keep that shirt?"

"G.J., I love this shirt. In fact, this is so comfortable I think I might have to wear it to sleep in tonight. And... ooh, better thought. I will wear it to wrestling practice." Adam laughs. "That is going to be priceless."

"You will not get your funky sweat all over my shirt."

"If you don't let me, I will walk around with my shirt off for the whole time you live here and do push-ups in your room."

"Dirty pool." I huff.

"Sweet dreams, G.J.."

"Goodnight, Adam," I grouse.

Chapter Fourteen

I go to school on crutches the next day. Jack drops me off by car since there is no good way for me to take the bus. Adam has wrestling practice before school, so he caught a ride with my favorite new neighbor. Crutches are meant to make it easier for you to get around when you're injured. They don't. Instead of your injured leg being your only source of pain, your arm muscles get tired, and nobody mentions how much your armpits hurt. By third period, I have lost feeling in my hands, and I'm sure I'm doing something wrong that is going to cause me permanent nerve damage.

Mr. Decker gave me a pass to get out of each class five minutes early to avoid being in the crush of kids in the halls between periods. This does save me the awkward ogling from my fellow students en masse. A hurt leg is one thing; a bandaged head is quite another. I feel like I'm a victim in a Civil War re-enactment. All I need is a flute. Desks, however, are hard to navigate. There is this awful pinching whenever I force my leg, which won't bend, into those plastic chairs found in most municipal buildings. I wonder if those chair folks have a monopoly.

Jack, in his attempt at being "Super Dad," drops off fresh Subway for Adam and me. Adam picks our sandwiches up at the office and brings them to our lunch table. "Thank you. That was so nice of your dad."

Sitting next to me Adam says, "After the other day, Dad doesn't want any of us eating from the cafeteria."

I feel so guilty. Those poor lunch ladies. I had inadvertently thrown them under the bus. Like they had the best reputation before I sabotaged them. "About that…"

"You don't know that it was you," Nat says as she joins us.

"What was you?" Drake asks as he sits next to the now disgruntled Nat.

Ignoring him and adeptly changing the subject, Nat says, "You know what is horrible about you living at the Wyfles'?"

Adam pauses with his sandwich halfway to his mouth.

Nat smiles at him and continues, "We won't be bus buddies anymore."

"Oh, man, you're right. Maybe I can walk over the hill every morning and get picked up at my old stop?"

Adam says, "How about we pick Nat up in the morning, and we can all ride together?"

"Not the same," I say, finishing my bite of sandwich. "No privacy with big brother around."

Adam slides an unhappy glance my way and says, "Derek sat in front of you on the bus. We always knew what you said."

I spin and gape at Adam and then at Nat. Her eyes narrow. "How did you not know we were being spied on?" I ask her.

"Right, like I haven't been busy listening to your thoughts?" Nat shoots back.

"Can't you scan the area or something?" I ask her.

She slides her eyes toward me in annoyance.

I spin back to Adam. "Why would you do that?"

He shrugs. "We wanted to know."

"Who is we?" I ask. Then I notice the blue of my t-shirt under his clothes. "Why are you wearing my shirt?"

Hamilton sits down on my other side. "Why do you have her clothes?"

"Oh, she gave it to me when we were in bed together last night," Adam says in all innocence.

I slant my eyes at him.

"Deny it," Adam challenges.

"Hey, um, Adam," Drake cautions, "You do recall what caused G.J. to end up in the hospital."

I spin back to Hamilton with fear evident on my face. He looks like he's ready to kill someone. "Why on earth do you want to hurt me now?"

Hamilton looks at me and something changes. "I won't hurt you again." Then he moves his eyes back to his lunch like it is the only thing on the planet.

The wave of intensity having passed allows me to get back to Adam. "Look here, big bro, if you keep implying we took a roll in the hay, I want you to remember I have a devious mind and now live under your roof. Don't push me or you could end up with an underwear drawer full of unwanted critters."

"See, big guy," Drake says, "she's good."

I turn back to Drake and see Hamilton nodding out of the corner of my eye.

Nat laughs. "G.J., for such a smart girl you really can be dense."

"Nice look," Sara's sour voice rings from behind me.

"Really?" I look at Nat.

"No, I mean the white gauze is an actual improvement over the way your hair normally looked." Sara puts enough syrup in her words you would think she had squeezed the whole state of Vermont dry.

"Hey, Sara," Nat says. "We know what you're trying to do. G.J. is just more powerful than you or your mom. So if you keep coming for her, she'll knock you to your knees. Give up now."

Drake puts his hand on Nat's back to get her to stop talking. *Great, now my team is working the sinister smack talk.*

"What are you talking about?" Sara has found her snotty again and is not afraid to use it.

"Leave it," Drake warns Nat.

"Doesn't matter. I didn't come to chat with the giant gimp," Sara dismisses me. "Hamilton, I was just coming by to say you can pick me up at six-thirty on Friday not six. I need time to change after practice."

I turn and gawk at Hamilton as Sara leans down and kisses him on the cheek right before she leaves. I blink. I would like to say I understand what I feel at that moment, but there are several seconds of just blank mind. I want to run, but in my present condition, there is no graceful exit. I can't understand my feelings. Doing my best to rationalize my strong reaction, I start to smoosh puzzle pieces together. Sara and her mom want to hurt me, and Hamilton put me in the hospital. Sara and Hamilton are dating. Gus mentioned that Hamilton liked Sara.

"G.J., no," Nat calls.

"Well now that makes sense," I say aloud, ignoring Nat.

"What?" Hamilton focuses on me. He sniffs the air.

Rage fills me to the point where I'm not sure I can hold on to my temper. "You disgust me." My face flushes hot.

The boy actually smiles. "Why are you so angry? Are you jealous?"

I move past rage and go into full-on fury. My eyes blaze.

"Adam, get her out of here," Nat says urgently. When Adam doesn't move fast enough, she yells, "NOW."

Adam tugs at me but Hamilton grabs his hands, trapping me between the two boys as they struggle. "Don't touch me." I am nose-to-nose with Hamilton as I spit the words through my teeth.

"Hamilton, let her go," Nat pleads. "You don't understand."

Hamilton still has this smug grin on his face. "I love this," he whispers in my face.

I can't believe he would collude to do bodily damage to me with my enemy and have the gall to tell me he loves seeing my rage when I figure it out. I am past fury and am about to hit apoplectic.

"Hamilton," Nat's voice snaps to get his attention. "She thinks you attacked her *for* Sara. Let her go. She is not messing around. Don't be this arrogantly stupid."

My chest is heaving, and Adam is still trying to extricate me from his opponent's grip. Hamilton glances from me to Nat. Seeing her intensity, he looks back at my face, which is maybe two inches from his. I'm breathing hard, not able to control my anger. "I wouldn't do that." His attempt to convince me is pathetic.

I will his hands off me. He tries to keep contact, but he is no match for me. "Stay the hell away from me."

"G.J.," Hamilton starts, but Adam has me up in his arms, and we are moving away. Nat follows with my crutches and backpack.

We are all quiet as Adam carries me to science. I'm seething. I'm so mad, and I don't even think about protesting that Adam shouldn't be carrying me until we are almost to the classroom. "Adam, put me down. I don't want you to hurt yourself."

"It's not an issue," he dismisses me.

We hear quick footsteps behind us, and I turn back to see Drake running to catch up. Reaching us, he says to Nat, "Good job back there."

"Mock me all you want, but G.J. was about to go postal." Nat shoves my backpack and crutches at Drake.

"Whoa, looks like G.J. isn't the only one who doesn't get someone's motives," Drake says to Nat's retreating back.

"Well, I finally figured out why he attacked me. Sorry it took me so long. If you knew what was up, you could have said something." I give Drake an accusatory stare.

Adam puts me on the stool at our lab station. "G.J., Hamilton did not attack you. He wouldn't do that."

"I know he is your friend, but don't defend him to me. This girl knows what time it is," I say gesturing back at myself with my thumbs.

"Time is relative," Drake adds dryly.

"G.J., trust me. The last thing I want is for you two to be on good terms, but Hamilton wasn't attacking you. He was going after Drake for touching you," Adam explains.

"What?" I am thoroughly confused and look at Drake.

Drake nods.

I look at Adam, waiting for him to explain.

"It is just the way he is… we are… about our things," Adam replies.

"Your *things*?" I ask.

"This is going to be good," Drake says in an arid tone.

Adam looks decidedly uncomfortable. "We…" his ability to find his way to the next word seems stilted, "are pretty territorial."

"Territorial?" Hamilton's word-repetition questions have contaminated me.

"This might need to be handled at another time," Drake offers as other kids and Mr. Alberts filter into the room.

"Yeah." Adam's relief with his escape is palpable. "I need to talk to my dad anyway."

"Your dad?" I ask.

"Miss Gardener, we are glad to have you back. I received your absentee work from Mr. Wyfle. I have every confidence you will be back up to speed in no time," Mr. Alberts addresses me from the front of the room.

"Thank you, sir," I reply, forced not to pursue the previous topic any longer.

"Hey, Adam, who is picking you guys up after school today?" Drake asks.

"My dad, why?" Adam replies.

"I searched the woods for those circles, and I wanted to talk to you guys and Gus about what I saw." Drake's words are full of unspoken meaning.

"I'll call him and tell him to be a few minutes late," Adam offers.

"Cool," Drake responds.

At five before the bell, I gather up my things and head out. Drake says, "Meet us in the auditorium after school."

I give him the thumbs up while still holding on to my crutch.

Chapter Fifteen

Because I have my five-minute early pass, I get to the auditorium before everyone else. It's dark, so I call out, "Hello?" as I finagle my way into the heavy doors, my crutches definitely not helping with grace or speed.

Out of nowhere Gus answers, "Hello, gorgeous."

I ease my way forward on my hobble sticks and search the room for Gus. "Did you get out of class early, too?" Gus just appears next to me. "Ahhh. For heaven's sake, you could scare a body out of its skin by doing that."

"I didn't intend to frighten you." Gus then scoops me up in his arms and whisks me to the front row so he can seat me with my leg having room to protrude. As graceful as he is in that motion, I am equally discombobulated. My crutches are all akimbo, and I really can't get used to all these people hefting me around like bags of groceries.

"Gus, sweet Betsy, give some warning when you are going to carry people. You might find it unnecessary and possibly unwanted," I huff.

"G.J., that is no way to say thank you."

"Thank you." I smile at him.

Gus sighs. "Fifteen." He shakes his head.

The final bell rings.

"How old are you?" I ask him.

"Unfortunately, too old for you just yet," Gus answers. "You are definitely a prize to wait for."

I shake my head and blush. "You are such a flirt."

Almost immediately, the auditorium doors slam shut and Adam comes in followed by Hamilton. My good mood goes kaplooey. Drake opens the door next before the two other boys make it to the front of the room.

"Hey, looks like the gang's all here," Drake says.

"Gangs are illegal." I sulk that Hamilton has come, too.

Hamilton just leans, staring at me with his back against the stage, boring holes though my skin. I try to look anywhere but at him. I decide to direct my angry attention at his accomplice.

"Don't look at me. Dad is his ride home today, too." Adam puts his hands up in defense.

"Trouble in paradise... again?" Gus asks, looking between Hamilton and me.

Drake says, "Dude, these two communicate with each other about as well as if they had two paper cups and a string."

"Can we just get on with this? I have a ton of work to catch up on." I just want to get away from the big jerk.

"Young pups are often clumsy in their attempts to woo," Gus says, waving off the tension in the room.

"Nope, I am pretty sure he made Sara super happy by putting me in the hospital. He got a hot date out of the deal." I'm so snappish and not proud of myself. I really want to take back my words, but they are free. So, I do the next best thing and change the subject, or try to. "What did you find out, Drake?"

That weird rumbling starts again and Adam says, "Easy."

"I did not..." Hamilton is clenching his teeth so hard it is an effort for the words to get past them.

"Deal with this later." Gus grabs my hand. "Nobody is in the right frame of mind."

"Right," Drake starts. "So I searched the woods last night. I think there are more Wiccans operating in the area than we think."

"What makes you say that?" Adam asks.

"Well, there are the circles that G.J. and Hamilton saw, and then there are the ones that have been closed. They are more respectful somehow. Maybe there is help to be had if we can find the Wiccans who aren't out to get G.J.," Drake offers.

"She could use some training to reach her potential, and I don't see Sara or her mom offering," Gus agrees.

"Why would I train? I don't have to do anything to make things happen. In fact, right now I am *too* powerful at times," I object.

"What about what the email from your dad said? Maybe these other Wiccans can help you with what he said," Adam suggests.

Gus, Drake, and Hamilton all look at me. "Thank you, Adam. Remind me next time I want to share confidences with you that you are a blabbermouth."

"I thought you said you didn't know your father," Gus says.

Listing off my objections I answer, "A—We don't know the email even came from my father; it's only a possibility. B—That was supposed to be a private conversation, and I am uncomfortable addressing my family woes with the present company." I glare in Hamilton's direction. "And C— How am I supposed to be helped by another group of Wiccans? Who is to say they aren't as crazy as the other crew headed by the sadistic Ackers' girls?" I glance at Hamilton and say, "Sorry to besmirch your sweetheart in your company."

"She is—" Hamilton begins.

"Can you guys track down who was at the other circles?" Gus asks.

"What? I think Nat would be a better thought. She can do her mind guru stuff," I say.

"It would be a significant amount of luck if Nat happened across one of these women at the exact moment they were thinking about their involvement in Wicca," Drake says. "But with all that has been said, I think it would not hurt for you to work with someone with some insider knowledge."

"Point taken, but how can they track them down?" I ask, regarding Hamilton and Adam.

All of the boys just look uncomfortable.

"Hey there," I say and wait. "Yoo-hoo," I try again. "Can we please quit playing secret, secret, I've got a secret?" I try to sound nice, but it is getting really hard.

The auditorium doors open, and Jack comes in. "There you are."

Well, there goes my moment of getting anything out of this crew.

"G.J., can you make it to the car?" Jack asks.

"Yes, sir." I grab my crutch and push on the handle to leverage myself out of the chair. Putting the crutches under my arms, I wince from the bruising that has accumulated there.

My face must really reflect pain well since Adam says, "I can carry her, Dad." At the same time, Hamilton just moves in and scoops me up.

Jack looks between the two boys, and I hiss, "I can get there myself. Put me down, or I will crack you over the head with my crutch."

"G.J.," Jack says shocked.

Hamilton just smiles.

"Oh sure, I look like the bad guy." I decide doing this in front of Jack would be just about as smart as sticking my finger in a socket, so I let Hamilton carry me to the car.

Drake says under his breath, "Man, you better be wearing a cup."

The whole way, Hamilton just keeps sniffing me. I really hate this boy.

We are almost to the car when Mrs. Ackers stops us with Sara right behind her. "Jack, how nice to see you. I didn't realize you were running a service for invalids."

Jack smiles broadly. "Have you met G.J.? I am taking care of her now." There is pride *and* warning in his voice.

Mrs. Ackers about swallows her tongue. But venomous beasts can switch directions with that appendage quickly, so I am not surprised she comes back saying, "A bit young for you, isn't she?"

Jack just smiles and unlocks the car. "Always a pleasure, Leslie." He dismisses the nasty woman. I'm really starting to like Jack. I can totally see what Aunt Celia sees in him.

"Hamilton remember six-thirty, not six." Sara calls over her mother's shoulder.

Jack looks at Hamilton, who then looks at me still in his arms. Hamilton says to Sara, "About that, I've made other plans." His gaze is still on me.

"Great," I mumble so low that only the boy holding me can hear. "That's gonna make her less P.O.'d at me."

Hamilton sighs.

"What? I thought you wanted to know more about me?" Sara's pout is so pitiful *I* almost feel bad for the girl.

"Why don't you put me in the car, and you two can continue this conversation?" I lean close to Hamilton's ear and suggest sotto voce.

Hamilton shakes from his head clear down to his toes. He hops to and quickly moves to put me in the car. Jack helps and soon they slide me into the back seat and watch through the window as Hamilton confronts Sara and Mrs. Ackers. There are a whole lot of hand gestures. At one point, I think Mrs. Ackers might just take flight. It is taking a while, and Jack finally has enough and calls Hamilton back to the car, so we can leave. Adam and his dad climb in the front seat, and Hamilton opens the door where my foot is.

"Well, um, I'm not sure how this is gonna work out," I say as Hamilton leans down.

He lifts my leg, and I squeeze my eyes shut in pain. I hear the door close. All of a sudden, he opens the door behind me and lifts me backward, so I am more reclined. Then he slides his body underneath mine with him sitting upright facing forward. Putting his hand on top of my head, he lifts me back upright until I am in the car, and he slams the door closed.

"You have got to be kidding me." I scowl at Hamilton, his nose a centimeter from mine.

"We'll be home shortly," Jack soothes from the front seat.

A low grumble sounds in the car, but it doesn't sound like the engine. Hamilton's chest starts to vibrate, too. I know because my body presses up against him. Now, I don't know if you have ever been forced to be snuggled up with someone who has ticked you off to the level I have reached, but it is about all I can do not to have a complete conniption fit. I kind of go into a blank place, like I am in a stasis. *Just get home, just get home.* With all the chanting I have taken to lately, I might want to think about making a yoga video or selling candles for a living.

"Boys." Jack's voice takes on an almost roar-like quality. I shiver.

Hamilton whispers in my ear, "It's all right." His hand rubs my back.

I turn my face to glare at him. Wouldn't you know it, the guy in front of Jack slams on his breaks, forcing Jack to do the same. Well, I am only going to say the front of my face smooshes up against Hamilton's. As soon as inertia will allow, I jerk back. But it is too late. I'm not a woman of the world, but I fear I'm gonna have to claim Hamilton Calhoun, that rotten twerp, is the first boy to ever kiss me. We're both kind of astounded. I know for a fact that, if someone gives it a try, they'd be able to fry bacon on my cheeks with how hot they are. Hamilton squirms under me, and I honestly can't think of anything on this green earth that will make this moment more uncomfortable. So I just say, "Pardon me." I start to think of all the ways my life would be better if I were a hermit.

"Not a problem," Hamilton mumbles back.

I pray to the good Lord above for space aliens to come take me away from this very moment and so thankful when Jack's car makes the bump, bump as we enter his driveway. Sadly, there will be no fast escape for me. Adam actually is the zippy one in this scenario. He is up and out of that car, so fast I think he's attached rockets to his hiney. My eyes track his movements through the window until I hear sniffing close to my ear.

"Will you please stop smelling me?" My tone lets Hamilton know I am not amused.

Jack has already gotten out of the car and is heading toward the house. And I can see Adam pulling the wheelchair out of the garage.

"Why?" Hamilton asks.

I level my evil stare at the huge boy-man. "Are you slow? Or high? For what sane purpose do you and all the other boys in this town think it is appropriate to go around sniffing at people?"

"Who else has sniffed you?" Hamilton asks.

Really, that is the part of my tirade he catches? "Who hasn't? Why are you still sitting here? We are home now. Get out of the car so I can." I am more commanding than the Queen of England, and I mean an old school queen like Elizabeth I. Somehow I just don't see the II as too overly pushy. Maybe it is the little square purses. They just don't scream authority to me.

"What if I don't?" Hamilton asks, taunting me. I will lay money down that if given an opportunity, this guy would poke an angry bear.

I survey my current options. Adam is halfway back to the car. Plan A—I could be patient and wait for him to come get me. I throw that choice out right quick. This situation doesn't call for calm waiting. Plan B—I could open the door behind me. This option seems good, but if I start to fall, I'm not sure if Hamilton will help or laugh. Plan C—I can try to reach the door at my feet. This, for some miscalculated reason, seems like my best choice. So, I go with Plan C.

Leaning forward and trying to reach past my feet in a bend, I grab for the door handle. "Ahhh, God what are you doing?" Hamilton hollers.

Getting enough air to force out my words from this contorted position is difficult, but I say, "I believe I have asked you not to say that."

"Fine, oomph. What are you doing?" He seems just as uncomfortable as I am at the moment.

Giving up on Plan C, I revert to Plan B: lean back upright on Hamilton's lap and grab for the door handle behind me. The door gives way, and I tilt back intending to put my hand out to stop my fall. But it gets caught in the front seat belt hanging near the door, and I head straight for the ground. Hamilton, I can only assume in his attempt to prevent this, twists his body to get his hand behind my already battered skull. In doing so, somehow when we hit the ground and—I really would like to examine the physics of how this is possible sometime—he lands on top of me. However, he does cradle my head, so there is no concussive impact.

No more blood could possibly rush to my cheeks. Hamilton lies on top of me. My injured leg is half in and half out of the car; our faces are maybe an inch apart. Sweet Jiminy, how do I end up in these ludicrous positions? "Get off."

His hand not holding my head wraps around me tightly as he says, "Make me."

I narrow my eyes. Is he totally insane? I have so much anger rolling around inside me I'm afraid if I let loose, I would be lethal. And while killing him might be a passing thought, I really don't want to have convicted of murder checked off my to-do list before getting a driver's license.

"Hamilton. What the hell?" Adam yells.

"Stay out of this," Hamilton shoots back, his green-gold eyes boring into me like he is surveying for oil.

"Screw that." Adam grabs Hamilton and tries to pull him off.

Unfortunately, this just jostles me further, and I scream in pain and frustration.

"Stop. You're hurting G.J.," Hamilton accuses his lifelong friend.

"Me? Just let her go, you dumbass. What the hell are you trying to prove? Damn it, Hamilton, use your brain." Adam is full out yelling at this point.

I am just about to go for unleashing my will on him as the earth shakes in a low rumble. This noise makes all my bones rattle together. Fear hits me like a tidal wave. The two boys stop their tussling, but my flight response is back big time. Pinned by Hamilton's body and my leg bound as it is, there is no release for my adrenaline surge, and my whole body trembles. Hamilton's fingers are petting the turban-like bandages, but his eyes are on something above my head. He seems not to be able to look away from whatever it is.

Adam is staring at the ground. He acts like he would not or could not look at whatever Hamilton is fixated on. Hamilton releases me gently and rises to his feet. "Take G.J. inside," he instructs Adam.

Without a word, Adam swoops in and has me up and halfway to the house. He too feels my tremors and tries to soothe me as we move quickly toward the house, the wheelchair forgotten. I look over Adam's shoulder and see Hamilton facing a huge wolf in some bizarre stare down. "Adam, we can't leave him out there."

"G.J., this is not our concern. Don't get involved," Adam says as we enter the house. I peek back at Hamilton one more time and see him take off his jacket.

"Adam, call animal control," I say, fidgety with my amped adrenal glands going into overdrive.

"We need to let them resolve this. It is the only way," Adam says.

"What?" I'm sure my hearing is on the fritz.

"Just calm down. Hamilton can't have," Adam stops and adjusts his words, "whatever he wants." The frustration in his voice is raw and personal.

"Adam, what does that have to do with the price of tea in China? Hamilton is about to get mauled by a huge dog," I yell at him.

"It's not a dog," Adam snaps.

"Oh for the love of Pete. Wolf. If you aren't going to help him, I will." I start to pull my body out of his embrace, but he seems to be part python. Every time I think by moving this way or that I will get free, his hold gets a little more secure. Damn wrestlers. I have a thought and yell, "Jack. Jack, hurry."

Adam shoots a hand up and covers my mouth. "Shut up. He'll hear you," he growls in my ear.

Through his hand, I mumble, "Mats ma moint," and I bite him to remove his hand.

"You really should not have done that." He starts to shake and seems to be doing some deep breathing exercises, but on every intake of breath, he seems more agitated. "G.J., you need to calm down," Adam says, but on cue, in order to prove that isn't going to happen in this environment, I hear a yelping scream from outside, sending even more heart-racing hormones loose into my blood stream.

"Dear Mary, how are you so nonchalant?" I say, "I hate the boy, but I don't want him dead."

Adam starts breathing harder. "G.J., I can't take how excited you're getting. Please, I'm going to lose it if you don't calm down. Is that my blood on your lip?" His eyes look like they are backlit.

"How, in the name of all that is holy, do you think anyone should be relaxed right now?" My adrenalin gives my anger a spike like a high-school punch bowl. I wipe at my mouth. "No," I say feeling my mouth. "I think you split my lip when you gagged me. The blood is mine." As soon as the words leave my mouth, I know something is very wrong. Adam is no longer Adam. The light hitting his eyes reflects a feral gleam like fireflies have crawled behind them.

In a voice with more gravel than Jack Palance, Adam says, "Your room." He moves me with a grace and speed my clumsy self has no ability to comprehend. Arriving he places me on the bed, sniffing up and down my body. That is it. I fling Adam backward, and he hits my desk, books flying everywhere.

"Adam, Jiminy Cricket, what has gotten into you?" My eyes widen in disbelief.

"You," he roars as he lunges for me again.

Again, I fling him back. More books dislodge with the jostling plus gravity. "Jack," I scream.

"No," Adam roars as he tries again to get to me.

I send Adam soaring for the door just in time for a winded, disheveled Jack to catch him. Adam actually snarls at his father. More surprising than that, Jack snarls back. Whatever that moment is, it makes the younger Wyfle man look down and away, but he still seems to be growling and breathing heavy. Seeing they have cleared my door threshold, I slam and lock it with my will.

I gulp in air. What? What? I can't even form an actual question in my mind. My flight reflex is still in control. Dear Lord, what about Hamilton? This is a mad house. I need Aunt Celia. How can I explain this to her? I can't even comprehend it myself, and I'm here. I pick up the phone by my bed and start to dial. A loud pounding knock makes me jump out of my skin and drop the phone; it skitters under my bed.

"G.J., I know you're scared. Please open the door." It's Jack.

I sit mute, hoping my silence will indicate I have mimicked the famous Elvis phrase, making it my own: G.J. has left the building.

"Please let me talk to you." Jack's voice is firm but cajoling.

"Jack, as of this moment, I just can't do that. Look, you seem like a very nice man, but I am pretty sure at this point, I cannot live with Adam. And, since he is your son and all, I think that means I am going to ask Aunt Celia to take me back to her house. No offense, but—" My sentence is cut off by something slamming up against the door.

Jack is in the broken doorframe. His eyes have that same feral look Adam's held a few moments before. In a soothing voice, I don't think someone leashing in that much ferocity can muster, Jack says, "I can't let you do that." He advances toward me.

Chapter Sixteen

Jack has his hands up, patting the air as if to cool the situation down by slowly pushing air at it. "Your aunt means the world to me. I just can't lose her over something so trivial."

My eyes move around the room as if to see if I'm still in reality. "Trivial? Jack, you weren't here. Had I not been able to do what I can do, Adam would have attacked me."

Jack appears dismissive. "Adam was just caught up in all the heat of the moment. When you both cool down, he will make it right."

The speed my heart rate had been racing is giving into the lethargy that inevitably follows so much urgent demand from the accelerated blood flow. I let out a deep sigh, trying to clear my head. "Hamilton…"

"Will be fine. I had no idea he was getting so aggressive with you. You are too young to be so worked up. He is so headstrong sometimes he forgets you are teenagers. He will give you some space now," Jack says trying to soothe me.

"No, he was outside with a wolf," I say, panic still clear in my voice.

"I saw him home. He is a little scraped up but fine."

"What about the wolf? What happened to him?" I ask immediately.

Jack smiles at me. "You are so caring, G.J.. You are definitely special. I can see I will be fighting all the boys away. I am going to have to start training. These young pups aren't as small as they used to be."

An inadvertent blush slides up my cheeks, and I force it back down. "Jack, what happened with Adam was more severe than that. It was a hare's breath from a *Lifetime* movie, or worse, a show on ID. I really can't say I will feel safe here. That was... intense."

Jack sits on the side of my bed and stares at his clasped hands. He blows out a breath. "I don't know what I can say to make you more comfortable. I know Adam is a good kid. He would not have hurt you. That was a wild moment for him, but he will get it together." Jack looks me dead in the eye. "He cares about you. You were upset, so he was agitated. That, I can promise you, won't change. Something set him into overdrive. Maybe hormones?" Jack offers.

"I hate to mention it, but we are just starting the joys of adolescence. If hormones are going to be an issue, then we have a long row to hoe yet," I point out.

Jack smiles. "You have Ceily's quick mind."

"Adam would not let me help Hamilton or call for you."

Jack nods as if that makes perfect sense.

"He went as far as to clap his hand over my mouth and draw blood." I point to the sore spot on my lip.

"Ah, that's what did it." Jack lets out a guffaw.

I tilt my head. Maybe Jack has been wondering why my lip is split?

"Well, that makes me feel better," Jack says, slapping his hands on his knees as he stands to go.

"Pardon?" I ask, thinking I must have fallen asleep when he actually settled things. I'm pretty sure I missed narcolepsy as part of my head injury.

"Why don't you take a quick bath, and we can all discuss this when you are cleaned up and feeling more settled?" Jack says as he moves to the windows and opens them as if it is a beautiful spring day and not the middle of winter.

He leaves me sitting there completely nonplussed and returns with my crutches and chair a few seconds later.

"I'll get your door fixed after you are done," he says, examining the splintered frame as he leaves me to do as he instructed.

Wow, do I need to get outside and out in the woods. I'm not sure how much longer I can take being out of commission. Hobbling to the bathroom, I try to rinse away the last few minutes, hours, days, and months. I'm not sure how far back I really need to go to get to a clean slate.

When done, I make my way back to my bed and sit down, trying to figure out how to get the new gauze back in place. From behind me, I hear a soft knock. I turn to see Adam in my doorway. "You need help?"

I don't answer. I just look at him.

He walks in the room. "G.J., I am so sorry. I have never done anything like that with a girl in my life. I have no defense."

"I've been thinking about this, and I believe you. But, honey, that scared the ever-living hell out of me," I admit.

"I know; boy, do I ever know." Adam glances down for a second then back up at me. "Never be scared of me. I swear I will never hurt you. I really cannot take your fear, especially of me. It drives me crazy." His voice is a sincere confession.

"Well, yeah I was pretty sure you hit nut job back there." I smile at him. This was the Adam I knew. I decide the other was an anomaly. I will keep a lookout for such a thing again, but I *want* this to be water under the bridge. So, I make my discomfort scoot.

Adam smiles broadly back at me. He is a handsome son of a gun. He puts his hand out, offering to take the bandages in my hand. "Let me help."

I hand him the gauze and say, "Okay, but if you make me look funny, I am super gluing your toilet seat down."

"It's a head wrap. What look were you going for?" he taunts.

"I'm hoping for more Greta Garbo and less *Girl with the Pearl Earring*." My face is completely deadpan.

"Not into the classics?" Adam asks.

"I want a smoother finish and don't like the idea of having a tail," I defend my choice.

Adam chuffed. "All right, no tails today, but no promises in the future. Some people think tails are hot."

I giggle. I can't help it. He is being absurd, and I need the stress relief.

****

Later, after Aunt Celia gets home, Jack is just finishing fixing my door. She kisses him then asks, "What happened here?"

"A little miscommunication," Jack dismisses her concern.

"G.J.? Honey, are you all right?" She comes to my bed where I'm reading my English homework.

"It was a little freaky earlier. But I've worked it out," I say not wanting to ignore what happened like Jack is, but not wanting to sound the alarm anymore either.

Jack narrows his eyes, assessing the conversation.

"What happened?" Aunt Celia asks me.

"The kids had a disagreement, but it was all straightened out in the end." Jack again seems to get out his industrial-sized broom to sweep the issue under the rug.

"How did the door get broken?" Aunt Celia asks. I tell you she is a sharp cookie.

"I did that. G.J. locked herself in her room, and I won't have that in this house," Jack says in the parent-of-the-year voice he's trying to master.

"Jack, she is a teenage girl. It is their God-given right to lock their doors when in the heat of an argument. If she wasn't locking people out, I would have to take her to therapy," Aunt Celia says.

I'm not sure how I feel about that. I think in this particular moment, it is not the irrational but the rational teenage girl handling that situation.

Seeing his way to make this about my age and not this environment, Jack says, "I guess you are right. I will try to keep that in mind."

Sneaky man. "I thought it was because I wanted to go back to Aunt Celia's house." I throw him a curveball. I would have played nice, but I'm staring up at him from under the bus he is throwing me beneath.

"G.J., we all agreed to give this a go. We haven't even been here a week. I know you have been through a lot but please, kiddo, we all need to *try* if this is going to work," Aunt Celia says with a soft note of pleading.

Set and match to the man with the wolfish grin. I sigh my defeat, and Aunt Celia takes it as a good sign.

"Besides, the house is always there if things don't go as planned," Aunt Celia adds as she turns to leave the room. "I'm going to get out of my work clothes. What's for dinner?" She walks out.

I will have to admit there's what my mama would call a touch of the devil in my promise of a comeback smile I give Jack. He scowls and storms after Aunt Celia.

****

On Friday, I have both of my follow-up doctor's appointments, so Aunt Celia picks me up early from school. It's nice not to have to worry about the car-pooling situation for a few days. After the neurologist examines me, he says, "You seem to be doing remarkably well."

Aunt Celia gives me a dirty look, and I blush a little saying, "I always do heal fast."

"Well, that is remarkable. If you continue to heal at this rate, you should be almost completely mended by the time I see you next month. The human body is a resilient thing. Wonders never cease to amaze me." After a few warnings of what to look out for, he sends me on my way and says he will see me in a month.

Leaving the doctor's office, Aunt Celia says, "Kid that was a close call. I hope we are as lucky with your orthopedist."

"I had to heal my head. No way could I handle all that has been going on with a dreidel spinning in my brain."

She smiles at me in the rear view. "I get it."

The leg doctor tries really hard to get us to sign off on me being in a study he is doing for a paper he's writing, but Aunt Celia is firm in her objection. He is so forceful that at the end of the appointment she goes to the front desk, insisting we receive my medical records; we will be seeking out another doctor.

After that appointment, she hands me the file and says, "Do what you gotta do, kiddo."

I love this woman. I spend the rest of the ride home healing my leg. I don't complain about how much it hurts because I'm going to be free again. I can't wait to tell Nat and to get back out in the woods.

Chapter Seventeen

The fresh air is better than sweet tea on a hot day. I walk for hours. I never want to go home. I come across only one of the dead spots and take the time to pull the energy back to it, replenishing what the Ackers stole. I need to get a hold of Drake and have him take me to the ones he'd found. While I admit the circles are strange, I also notice pairs of jogging pants and shorts left all over the woods. I pick up the first pair with a stick, thinking someone had carelessly discarded it and take them home to throw away or give to charity. But I find more than a few misplaced items. And they are scattered everywhere. I wonder if some sports team was flying over, lost their luggage in a cargo door malfunction.

Arriving back to the house, Jack and Aunt Celia are cooking in the kitchen together, and Adam is doing homework at the table with his ear buds in. I don't blame him. I try to find all kinds of ways to ignore the mating rituals of Jack and Aunt Celia, and cooking is definitely one of them.

"How was the walk?" Aunt Celia asks, her focus on the onion she's cutting.

"Good, but does anyone know if there's a missing soccer team's airplane around here?" I ask. That brings everyone's attention to me and the stick I'm holding with the pair of sports shorts I found.

"One pair of shorts makes you worry over a soccer team? I don't follow," Jack says.

"One pair? No. But the dozens I found have me concerned that just over the next hill there is a hopeless crew of athletes speculating over which one tastes the best," I say.

Adam jumps in before Jack can say anything. "We workout back there. That hill is a beast. Sometimes we discard layers. It's been going on for years."

I don't miss Jack smiling and nodding at his son.

"You take off your shorts?" I ask skeptically.

"Young lady, I don't think it is appropriate for you to discuss what Adam chooses to wear or not wear while working out," Jack reproves.

"Jack." Aunt Celia throws a piece of chopped onion at him. My lips roll in and I close my eyes to avoid expressing my own embarrassment.

I take the stick holding the shorts and drop them on Adam's book before exiting to my room.

****

A few minutes later Aunt Celia knocks on my door. "You okay?" She gives me a smile.

"I think I am going to find a new level for what all right means. My old standards don't seem to apply." I decide now is as good of a time as any to tell her what is happening with the other nonsense. "Just so you are up to speed, and maybe if you have another chat with the mystery P person, I wanted to let you know Sara Ackers and her mama are out to get me. And Hamilton and Sara are dating. He says he didn't attack me for her, but I'm not so sure. Yesterday, they chatted after school and he tried to attack me again that afternoon. Now, I know I am going to sound like I dropped acid on this next part, but it happened. The only thing that stopped him from whatever he was intending to do was an enormous wolf growling at him. Adam took me in the house, so I don't know what happened, but Jack said Hamilton was fine, and he saw him home."

"Another wolf?" Aunt Celia is terrified. "JACK," she calls, fear clear in her voice.

"That was not the main point," I mumble.

Jack is at the door in a flash, searching the area like he is on a S.E.A.L. team. Clearing the room mentally, he goes to Aunt Celia, making her his only focus. It was clear to me, if not to Aunt Celia yet, that Jack is all in.

"Jack, G.J. said there was another wolf here yesterday. Why neither of you have chosen to tell me this until now, I am not clear on." She is hot. "Particularly since G.J. just got back from romping in the woods where these things must live."

Jack takes her by the arms and rubs his hands up and down. "It was no big deal, and I took care of it." He shoots me a look telling me he thinks I'm a rat.

I put my hands up. "Look, I'm not worried about the wolf. Wolves don't scare me. Having a neighbor who has now attacked me twice and has a girlfriend who seems to want me to star in her home video of how to bully so she can teach people by YouTube *does* make me uncomfortable."

"Not worried about wolves? G.J., you are not invincible," Aunt Celia says.

"The wolves don't hurt me. Hamilton and his bitchy Barbie are the issue," I try to redirect.

"Listen, kiddo, high-school bullies are only as powerful as you make them. Wolves are wild animals that you cannot control. You have your levels of concern backwards," Aunt Celia scolds.

"Hamilton has apologized, and I am sure he is not working with Sara against you," Jack tries to intercede.

Aunt Celia turns on him. "If this young man has attacked G.J. twice, I agree with her that she should be concerned. I know you have known him for a while. And I was willing to take your word after the first time, but now there have been two attacks. I won't have her in danger." Aunt Celia puts her foot down. "Not from wolves and not from Hamilton."

"I am not in danger from the wolves," I say.

"G.J. is right. Wolves are just a part of life around here. They won't attack either of you," Jack supports my argument. I'm not expecting help from that quarter.

"Jack? A wolf almost came through the window the other day. Now you've had to run off another one. I have lived in this area for years, and I have never seen a wolf. Now they are everywhere. I don't care what you say; this is not safe." Aunt Celia is not letting go of her argument. "Add to that, the neighbor boy keeps attacking G.J. I think we need to go back to my house."

If she had taken a two-by-four to his head, she couldn't have struck Jack any harder. "Ceily," Jack breathes out her name in a pleading tone. "Please, babe, don't."

I really want to be a water droplet that can evaporate into the atmosphere at this moment. Even though this topic concerns me, I just know this is a private issue for the two of them.

"Jack, she has been through so much. I have to keep her safe. I love you, but this has to be my priority right now." Aunt Celia is easing his pain somewhat but is holding firm.

Jack pleads to me for help. I have to try. Whatever issues I have with Jack, he loves Aunt Celia. I don't want her to lose out because of me. That just seems wrong.

"Aunt Celia, I wasn't telling you any of this so we would move. I was trying to make a different point. My friends and I think maybe there is more than one coven in the area. Gus thinks another coven might be able to help me learn to defend myself and do what P said I could do in the email. I thought you might ask him for me."

"Who is P?" Jack asks.

Aunt Celia gives me a cautioning stare. "Don't worry about it."

"Too late. Who is P?" Jack swings his eyes from Aunt Celia to me.

"I don't know. I just know he has information about me," I say, not comfortable under Jack's scrutiny.

Aunt Celia levels me with her gaze. "Not helping, kid. Jack, I can't tell you that."

Jack's eyes flash, and I'm pretty sure I now know what jealous rage looks like. "Who... is... P?" Jack's an intimidating man.

"Don't push me right now. If you decide to make this an issue, you will be picking a losing fight. You can trust me because I am keeping a promise by keeping this from you." She lays down the law.

"I don't like you keeping things from me," Jack says, still very angry.

"Here, Jack." I give him the email.

"G.J.," Aunt Celia says in exasperation.

After he finishes reading the email, he hands it back to me. "Can you do what he says in the email?" Jack asks me.

"No. That was what I was trying to talk to Aunt Celia about." I switch from talking to Jack to Aunt Celia. "I want you to ask P if they know who's in these covens or how you go about finding a coven. I don't know the first thing about this whole underbelly. How do you get involved? Drake said there seems to be different covens operating in this area."

"I'll find out," Jack volunteers.

"This does not address that Hamilton boy. I don't think G.J. is safe with him next door." Aunt Celia is back on her point. She's better than an English setter.

"I will handle Hamilton. G.J. is safer here than anywhere." Jack's trying to convince Aunt Celia not to leave.

Adam walks up to the door and pulls his earphones out as Aunt Celia puts both her hands up in a "stop talking" motion to Jack. "What if he attacks her again? We can't be with her at all time and with him right here, I cannot take that risk."

"I won't do it again," Adam says from the door. "I promise. I won't lose control like that again."

Aunt Celia spins toward Adam. "What?"

Jack puts his hands over his eyes.

Aunt Celia now turns on me. "What is he talking about?"

I look down. "It was no big deal." I try to dismiss her concern, but I know there is no good direction out of this mess. I can actually sense Aunt Celia's blood pressure rise.

Adam apparently has swallowed his tongue, because he loses all ability to speak. So Jack, that poor stupid man, tries. "I told you the kids had a disagreement when G.J. locked me out."

Aunt Celia's narrowed eyes and disgusted stare let Jack know that was the wrong answer. She slams the daggers she is glaring at him home and in a scary, low voice I have never heard her use she says, "You mean to tell me after your son attacked my injured niece, you felt the need to make sure she did not even have a locked door as a defense?"

The room gets the kind of quiet you would expect in the vacuum of space. As dangerous as the men in this area tend to get, they have nothing on Aunt Celia at this moment.

"G.J., pack your things. We leave in one hour," Aunt Celia says as she moves out of the room.

"Ceily," Jack pleads.

"Don't, Jack. Don't even try to talk to me right now." Aunt Celia is brooking no argument.

"Jack, I am so sorry," I say to him. If you have ever seen a heart shatter, you know, as a human being, you feel a ripple of the energy as it happens.

"G.J., help me make this right," Jack pleads.

"I will. I promise." I know this vow is vital.

Jack seems to cling to my words as his only hope. He nods and says, "You better get packed, kiddo." Taking a deep breath, he pushes past Adam, who stands there with his head hanging in shame.

****

It's dark outside as we load the last boxes into the car. Aunt Celia has not said one word to Jack. He moves like a zombie, helping us get things into the car. Adam looks like he's going to be sick. I rub a hand down his arm. "Hey, I'll see you at school, okay?" I'm trying to remind him we said we would still be friends.

A car pulls up next door and Hamilton emerges, glancing over at what's happening. I know this is the last thing that is going to make this moment better. It's like dropping a Mentos in a Coke to make it less bubbly. But no matter how much I try, I can't turn away from this train wreck about to happen. To make this moment the perfect culmination of just plain old awful, the person driving the car is Mrs. Ackers, and Sara is sitting in the passenger seat. What fates have brought these people to witness this horrible act in our life stories?

The wicked women find it necessary to get out of their vehicle and insert themselves in this private matter. Hamilton starts toward us. "What is going on?"

"Stay away from G.J.," Aunt Celia warns, making it seem like Hamilton is about as big as a flea.

"Celia, he won't harm her," Jack says. I'm not sure if he's cooling her temper or warning Hamilton not to try it.

"Jack?" Mrs. Acker's asks. "Trouble in paradise?"

Aunt Celia turns on the evil woman. "I don't believe you have any business trying to insert yourself in our lives. Please go."

"Adam? What the hell man?" Hamilton says to his friend.

Adam just shakes his head and studies the ground.

"Jack?" Hamilton asks.

"The girls are going back to Celia's house," Jack explains. The pain the words cost him moves across his features in the light of the street lamp.

Hamilton looks dumbfounded. "Why?"

"Well, Mr. Calhoun, it could be because you and your friends keep attacking my niece. Why would I put her in your vicinity after what you have now tried to do at least twice?" Aunt Celia rails at him.

"Aunt Celia." I give her a look to drop this right now.

"You think moving out of Jack's house is going to keep me from her?" Hamilton says in a menacing tone.

Jack makes that same growling noise he had made to Adam when he'd stopped Adam in my room. Aunt Celia looks at Jack rather shocked. Hamilton looks down like he has been cowed. Aunt Celia turns on the admonished young man. "Don't you ever threaten G.J. again." Aunt Celia is back to making Jack seem like a small puppy when it comes to aggression.

"Celia, as long as you have the car packed, why don't you take your niece and leave town?" Mrs. Ackers chimes.

"Leslie, what is your problem?" Aunt Celia levels her gaze on the other woman.

"G.J. is the menace in this situation. That girl has attacked Sara twice. I understand she has a troubled past and was possibly responsible for her mother's unfortunate demise. Maybe you should think about reform school for her." Mrs. Ackers is trying to push Aunt Celia's buttons.

"Leslie, I don't think you quite grasp the situation. You have raised a vindictive little twit who does everything in her power to belittle and bully others, including intimidating and lying. This is the nasty, selfish child you are unleashing on the world. Her level of entitlement is only rivaled by your own. I believe I indicated earlier that you have no business here or involving yourself with us. Have some manners, and for pity's sake, teach your daughter how to behave by leaving us alone." Aunt Celia doesn't raise her voice. She doesn't point a finger, but she fells Mrs. Ackers like a sickle through hay.

That is the first thing to bring a smile to Jack's face since Aunt Celia said she was leaving. He walks up behind her and crosses his arms. She doesn't need his intimidating stance, but it's nice to see he wants to show solidarity.

After a few huffs and puffs of outrage, Mrs. Ackers finds her mental handbook of villainous sayings and comes up with a lame gem. "You have no idea who you are dealing with. You will regret ever having said those words, Celia. You should have learned by now. We can make your whole world one of pain."

I have to ask. "Do you write for the W.W.E.?"

Aunt Celia sends me a "stay out of this" glare. "What I have learned is you are absolutely a bore. You have deluded yourself into thinking your opinion matters to the rest of the people in this town. Live in your world of hate, Leslie. Burn up your energy. I won't waste any of mine on you."

Mrs. Ackers turns to Sara and says something I can't hear. Sara and she start to chant in murmured tones. This time I feel the energy they are calling. I feel it flowing down from the hills. I have called the same energy back to the circles. They are gathering it to do something to Aunt Celia. I'm watching two Wiccans in action. I pull the energy to me. I can't let them have it. The more I draw it to me the more they try to call. My body is pulsing with power. I'm not used to holding it like I'm a battery. Power whips at me almost like I'm a superconductor.

"Adam, get G.J.," I hear someone call.

I feel large arms wrap around me and pull my vision away from the Ackers. But that won't stop me from absorbing energy. "Make them stop calling power." My voice is not my own. I sound possessed.

"Hamilton," someone screams.

The draw of the power stops. I have energy everywhere. My teeth are vibrating in my head. I hear Sara and her mother yelling in protest, but I can tell none of the power has reached them. They are as weak as fresh-born kittens. It takes energy to draw energy, and they've gotten none of the payoff. I, however, feel like I can wipe out all of Spokane.

"Jack." Aunt Celia's terrified voice rings in the air. I pull that power to me as well.

"No more…" I plead. I'm half-drunk and half-terrified from the power I am holding.

The person holding me tries to soothe me by cradling me to his large chest and rubbing my back.

I hear the Ackers continue random objections. I unleash a small bit of power. "Gone," I command. In my mind, I will them in their car and several streets away. I know I have to be careful.

"G.J.? Where did they go?" the person holding me gently asks.

"I am trying to be careful." My eyes fill with petrified tears. I look up through the blur to what I think is Adam.

"I know you are. You are doing such a good job, sweetheart," the blurry face says. "Where did you send them?"

"A few streets away," I say, trembling.

"Good girl," the deep voice says.

"Oh, my God. What is wrong with her?" That's Aunt Celia.

"I don't know," says the person holding me.

"She was stupid enough to pull the energy they were trying to draw to herself." That's Hamilton, I'm pretty sure.

"She is doing great," says the voice holding me, but it isn't Adam.

"Great?" Aunt Celia shrieks, making me jump.

"Easy, G.J., easy," the voice says. I'm trying so hard to drop the energy instead of pulling everything available to me.

Hamilton somehow moves close. "G.J., send it back to the circles. You can do it. Push it back."

"I don't know where the circles are," I scream, anxiety riding my voice.

"Push it back up the lines, the ones from the email. Look for the lines." That's Adam, who is farther away now.

"There's too much. They called so much." I am louder than I need to be, but I can't help it any more than a redneck can resist hollering at a girl in an American flag bikini.

"Jack, let her go. She could hurt you," Aunt Celia's voice is quivering, but her fear isn't for me.

I blink to clear the water in my eyes and realize it's Jack holding me. "She's right. Let me go."

"No way, kiddo. We're in this together. Tell me what you need." Jack is using a growling voice; it somehow tells me he is trying to contain pain.

"Oh, Jack, am I hurting you?" I sob at the man. "I don't want to hurt anyone."

"I know, sweet pea. Find somewhere for it to go. Let's just send all that you are holding away somewhere. Where do you think it should go? Can you follow it back the lines it came from?" Jack is so calm. Even though I'm scaring the hell out of Aunt Celia who has seen me use power, Jack is holding it together and trusting me. I instantly trust this man. I know we are safe with Jack. Not just Aunt Celia, but me too.

"I don't know how yet. I'm so sorry." I have to close my eyes.

"Jesus. Stop apologizing. It is making me insane." Hamilton's voice sounds behind me, and I can sense he's pacing.

"Hamilton. Stop. She is drawing all excess energy right now. You are adding to the problem." Jack seems to grasp more than I do at the moment.

I hear a growl.

"Leave." I feel a wave of energy leave Jack, and it flows into me, making me feel even higher.

"No." I feel Hamilton's energy in his response.

Nobody will attack Jack in my presence. This man is holding me together. I turn on Hamilton. I honestly have no idea what I look like, but it must be something out of *Avatar, the Last Air Bender* because everyone shies back.

Jack rubs my arms, trying to get me to turn around. "G.J., can you stop pulling the energy?"

"Jack?" Hamilton yells at the man trying to talk me through this unknown moment for both of us. "Is she calling your command power?"

"Yes. And I did not feel your defiance so she is getting that too, I think. For G.J.'s sake you need to cool it," Jack says.

"I have never seen her like this," Aunt Celia says, panic holding her voice like a vice.

"G.J., follow the circuit." Hamilton tries to get my brain to kick on.

"There's too much. I'm overwhelmed. What was your girlfriend trying to do?" I feel power spike from somewhere, and again I call it to me. I shiver as it comes into me.

"Hey, G.J., calm down or I am taking my shirt off," Adam says.

"What?" comes a chorus of voices including my own.

"You know you want me to," Adam continues. "Remember manly goodness?" He rubs his chest in an "I'm too Sexy" manner.

A laugh escapes me. That idiot is trying to ease my mood by making light of the situation.

"Remember my yummy abs?" Adam continues to taunt.

Embarrassed laughter bubbles from my chest as I picture him shirtless in my mind.

"Hey, dirty mind, it's cold out here," Adam says, an arrogant smile lighting his face as his shirt disappears.

I'm so embarrassed all I can do is giggle. Here this guy's daddy is holding me, and I just undressed him with my mind.

"Put some clothes on, you idiot," Hamilton snarls at Adam.

Adam runs inside the house.

"G.J., where did you send Adam's clothes?" Jack asks from behind me, a rumble of laughter heaving his chest.

I shake with contained embarrassed amusement. I look up at the sky and shake my head. "I don't know."

"I wish your aunt could do that," Jack says.

"Jack." Aunt Celia joins my mortification motor train, but she doesn't find it funny at all.

Adam comes back wearing the G.R.I.T.S. shirt he stole from me, doing some horrible impersonation of a Miss-Jay runway stomp.

"You are an idiot." I giggle.

"Oh, yeah?" Adam says as he rushes me. Jack almost throws me behind him, but something makes him hold me in place for whatever his son is trying to do. Adam begins tickling me. "I'm an idiot, huh?"

"Ahhh." I playfully scream. "Stop." Great rolling hollers of laughter punctuate my words.

Jack picks up on what his son is doing and puts me over his shoulder, playing a halfhearted game of keep away, letting Adam tickle me for a moment then parrying to give me time to breathe.

"Have you all lost your mind?" Aunt Celia is still full of concern, unable to shirk off the fear that still has its hands around her heart.

Seeing her distress, Jack throws me into a waiting pair of strong arms so he can go to her. Hamilton cradles me, staring down at my face as the giggles start to die on it. But Adam digs his fingers into my ribcage, making me contort to escape him in Hamilton's arms. Hamilton spins and begins to play keep away with Adam. I laugh. I forget how much I hate this boy as we swing this way and that, trying to avoid Adam's lightning fast fingers.

"Dude, if I had a snowball, you would be toast." Hamilton laughs as he dodges Adam again.

Snow starts to fall in huge clumps from the sky. Hamilton looks up at the sky and then at me. He has this expression of wonder on his handsome features. I shrug.

"Hey. Whose side are you on?" Adam complains.

"Are there sides?" I ask, trying to play it cool. Hamilton tickles me. "No." I scream, unable to keep from laughing. I twist this way and that, trying to avoid the zing of his fingers reaching my ribs. "Hamilton," I squeal. There is just no ladylike way to be the recipient of a good old-fashioned tickling. I try to tickle back, but it just isn't working. All it does is give my fingers an excuse to travel over all those muscles. I shut those thoughts down right quick. Heaven only knows where that would lead.

"Put her down," Aunt Celia objects.

"The boys are trying to help her let off some of that energy by laughing," Jack explains. "They are just playing; we do it all the time. It helps release the tension."

"They play too rough with her." Aunt Celia has now gone into overprotective mode.

"Ceily." Jack is trying to sweet-talk her into understanding I need this. "Look at her. She is already better."

Jack is right. I can't tell if I am assimilating to the energy or if I am releasing it somehow. I am really starting to like that man. Hamilton sniffing my neck interrupts my happy thought. Adam gets close and begins doing the same. "Bwah." I thought poking my ribs tickled, but having two people stick their cold noses on my neck is worse. "Put me down," I scream. I am instantly upright on the ground, but Hamilton hasn't let go of my waist.

A pitifully small snowball hits Hamilton on the side of the head, and he releases me in order to give chase to Adam. They begin to playfully wrestle on the ground, just beginning to turn white with accumulated flakes. I take the opportunity to head off to the trees behind the house for cover. Aunt Celia calls out, "Freeze, young lady. We are leaving. Get in the car."

"Celia." Jack's broken heart rings in his voice like someone rubbing their fingers around the rim of a wine glass.

I wish we did not have some other place to be. I want to stay with Jack and Adam. I realize I am beginning to actually accept us all, as wacky as we are, as a family. But I trudge back to the car, slipping a little in the quickly falling snow. Aunt Celia is doing her best to protect me. She has to be onboard with this or it is never going to work. I look back over my shoulder. The two gigantic kids have stopped their scuffling and just watch as I walk away.

"See you in school, G.J.," Adam calls out. I hope I am right to read that as a promise we will still be friends.

I put up my hand as a farewell. Leaving these people actually hurts. I look at the desperate sadness on Jack's face. I can't help it. I run over and hug the huge man. Wrapping him up, I let him know how I feel by squeezing it into him. I hold so tight I am sure I would have given a mama bear a run for her money. Jack pats my back and kisses the top of my head. I've never had a daddy but, boy, I feel like Jack would make a good one. He gives that telltale double pat on my back that signals for me to go on.

Aunt Celia is already in the car, her face averted. I climb in and close the door. "I can't have you in danger all the time. Let's go back to my house, and we will work out where we go from there." I think she's trying to convince herself more than me. This is killing her too. I can tell by the water pooling up inside the rims of her eyes. As we pull out of the driveway, I look back. Something behind the house has caught the attention of all three men, and as we move out to the street, they begin to run in the opposite direction.

Chapter Eighteen

We stop for takeout and head to the house. We're both quiet as we wind through the streets back to Aunt Celia's. I honestly think we've forgotten patterns of speech and will have to start from scratch. I wonder if we will be reduced to Dr. Seuss level reading in order to develop language again. I hear the howl of one wolf and another and then more. Several sirens soon accompany those wails. I'm so distracted by my own morose feelings of loss that I don't catch that colored lights are bouncing off my retinas until Aunt Celia breathes out, "Oh my God."

My brain plugs the images before my eyes into a functioning thought process. There are fire trucks up and down the street where Aunt Celia's house sits. They are blocking the view of the exact structure we've been headed for. Aunt Celia throws the car in park where we are in the middle of the street and flies out the door. She is at a dead run in the blink of an eye. I'm horrified. I get out slowly. I know what we will find. Hadn't I wished we had nowhere else to go?

I somehow move forward, although my legs are so numb I'm not sure they are actually being used to propel me in any direction. A firefighter holds Aunt Celia back. She is screaming. I can tell she is. But my ears seem only to be picking up a rushing sound that blocks all other noises. I stare dumbly at the inferno that had once been Aunt Celia's home. The light of the fire and the emergency vehicles bounces off the glittering snow crystals falling relentlessly from the sky. It is beautifully macabre, and I stare in fascination; my thoughts shift into place like the gathering snow. You can feel the heat from the fire beating back the chilly night air.

Aunt Celia is distraught. I have ruined her life. First Mama now Aunt Celia. She would have been so happy if I weren't around. Mama would be alive. Aunt Celia would be with Jack. Maybe they would already be married. I throw Jack on the pile of people I am making as miserable as an animal caught in a snare.

As if I've conjured him by my thoughts, Jack stands in only sweat pants at the edge of the crowd, working his way over to Aunt Celia. Reaching her side, he just holds her to his chest as she rails. I stand watching it happen, disoriented with guilt of what I have done. Mrs. Ackers is right; I am a menace. I see her, too, then at the edge of the crowd. Am I pulling these people out of thin air every time I think of them? Jack searches the crowd with his eyes. As they fall on me, I send back a confession with my eyes. Jack shakes his head and mouths, "No."

I turn and run. I can't face what I've done to everyone. I can't take Jack being confident in me. I have no idea where I am heading. Away is my only thought. The wind pulls the tears from the corners of my eyes. I wipe my sleeve under my runny nose. My ears finally process the sound of my name being called, but I can't stop. I hear it again, but I just kept going. The snow is making things slippery, and I am cold and wet. But I care as much about that as a starving man would care there was a hair in his food. For some reason Ms. Stontz, my English teacher, is sitting in a car at the end of the road. I know I haven't brought her here since I didn't even remember she inhabits the planet with everything that is happening.

A big hand grabs my arm, jerking me to a halt, and I slide to a stop on the icy snow. As I spin into him, Adam appears mad at me. He also looks cold as snow hits his naked torso. Have I made it so this poor boy will lose his shirt all the time? "Why are you running away?" He has a snarl in his voice.

"Adam... I..." I shake my head, my mouth unable to form the words to confess what I have done.

Seeing my distress he pulls me to his chest much like what his father had done earlier that evening. "Hamilton's father is heading back to get the car. He will pick us up and take us back to our house. Dad will stay with Celia until the fire department finishes up. Come on," he commands. Adam takes my hand and walks me to the end of the street. People are everywhere. The fire must have roused them from sleep since there are several shirtless men of all ages. They seem to be staring down and circling the area more than even the fire team who are still trying to put out the blaze.

"I should make it stop," I say quietly.

Adam squeezes my hand. "Don't. Not with so many people around."

We stop walking, and Adam put his arms around me. He is so warm he keeps out the chill, and I marvel at how he can produce such immense body heat. I admit my sins to his bare chest, unable to bring my eyes up to meet his. "I did this, Adam. I wished we didn't have to leave you and your dad. I made this happen."

Adam grabs my face, pulling it up to lock his eyes on mine. "You didn't do anything wrong." He gives my head a little shake. "You hear me, G.J.? Not a damn thing."

A horn sounds as a car pulls to a stop next to us. A man at least as large as Mr. Wyfle gets out of the car. "Adam? What are your dad's orders?"

"We need to get G.J. back to our house," Adam says. "Dad will bring Celia when they're done here."

"Where is Ham?" the man asks, and I think that is such a silly nickname for the proud boy I know.

We all turn back to the gathered crowd. Hamilton stands with his back to us, full of tension. He, too, is shirtless. Adam points him out and says, "Over there."

Mr. Calhoun lets out an ear-piercing whistle, and Hamilton turns to reveal he is talking to none other than Sara Ackers, annoyed that he's interrupted He says something briefly to Sara and leans down. I have no interest in watching him kiss her goodbye, so I turn my head.

While he makes his way over to us, Adam introduces me to Hamilton's father, who gives me a smile full of genuine warmth. "So you are what all the hubbub is about."

I look at Mr. Calhoun, not understanding what he is referring to. I also decide there must be the need for some sort of secret decoder ring in order to decipher what most folks around here are saying.

"I apologize for Hamilton's behavior. I don't get out much with all my responsibilities, and with no mother I guess I have left Hamilton to be raised by the pack of us. It does not lead to the strongest skills with girls."

Hamilton jogs up to us, catching the tail end of what his father is saying. "Dad." Hamilton has a horrified note in his voice.

Adam laughs at him. "Your dad is trying to help your cause."

Mr. Calhoun's demeanor changes after his son arrives, and he begins shooting questions at him as we all climb in the car. "Could you tell what it was?"

"Kerosene," Hamilton answers.

"Was it what you had suspected?" Mr. Calhoun asks as he navigates the quickly deteriorating streets.

"I'm not positive now."

I see his father shoot him a look from the side of his vision. "Right. I'll tell Jack and the others. Let everyone know their assignments. You stay at Jack's until he brings Celia back. I don't want to leave G.J. without enough protection." It sounds like a military campaign.

"Mr. Calhoun, that is right nice of you, but I can take care of myself. And, to be honest, Hamilton is one of the people I need protection from." It might be rude to call out his son like this, but I am not going to have Hamilton as a bodyguard.

Mr. Calhoun brings the car to a stop as Hamilton spins his head to where Adam and I are sitting in the back and partly shouts, "What?"

I'm tired and at the end of my rope. "You have attacked me twice, putting me in the hospital once. You are dating a person who just tried to summon enough energy to send my aunt away in a bubble made out of Bubblicious on a slow drift to Mars and hates me with a passion only equal to your own. You have found every possible way to insult me in the short time that you have known me. In light of all that, I would prefer not to be placed in your care. Not that I need to be placed in anyone's care. People should be trying to find ways to ward *me* off."

Mr. Calhoun looks to his son, who just keeps opening and closing his mouth like a fish does when you're trying to get the hook out. "Who are you dating?"

"She thinks I'm dating Sara for some dumb reason," Hamilton mumbles.

"Over my dead body," Mr. Calhoun says with a seriousness that makes me think he is actually readying for the death match.

"Dad, I'm not dating Sara."

"Then why did you just kiss her?" I shoot, trumping his denial.

Mr. Calhoun growls. "You went against Jack?"

That's a weird thing to say.

"I did not kiss Sara," Hamilton says in stunned defense.

"I just saw you lean down to kiss her back there," I say.

"I did not. You are deluded," Hamilton dismisses me.

"I am not. You may not want to admit it to your daddy, but you should just fess up. If you like her, hiding it will only make things worse." My advice is completely unwanted.

"Do you have feelings for this Ackers girl?" Mr. Calhoun asks.

"What? No. Dad I told you…"

"You just came home from a date with her earlier when all the brew-ha-ha started." I don't know why it's so important to me to make him confess. "And I saw you lean down to kiss her goodbye just now."

Hamilton's face gets red, and he twists so he is poised to come over the seat at me. "I am not, nor have I ever, dated Sara. I smelled her right before I left. And the only girl I have ever kissed is you," he shouts in my face.

"What?" Both Adam and Mr. Calhoun shout at the same time.

"You did not kiss me." I'm horrified. "Our mouths bumped."

"What the hell, Hamilton? Dad said not yet," Adam says.

I glare at Adam. What in the world does "not yet" mean?

"Whatever." Hamilton glares at his friend. "It was before that, and you run around with your shirt off in front of her all the time. Hell, you're even wearing her clothes."

"Yeah she gave it to me when we were in bed together. Remember that," Adam jibes at his friend.

"Adam. You said you wouldn't say that," I yell.

His father putting his hand on his shoulder only stops Hamilton from launching himself over the seat. Mr. Calhoun says, "It sounds like there have been a couple breaches of Jack's orders. We will address this later. Young lady, having you around might just get one of these boys killed."

"What am I doing? Of all the things that are my fault, this nonsense has nothing to do with me. I did not kiss Hamilton, and Adam was only in my bed *talking*. I am not some floozy, and I will not have it implied by anyone that I am. My mama raised me right. Why do the two of you want to pretend you have some sort of faux-mance with *me* of all people? I'm nothing special." I finish a touch louder than is needed for the size of the SUV. "Dear gussy, you boys will compete over things you don't even want."

Mr. Calhoun laughs. "Good luck, boys. She is a live one." He shakes his head as he begins moving the car toward Jack's house again. "G.J., I will have to say, you, my dear, are definitely special."

Adam and Hamilton sit in silence, and I fall back into my thoughts for the rest of the ride home. The thought of Jack's house as home is right. It fits the way the right pillow helps you curl into the perfect position for you to get a good night's sleep. As we pull up, some of my tension leaves my body. Adam rubs my shoulder, somehow sensing my relief and letting me know he feels the same.

"Stay here." Mr. Calhoun says as he hops out. He circles the house, scoping it out like the queen is coming for a visit. He waives for Hamilton to come over. Hamilton then circles the outside again while Mr. Calhoun goes inside, and I assume he is checking the inside as thoroughly.

"Adam, why are they acting like they are an advance team for the POTUS?" I ask, watching for the two men to reappear.

"Someone just burned down your aunt's house. We take that seriously. Dad said he would protect you, and someone chose to cross him. We all just went on alert."

"Who are you people, the Spokane Mafia?"

"Dad means everything to the people around here. Nobody can strike out at the ones he loves without ramifications. Challenging Dad is a mistake."

"Nothing you just said makes me feel like we are not 'going to the mattresses.' Seriously, what does Jack do for a living?" I ask, expecting him to be straight with me.

"Dad runs a lot of things," Adam responds with mysterious vagueness.

"Yeah, still feeling like Jack has a mouth full of cotton balls," I say, referencing Marlon Brando's method of achieving his greatest roll.

A knock at the window makes me jump out of my skin, and I make one of those embarrassing squeaks I am apparently doing my best to bring into style.

Adam laughs. "Let's get inside." Hamilton and Adam flank me with their heads up, searching the area.

"Who do you two think you are? Do you think your high-school sports prepare you to take on ninjas?" I ask.

"Ninjas have nothing on our mad skills." Adam shoots me his sly grin.

"Shut up," Hamilton growls.

"Problems boys?" a voice sounds from behind us.

Hamilton shoves me behind him, and he and Adam form a wall. "Damn it, Gus. Where did you come from?"

"Originally?" Gus mocks him. "My mother's womb."

Hamilton snarls.

I peek from behind the muscled mass of man flesh.

"Look who is up and about. Feeling better, G.J.?" Gus asks.

"Well, if we're talking about physically, yep I sure am. If I only had hair, I would be right as rain. But if we are going to address anything else, I am going to have to use the Fifth Amendment and not give evidence against myself." I chat with Gus like we are at a coffee house instead of standing in the snow in front of Jack's house.

"Gus," Mr. Calhoun says from the doorway. "Been a long time. You look good."

"I try," Gus says with a nonchalance I could never pull off with one of my elders.

"What brings you around tonight?" Mr. Calhoun says, and with an unseen gesture, he somehow indicates that Adam should hustle me inside.

Gus is just in front of me. I mean, it's *poof* and he's there. The only thing missing is the smoke pellet screens magicians use. "I am here to talk to G.J.." Wow, he has some lovely eyes.

Adam swings me over his shoulder, and Hamilton moves to confront Gus. "What are you doing?" I holler. "I need to talk to him. What is with the two of you? I am not a Raggedy Ann doll. Put me down."

"Just a sec," Adam answers as he runs toward the door. I hate it when I'm indignant and someone acts like what they are doing is no big deal? I feel like between Adam and Hamilton tossing me around like I am a ball in keep away, and acting like I am defenseless; I am about done. However, holding a conversation while your behind is pointed toward the sky makes you lose some authority to say the least.

I'm about to use my will to T.P. his head as he drops me inside the door of his house and Mr. Calhoun's back is in front of me. "Forgive me. Do I have Samsonite stamped on my derriere? Are you the missing link between man and caveman? Maybe I need more supportive undergarments so you all stop confusing me for a sack of potatoes."

Mr. Calhoun goes out to talk to Gus and Hamilton. As soon as he does, Adam closes the door behind him. "We just want to make sure he is alone. Hamilton's Dad has known Gus for a while. With what happened at your house, do you think we shouldn't be concerned about what might happen to you?" Adam asks calmly.

"I think you people need to have a conversation with reality. Gus is a friend of mine. He would not hurt me. You all think Hamilton is hunky dory, and yet he made me get an awesome yet unwanted 'vaca' at the Lysol kingdom. I was most likely the cause of that fire. I am wholly capable of sending every one of you flying with a thought. There is absolutely zero reason for any of you to act like you have joined S.H.I.E.L.D. or the Justice League. I am not in danger. Everyone else is in peril from me. Were you not paying attention earlier when I lit up like a human firefly?"

"Okay, Super Girl, if you are your own hero, I expect you to wear a lot more spandex." Adam looks at me as if he is playing dress up with me in his head.

"Ugh." I throw my hands up and turn to go out the door. As I reach it, Mr. Calhoun walks in with Gus and Hamilton.

"Going somewhere?" Mr. Calhoun asks, looking from me to Adam.

"She's not sure she needs our protection," Adam explains.

"G.J., we are taking care of you for Jack. If you are concerned, just wait for him to get back, and you can bring it up with him. Gus wants to talk to you for a few minutes. Why don't you all have a seat in the living room?" Mr. Calhoun's invitation is more of a command. I swear all these men shop at the bossy-pants store.

"Look at all the attention you're getting. You must feel so loved," Gus says as we walk to the living room.

"There is a fine line between loved and kidnapped," I reply.

Gus and I sit on the sofa. Adam stands by the door, and Hamilton takes up a post by the window.

"Welcome to Fort Knox," I say, letting my gaze move from Hamilton to Adam.

"So it seems someone was worried about the heating bill at your aunt's house," Gus says.

I sigh. "Today has been busy. It started off all right. I got out of school early for a couple of doctor's appointments, healed my leg, went for a long walk outside..."

"You went on the steep side of the hill by yourself?" Hamilton interrupts.

I ignore him. "Then things kind of went downhill. I caused Aunt Celia to want to move out of Jack's."

Adam takes his turn breaking into the conversation. "I think that honor is mine."

I keep rolling. "There was a run-in with the Ackers, where I did one heck of an impersonation of a power cell. Oh, I mentally zipped them a few streets over along with their vehicle. That was fun. And then I set Aunt Celia's house on fire by hoping we wouldn't have to leave Jack's. But enough about me. What's new with you?"

"You did not set Celia's house on fire," Hamilton snaps.

"How do you know?"

"You are impossible." Hamilton gives yet another non-answer.

"Are you sure, Hamilton?" Gus asks.

"That she is impossible? 100 percent." Hamilton smirks.

"You're an idiot," Adam slings at his friend. "Keep it up. You're going to make things so easy."

"You both are so full of it," Gus says. "You said you thought you knew who started it. Who was it? Don't say Aldrich."

"Drake? Why would Drake burn down my aunt's house?" I ask, completely taken aback by the random accusation.

"Nah. Not this time," Hamilton says, vaguely referencing something that makes me worry Drake's hobby is arson. "Sara was clean too but, man, was she freaked out."

"G.J., were the Ackers summoning to attack you?" Gus asks.

"No, they were pulling the energy to go after Aunt Celia. I just reached out and directed it to me."

Gus flops back on the sofa. "You are truly remarkable." His incredible eyes fix on me like I am hung in the Metropolitan Museum of Art.

"I couldn't let them send that power after Aunt Celia."

"Why do you keep saying she is so special?" Hamilton asks with annoyance in his voice.

"Dude, do you have any idea what it would take to do that? To pull power away from the person drawing it is not something anyone I have ever known, who works with natural energies, can do. I thought you said you didn't call it intentionally," Gus says.

"Well, I hadn't before, but I just knew somehow what those two were up to. I felt for the line they were pulling and made it come to me."

"Wow," Gus says. "G.J., that is awesome."

I feel like I have just performed a super move in a video game. "Well, you might think it was, but it got weird. I couldn't shut it down. I started pulling in energy from everywhere. The colossal temper of *that* guy even." I jerk my thumb toward Hamilton.

"Temper?" Hamilton asks like he has never heard the word.

"How did you get it to stop?" Gus asks.

"Adam distracted me and made me laugh."

"My nudity distracts you?" Adam asks with his stupid flirty grin.

"Your clowning around," I primly correct him.

Hamilton coughs out a word that sounds like "Comega."

Adam tenses and says, "We'll see."

"Eat your Wheaties, tough guy," Hamilton taunts.

"Does this get as old for you as it does for me?" Gus asks.

"I'm not even sure what they're talking about," I answer.

"You said they pulled a lot of energy. How do you know? And why did you think it was directed at your aunt and not you?" Gus asks.

"I can answer that," Adam says. "She could tell it was a lot of power because she looked like the cartoon version of Storm from the X-men, and Celia laid Sara's mom out with a verbal MMA smack down." Adam grins with pride at Aunt Celia's mouthy mojo. Hamilton chuckles, too.

"Would have loved to have been there," Gus says. "Especially if these two were impressed with someone using words to fight."

I smile. "She does have a talent."

"You couldn't stop the draw?" Gus asks, getting back to my part in this mess.

"No, it was like I filled the cup, but couldn't move it or turn the faucet off. I was so worried I would hurt somebody. I'm pretty sure I zapped Jack a few times. It was an unsettling amount of power. If I had wanted to, I could have lit up New Orleans at Mardi Gras," I say. "I am just plain old terrified to find out what they planned to do with all that juice."

"Huh?" Gus says contemplatively. "We should find out."

"Hamilton can ask Sara," Adam says with a smirk.

"Me?" Hamilton asks.

Adam makes kissy faces at him.

"I did NOT kiss Sara," Hamilton objects.

"Well considering you thought *we* kissed, I'm not sure you quite get the idea of what smooching is," I joke.

In the matter of a heartbeat, Hamilton is right in my face. "Wanna test that theory?"

"HAMILTON." The boom of Jack's voice shakes the whole room.

My skin feels electric, and I can't tell if it's Jack's sudden appearance and lack of volume control or Hamilton and his… whatever that was. Hamilton is back across the room like I've thrown him and finds a very interesting knot in the wood floor he just cannot take his eyes off.

"Hello, Jack." Gus stands to shake Jack's hand.

"Gus, this is a surprise," Jack says, shaking his hand and clearly admonishing the room for the fact that we have company. Aunt Celia comes in behind him, soot-stained and stunned.

Jumping up, I run to her. "Aunt Celia, are you okay?"

She nods dumbly. I think she would have made a great extra in *Awakenings* before the big wake-up scene. Then she catches sight of Hamilton. That snaps her out of it. She looks at her watch and then back at all of us. It has to be past eleven PM. "Hamilton, I see absolutely no reason for you to be here at this hour. And let me make this perfectly clear. At no point in the near or distant future do I expect to see you, unsupervised by an adult, with G.J.."

Adam makes the mistake of chuckling.

"There are going to be serious ground rules for you as well, young man." Aunt Celia channels an old bitty like she has a Ouija board master's degree.

"Celia, I understand Ham has been a bit aggressive with G.J., but he didn't mean it," Mr. Calhoun says, coming up behind her.

"Lucas," Jack says, "if these rules make Celia feel more comfortable here, we can make sure they happen while they are in the house." Jack puts his arm around Aunt Celia in a show of support. With that simple action, he puts an end to any discussion.

"Luke, I appreciate that you trust your son, but currently his average with G.J. is a failing grade. He needs some serious work on his manners before he gets back in my good graces," Aunt Celia says.

Hamilton makes this pitiful noise, and his Dad looks away. Jack says, "Easy, sweetheart. You are tired, and we have all been through a lot today. We will work out some guidelines as to what is appropriate. The boys have always had an open door policy. We haven't had women around for too long, apparently. Your insight and help with this kind of thing will be very valuable to all of us." I'm kind of wondering if Jack has a background in politics.

"You're right, Jack. I am exhausted. Hamilton, Luke, I apologize. We will talk tomorrow. Why don't you come over for breakfast, and then we can sort things out then." Aunt Celia is too nice for her own good.

Hamilton looks up hopefully, and Mr. Calhoun smiles at her. "You've got a keeper here, Jack. Sounds good, Celia." He takes Aunt Ceila's hand and pulls her close to kiss her cheek. He then returns her to under Jack's arm. If Jack had feathers, I swear they'd be settling with Aunt Celia close to him again.

"Are you all right, G.J.?" Aunt Celia asks.

"This is not about me, at least I hope not," I say.

"Kiddo, there was kerosene and footprints in the snow. You had nothing to do with this. Unless you count the storm, which may just help track down who is responsible. By the way, Gus, it is getting bad out there. If you are going far, I suggest you call your parents before you head home." Aunt Celia's fatigue is hitting her hard now, and she suppresses a yawn.

"Yes, ma'am," Gus says, and Mr. Calhoun can't hide his smile.

"Why don't you head up to bed, Ceily? I'll check on you in a bit," Jack says.

"You'll get no fight from me right now." She kisses me on the cheek. "Goodnight. We will work out life tomorrow. Oh my bags." Aunt Celia seems to have just remembered we were packed to leave.

"I put them in your rooms," Mr. Calhoun says.

"Oh, you are a godsend. Thank you, Luke." Aunt Celia smiles at him. It looks like he is going to kiss her cheek again, but Jack lets him know that isn't going to happen if he intends on keeping his lips. Aunt Celia turns to Jack. "Thank you for being there for me again, Jack."

Jack kisses the top of her head and watches with purpose as she leaves the room. Once she has gone, Jack turns to Mr. Calhoun. He doesn't actually ask a question, but with his eyes he dictates for Mr. Calhoun to speak.

"No issues. We will work in teams of four by two. I was going to leave both boys here, but I think that might be an issue. You and Adam will have to handle that alone."

Jack nods once. He looks to Hamilton, who won't look at Jack but says, "I caught the kerosene too. The footprints were too small for Aldrich, but with the perimeter set up, I could not get close enough to pick up the trail. Sara is out, but I couldn't get close enough to rule out her mom. No indication of a second. No issues here."

Jack's gaze moves to Adam. "The fire department knows to make it a priority, and as you can see I caught up with our runaway."

Jack nods again. I am fascinated. I feel like I am in the middle of a G.I. Joe filming. It takes me a second for my saucer-sized eyes to take in the fact that Jack focuses on me.

"Yes, sir?" I ask like the man has spoken.

"Did you pick up anything with what you can do that might help us nail down who did this?" Jack questions me, and I think, for sure, he has been a drill sergeant in his life.

"Well, until I heard about the footprints and the flammable liquids, I kind of thought I had done it," I answer.

"You? Why would you think you had done it?" Jack asks, surprised.

"Because I didn't want us to leave." While I am not a shy person by nature, I feel like a four year old confessing I broke a priceless vase.

Jack's smile takes up his whole face, and he pulls me into his huge arms. It is so sweet I about cry, until Mr. Calhoun, Adam, and Hamilton make it a group hug.

"I'm not sure she is there yet, guys," Gus says from his seat on the couch.

The other men back off, and I look up at Jack with the called-for expression of a wary "you all are crazy" plain on my face. Jack laughs and says, "It's just something we do. It means we think you are one of us now."

"That right there is something you need to warn a person about. Otherwise, it would be a mite too easy to get the wrong impression," I instruct them.

"I like her too, Jack." Mr. Calhoun double squeezes my shoulder in two short bursts. That is an innocent sign of affection I recognize.

"Gus?" Jack asks. "What brought you around tonight?"

"I was checking on G.J. She is rare, Jack. Keep her safe or I will," Gus says without batting an eye. He just throws out the statement to this enormous man, who obviously has some sort of combat training, and then keeps talking. "I think she needs to get trained. From the sound of it, she could have had an issue earlier tonight, and I don't know what to do to help her. Can you guys track the Wiccans around here?"

Jack stares hard at Gus. I guess he doesn't like the threat at all. "We are already on it."

Gus nods and stands up. I think he senses what we all do—Jack is done with him. On his way by us he asks, "You thought it was Aldrich?" He laughs and says, "That would have been interesting."

Mr. Calhoun follows him to the door.

The door closes behind Gus, and Jack turns me to face him with intent. It is unusual for me to be the shortest person in the room by a few inches. The feeling only adds to the daddy-daughter vibe Jack is going for as he says, "Be careful of that one, G.J. His kind is incredibly dangerous. While we have known Gus for a long time, you are too important to us to have you run off with anyone like him."

I wonder when the drama kids became the big bads for parental types. I blame it on the likes of Johnny Depp. His career started off as an innocent NARC, and now he looks like he horded all those drugs he busted people for on, a show my mama loved called, *21 Jump Street* and started using them to make himself more creative later in life. What possessed anyone to make Hunter S. Thompson more accessible to kids with a movie like "Rango" if there were not narcotics, and I mean a lot of them, involved.

"I have no intention of running off with anybody," I say to calm his nerves.

"You tried to run away today," Hamilton says.

"Yes, but I was by myself." I stick my chin up as I answer him to look down my nose at the taller boy.

"No running. With or without people," Jack commands, using just a touch of the roar his voice can get in it.

"Can I get a note for P.E.?" I tease him.

"G.J., it has been a long day. I'm tired. You need to go to bed," Jack says.

"If you are the one who is tired…" I start but peter off as Jack raises his hand.

"Adam," is Jack's only word.

"How come…" Hamilton starts to say something, but Jack just points to the door.

I kiss Jack on the cheek. "Goodnight, Jack."

Jack rubs the back of my head. "Goodnight. We've got it. You can rest easy. Tomorrow we will move you to a permanent room."

I guess Jack wants his office back. Adam walks me back to my room, goes inside, and searches it. Then he closes the blinds and turns back to me. He looks annoyed. "Why didn't you wait at the door?"

"I'm sorry. Please give me the instruction manual for hyper paranoia, and I will study up," I say.

Adam gives a soft whack on the back of my head.

"Ow." I complain, more in surprise than pain.

"G.J.. God, I'm sorry. I forgot." Adam is encircling my head with his hands like he is making a protective bubble.

"Call the doctor. I live with a dumbass, and I need it removed," I say, giving Meryl Streep a run for her Oscars until I smile at the end.

"Woman," Adam mock shouts.

"Goodnight, Adam."

"Night." He leans in, kisses my cheek, and leaves me to get ready for bed. I'm wiped out with all that's happened. My mind is so full it just stops wanting to operate and shuts down almost the instant my head hits the pillow.

Chapter Nineteen

The next morning Aunt Celia comes to get me. "Up, up, kid. I need you to be in charge of the French toast."

"You're going to have to let me get broken in on coffee in the morning if you're going to wake me on weekends," I say, trying to burrow under my pillow.

"You have always been a morning person. Have the teenager morning comas finally hit? The Calhouns will be here shortly. We need to get moving. I'll make you some hot chocolate," she tempts me, knowing chocolate is my happy place.

"Deal," I say as I struggle out of bed. I wander into the kitchen in my sleep gear, which consists of sleep shorts and an oversized t-shirt.

I'm a fairly good cook. I have always just known how much of this or that to put in a recipe. I think it is the science of it. Alton Brown is a hero of mine. I love knowing that I am causing a chemical reaction when cooking. And my French toast, pardon the brag, is super yummy.

I get everything prepped and then slide it in the oven then I help Aunt Celia chop fruit. "How many people are coming for breakfast?" I ask, eying all the food she's preparing.

"I think there will be six of us. But have you seen these guys eat? I think Jack could pull a chair up to a buffet and ask for seconds."

"Really? I hadn't noticed." I shrug.

We have just put on a side of bacon as Adam comes in wearing just his sleep pants again. He stands frozen in the doorway, staring. I glance to Aunt Celia, who looking back at Adam and asks, "Is there something wrong?"

Adam turns and walks out. Aunt Celia shrugs, and we go back to working on breakfast. A few minutes later Adam comes in with a shirt on and holding something in his hands. Aunt Celia is in the pantry collecting things to serve. Adam walks over, staring at the ceiling, and hands the bundle to me. "Fair is fair. Put them on."

I grasp the item he's holding out to me and find they are sweatpants. I peek at my bare legs, shake my head, and blush. Without a word, I slip on the oversized pants, rolling the waist down so they will fit. After finishing, I spin for him. "Did you pull these off a tree out back?"

"Phew. Your legs and bacon at the same time might kill a man," Adam says after Aunt Celia has gone into the pantry.

"I heard that," Aunt Celia calls.

Adam turns beat red. "Sorry, Celia," he calls back.

"Sorry for what?" Jack rumbles, walking into the room clearly having just woken up. He wears what Adam wears to bed, and I think to myself, *Go, Aunt Celia.*

Adam's head drops on the counter. I just laugh at him. "Adam is uncomfortable with sleep shorts and pork products," I offer helpfully.

Jack looks like he doesn't even want to try to figure out what I'm talking about and heads for the coffee. Aunt Celia walks back in and Jack perks right up, passing the caffeinated carafe and sliding his arms around her instead.

"Good morning. Finally decided to join the living?" Aunt Celia kisses him and reminds him there are other people in the room by pushing him away. He just watches her for a minute and then goes back to his morning coffee ritual.

"This place smells great," Mr. Calhoun says, coming into the room followed by Hamilton.

"Good morning, Luke, Hamilton," Aunt Celia says invitingly.

Mr. Calhoun comes over and kisses Aunt Celia on the cheek. Hamilton follows and hesitates but clearly wants to do the same.

"Let the boy kiss you, Ceily," Jack encourages.

"What? Oh…" And Aunt Celia offers Hamilton her cheek, which makes him stupidly happy.

What a weirdo. I grab hand mitts and have to get past Hamilton and his dad in order to get the French toast out of the oven. As I move past them, Mr. Calhoun kisses my cheek as well. Hamilton leans forward, but I just glare at him. Then I bend over to check on my concoction. While my head is down in the oven, I hear Adam say, "Thank God for the sweat pants."

I twist so my back is facing the other way and shoot him an evil look. Am I really going to have to worry which direction my fanny aims from now on? I pull the dish out of the oven and make my way over to the table Aunt Celia has set. We have a ton of food. In addition to my delightful toast, there are two pounds of bacon, ham, scrambled eggs with sausage, fruit, yogurt, muffins the size of your head, and all the fixin's. You would think we are down south, but there are muffins and no biscuits or grits.

I go back to the cooking area to get a serving spoon and grab the pitcher of O.J. "I think we're all set."

"Jack, no shirt, no food," Aunt Celia says.

He grumbles but heads out of the room in a hurry so as not to miss out on anything. I sit down and pour some juice. Adam takes the chair next to me, and Hamilton sits across from me. Luke waits for Aunt Celia to sit then sits next to her.

"Please, boys, get started," Aunt Celia prompts.

They all just look at her. Jack comes back in and sits opposite from Aunt Celia. He takes a plate full of food and passes it to Hamilton, who passes it to his dad. His dad puts food on Aunt Celia's plate then takes some for himself. Next, he passes it back to Hamilton, who just holds it for a minute.

"Hamilton? Is something wrong?" Aunt Celia asks.

"I just don't know if G.J. should get food before I take some," Hamilton says.

"That is so thoughtful. G.J. can wait until it is passed to her. Go ahead and take some while you have the plate," Aunt Celia instructs, seeming to fall for this Hasklesque move. If Hamilton thinks that is all it will take to be trusted, he has another thing coming.

"Just wait until she has started to eat before you begin eating. There is plenty on the table. Everyone will have their share," Jack clarifies.

I'm so perplexed. What in the world is that about? Hamilton passes the food back to Jack after he is done. Jack puts food on my plate and passes it on to Adam. "Thanks," I say, wondering what all the food issues are about.

Jack takes a bite. Then Aunt Celia takes a bite. Next Mr. Calhoun takes a bite. I wait. Jack, Aunt Celia, and Mr. Calhoun all are eating without an issue, making happy food noises and comments saying the food is a success. I love watching people enjoy my cooking. Jack stops and asks, "G.J., are you not hungry?"

"Oh," I say and then take a bite of bacon.

After that, it is like a race to see who can get the food to their mouths the fastest between Adam and Hamilton. Hamilton apparently thinks he wins, because he chews with a victorious grin on his face. One more thing to indicate Hamilton belongs on a funny farm. Adam appears truly disheartened, so I pat his knee. Hamilton's face falls, and Adam now wears the grin.

"Boys," Jack scolds, and I have no clue as to what for.

"This French toast is incredible," Mr. Calhoun says.

"Thank you," I reply.

"You made this?" Hamilton says, gesturing to the food on his plate. I nod.

"You can cook?" He huffs out a short laugh.

"G.J. is a wonderful cook," Aunt Celia defends me. "When she was four or five she made a cheesecake I still have happy dreams about."

I roll my eyes and shake my head at the compliment.

"I can't wait to try some more, if this is any indication," Mr. Calhoun says.

"This gets better and better," Adam says like he is winning prizes on a game show.

"Well, you are welcome to dinner any night, since it looks like we will be staying." Aunt Celia lets out a sigh, reminding everyone why we are still here.

"Celia, I hate that it happened, but I am not sorry it brought you back here," Jack announces.

Aunt Celia looks at Jack with murder-mystery suspicion on her face. "How did you all get there so fast?"

"We went over the hill," Jack responds. "I told you last night."

She keeps looking at the men at the table.

"You think *I* did that?" Jack makes the Hulk look like a snuggle toy.

Aunt Celia says nothing.

"Aunt Celia, I have been over that hill. No way could they have had time to set the fire and have the response teams there by the time we made the drive," I defend Jack.

Aunt Celia stares down at her food. "I'm sorry. I feel attacked, and I am taking stabs in the dark. Thank God G.J. has a rational head on her shoulders." She sighs again and considers Jack, who just about melts the second her sad eyes make contact.

"I know. It's a hard time for you right now," Jack says, which makes Mr. Calhoun look at the man with a "you are done for brother" smile on his face. Jack throws a piece of muffin at his friend.

"What about P?" I ask.

"G.J., do you have to bring this up now?" Aunt Celia's exasperates.

"No, Ceily. G.J. might have a point. You said it was dangerous for you to let anyone know about this P. Maybe by you contacting P, the danger became real." Jack hops on my thought train and rides it to the last station.

"Man, what if they didn't know you were out of the house?" Adam wonders.

"You think they were trying to kill Celia?" Mr. Calhoun asks Adam and looks at Jack.

The room vibrates with that noise but lower and louder. Aunt Celia looks up and around like I had when I'd thought it was an earthquake. But, I eye Jack, realizing for the first time the sound isn't natural; it's coming from these men. Jack notices my gaze and turns off the rumbling noise.

"What now?" Aunt Celia says with her hands braced on the table to steady either it or herself.

Mr. Calhoun pats her hand to reassure her. "Nothing's going to harm you."

I stare at Jack. All my warm fuzzy confidence in him goes on a little trip away for the moment. Jack sits, watching me, assessing if I have put something together and if I will be a threat. Our little eye sparring cuts short as Aunt Celia says, "G.J.."

I look over at her.

"Kiddo, I am so sorry," she says, tears filling her eyes.

"What's wrong?" I ask, upset because she is.

Aunt Celia covers her face and can't talk, so Adam guesses. "They wouldn't be after Celia. They would be after *you*." Everyone looks back at me.

"Me? Why me?"

"Because you are you," Hamilton says.

I roll my eyes, letting Hamilton know he is as big of an idiot as he always is whenever he opens his mouth.

"What Ham is saying is, it's because you have the abilities they have told me about," Mr. Calhoun clarifies. "You really do have an issue with this?" He directs at his son.

Adam laughs.

"When I emailed... I didn't even think. The IP address. How stupid can I get?" Aunt Celia is mentally beating herself up. "Jack, I have to get her out of here. We have to leave town."

"No." Jack's emphatic. "You are safer where we can protect you."

"Jack, they just burned down my house. I can't see you get hurt because of this. This is my promise to keep."

"Celia." Jack's voice is sharp. "When are you going to understand? I intend on everything we have to go through from now on to be something we do *together*. You are not going to be able to get rid of me. So start letting me carry my share of this load." Okay, I have no idea what makes the large machinery noise in Jack's chest, but I'm a Jack fan. I have pompoms and the foam finger.

Aunt Celia gets up and leaves the room. Jack is right on her heels. This leaves me with the knowledge that somebody is actually trying to end my existence. My eyes focus on a piece of cantaloupe on my plate. My eyelids shutter like I am taking frame after frame of film in my head of that piece of fruit. Adam puts his hand on my shoulder. I look at him. He pulls me into his chest again, which is awkward sideways, so I just fit my head under his chin and stare at the table again. "Somebody is going to kill me?" I ask in a small voice, which is all I can muster.

The place settings all shake with the force of something slamming down on the table. I jerk away from Adam, surprised. Hamilton has his hands flat on the surface of the table. In a low grumble, he says, "Nobody is going to kill you." He seems so mad at me.

Mr. Calhoun puts his hand on his son's arm, holding him back. "Ham," he says, calming his son down.

"Do you have to be such a jerk all the time? I just found out someone besides you wants me dead. Forgive me if I need a sec to adjust," I yell in Hamilton's face as I get to my feet.

Hamilton starts breathing really hard. His eyes look like they have glow sticks in them. This isn't a trick of the light. This is not fake contacts. This is… another clue for me that these guys are not on the normal chart.

"What are you?" My inner scientist is assessing the test subject.

Hamilton leaves the room so fast I'm unsure how it happens. Mr. Calhoun looks at me hard. "You may have just caused more harm than good by being so observant."

Adam is up. "Don't even think about it."

"I have to enforce the law," Mr. Calhoun says.

"G.J. is under Dad's protection," Adam warns.

"Your dad knows the law." Mr. Calhoun is breathing hard now.

"DAD," Adam screams.

"Are you challenging me?" Mr. Calhoun is tilting his head in a predatory way, looking through Adam. Adam cowers back.

"If he won't, *I* will. No wonder your son is so violent," I say, drawing this man's attention to me. Sometimes "uh-oh" does not even come close to covering it.

"You challenge?" The low rumble starts again, and his eyes are glowing just like his son's had.

"She doesn't know what that means," Adam appeals.

Somehow, I know backing down isn't going to make this situation any better. I feel amped like I did the night before when I had drawn power. I'm not sure where it is coming from, but what starts as a tingle is a full-on prickle of power now. "I challenge," I say with a confidence I am pretty sure I don't really feel.

Mr. Calhoun lunges for me, but Adam jumps in the way. "Adam, stay out of it," I yell.

Mr. Calhoun makes quick work of the younger man with punches and kicks. Adam falls to the floor bleeding. The big man comes for me again. Up until now, I've always thought that adrenaline is meant to make you hightail it out of there, hopefully faster than the thing giving chase. But I can see this is not its true purpose. My heart is racing with the anticipation of the fight. I am going to own this guy. I have a heady sense like this is a fait accompli.

I draw power to me and strike Mr. Calhoun in the chest. He roars with the pain, not expecting me to pack such a punch. He paces in front of me, looking for a weakness. I stand my ground, waiting for him to come to me.

He charges at me again, and again I slam him back. This time he hits the wall with such force he leaves an indent in the drywall. He's lucky to have missed a stud. This really makes him mad because that is the tipping point between anger and unreality. He drops to his hands and knees and stares at the ground. I think I've just rung his bell, and he needs a second. I focus on Adam and heal him while I stand there. Sitting up slowly, Adam looks around. His eyes grow in horror as he finds where Mr. Calhoun had been crouching. Only Mr. Calhoun is gone. For those of you who saw this coming, Bravo. If this was really happening to you, I guarantee you wouldn't have actually put this in the realm of possible. Mr. Calhoun has turned into an enormous wolf.

"Peas and carrots," I say in shock. Maybe I actually curse. I guess I have some inkling that these guys were different, but who would have thought werewolves are real? It takes me a split second to run through everything and click the pieces in place. So my wolf is a person? If so, who? Oh lordy. I don't even want to know.

"What in the hell is going on?" Jack says as he comes back in the room. He stops dead in his tracks.

"Dad, you can't get involved. G.J. challenged him," Adam warns.

Aunt Celia comes running in now. "Dear God. A wolf. In the house."

That draws my attention for a second, and that is all the wolf—or Mr. Calhoun, whatever—needs. He pounces and knocks me on my back. "No kill," Jack yells out his command.

The wolf looks down in a snarl. I sling that sucker up so hard he bounces off the ceiling in a yelp. Poor Jack, I'm putting dents all over his beautiful house. Power feels like it has replaced the blood in my veins, and I slam the wolf from one wall to the next. Ushering the beast to the back door, I dominate him with power. Every time he attempts to get up and fight, I put him back down. Finally, when we are outside, the wolf gets up, but keeps his head down in submission. I've won.

Jack confirms it by wrapping me up with his arms from behind, leaning down, and telling me so. "You beat him, G.J. It's done. Let him go lick his wounds."

"I hurt him," I say horrified. I know it sounds strange but I just wanted to win. I didn't want to hurt him. "I need to heal him."

"No sweetheart. He needs to feel this, so he can accept it," Jack says. "Calm down and come back inside. Your aunt is about to have a heart attack, I think."

"Jack, does she know what you are?" I ask him quietly.

The big man just shakes his head.

"Wow. Are you going to tell her?" I ask.

"I can't until we are married. Pack law."

"You know I have about a million questions."

Jack nods.

"Are you going to answer them?"

"I have to." He gives me a sad smile. "You are my new Beta. Can't enforce laws you don't know. Get ready to study."

We have reached the kitchen. There is no worry about me talking about what he just said because I'm speechless. Aunt Celia rushes to me, looking for injuries. "Oh my God. G.J., are you all right?"

I nod.

"I told you those wolves were not safe. No more woods." Aunt Celia is putting her foot down, and I am all tuckered out on fighting for the moment, so I just put my head down. What everyone in the room realizes in that moment is that nobody can stop me from doing anything anymore.

Chapter Twenty

Jack is going to call in workmen to repair the damage we had caused in our cage match, so he tells me to go pick a room upstairs, so the workmen can decorate it while they're here. Adam offers to share his, to which he receives a smack on the back of his head from his father. This comes with instructions I'm not to choose the room next to Adam's either. In fact, Jack isn't happy with any choice that doesn't require Adam to pass Jack's room before he can get to mine.

****

The next day Aunt Celia has to go meet up with the insurance adjuster at her house. Surprisingly, Jack calls Luke to take her. I feel like after beating him senseless I've earned a first name basis with Mr. Calhoun. Jack takes this time without Aunt Celia to call a mini pack meeting. Jack is not the head of just one town. He is in charge of the whole territory, which includes parts of Canada. What he calls on this occasion is just the local pack.

Almost all the boys in letter jackets appear with their fathers. Adam explains most of the pack's young is on athletic teams. It allows for competition and teaches them to work together, so it is accepted as a natural course. They have to pull back on their strength if the other competitor is human and not wolf. But, in this area, that's rare. Jack's house is big, but the room is to the brim with manliness. What I notice is there are no women. At all. I'm it. The only bit of estrogen as far as the eye can see. Hamilton is there brooding as usual, and I'm just sure as can be my kicking his daddy from here to Texas and back has done nothing good for our relationship.

Jack calls the meeting to order. "You may have heard yesterday morning there was challenge fight. G.J.," Jack puts his hand on my shoulder, "won. She is your new Beta according to pack law."

A murmur moves across the room. "What did she do, hit him on the head from behind with a frying pan?" One of the older men calls out.

"It was skill versus skill as the law states. I witnessed it, and Luke has submitted. That fight is over," Jack says, letting the men in the room know his ruling will stand. "Now, you all know no one can challenge a new Beta for one full moon cycle. We are halfway through this cycle. So that gives you about six weeks to think about challenging G.J.."

My eyes look at Jack like he has just marked me for death. Hamilton laughs. I truly cannot stand him.

"I strongly advise against that for two reasons. One, G.J. is the whelp of my prospective bride. Any attacks on her I will see as a challenge to my authority. I will kill you should you harm a hair on her head," Jack says, rumbling his words to let them know he is serious. I would say "awww" but for the violence associated with the sweet statement. "Secondly," Jack continues, "G.J. is a natural Witch. We are not talking Wiccan, gentlemen. And some of us have had trouble with Wiccans. So, we respect that kind of power. She is a Witch. This girl is powerful. Luke is a strong wolf and could not beat her. Don't challenge her thinking she will be an easy mark.

Some of you know the history and what she can mean for our pack. I urge you to share the oral traditions, so our young understand what she may be able to do for us—should G.J. be willing, when the time is right." He looks at the group of men. "No one gets to make that call but me or G.J. NO ONE." The whole room shakes, and I feel the power of his command without even trying to pull it to me.

I rock back and then settle forward again. Every person in the room has their eyes on me, which makes me give a little wave and say, "Hey y'all," my southern hanging out like laundry on a line.

"Why doesn't she have any hair?" an old man asks. "How can we harm a hair on her head if she doesn't have any?"

I shoot a glare at Hamilton. Jack takes in a deep breath like he will speak, but I'm faster with my chitchat and beat him to it. "I come fully equipped with hair. I just had a little run-in that caused me to need doctors, but I promise you that's not the norm. I heal up right quick all by myself usually."

"What does that mean?" another man asks.

"Well… let me show you," I say, and I call a knife in from the kitchen. The handle floats right into my palm, and I hand it to Jack. Murmurs have followed the knife, and that display alone dumfounds the men. "Go ahead, Jack. Slice or dice, your choice." I smile at his unhappy expression.

Someone in the audience lets out a growl. Jack's head shoots up searching for the challenge, which is quickly silenced. "G.J., drawing blood in here is not a good idea."

"Well I don't want you to punch me so chop-chop," I say.

Jack looks hard at the crowd. "Don't inhale." he yells and then slices through the skin on my arm in a lightning strike with the blade. I know I told him to do it, but gosh, give a girl some warning.

Another growl erupts from the crowd, and I figure Hamilton has inhaled because he is trying to get to me. Realizing my blood fascinates everyone and everyone is holding their breath, literally, waiting for me to heal, I do so. The skin on my arm fastens itself up like a zipper closing. Hamilton gets to me as the crowd responds to what I have just done with awe. He grabs my arm and studies the healed skin. He looks at me before dropping to his knees and, of all the gross things you can imagine, he begins licking the blood off my arm.

Jack has him by the throat and pinned on the ground. "NOT NOW." Jack gives Hamilton a little slam to tell him he means what he says.

You know, I think I am pretty accepting of all this. I mean I can do Witchy Poo things, so I understand more than most that there is the possibility for different *people* in the world. But that moment right there brings it home to me that *people* does not always mean human. These men are all part animal. They have instincts of which I have no comprehension. I don't see how I *can* understand. And I'm the second in command to Jack? Chalk up another ridiculous error in judgment to G.J.. What I know is, right now is not the time to face this welling fear inside me. Most likely these folks sense it, but I'm going with bravado until otherwise specified from Jack.

Jack stands, and Hamilton gets up. He is still ruffled but has no interest in challenging Jack any longer. Adam comes up and slaps him on the back, easing the tension. I realize Adam does that a lot. He makes sure things don't escalate by joking around. What a neat talent to have.

"My mate will be back soon. Come meet your new Beta. You will always defer to her when I am not present," Jack says imperiously. I'm not prepared for the swarm of people who surround me and do what the men around here do best—sniff. Lordy, it is so hard to just stand there and let that happen. Some get right in my neck and others find other places to try to catch a whiff. All above the waist, thank heavens, but still it is all I can do not to squirm. I hear a few say a mumbled "Beta" showing deference by lowering their gazes, and soon the room is emptying as they get what they came for and leave.

When they're all gone, with the exception of Jack, Adam, and, of course, the ever-present Hamilton, I flop on the sofa relieved it is over. "Well… that went well, I think."

Jack laughs. "Yes, it did. I don't recommend drawing blood in the presence of them again if you can help it."

"I like to keep all my blood in its original container, thank you very much," I say.

"Too bad," Adam says. "You taste really good."

I shoot him a dirty look. "Sicko."

"It is not sick. That is part of who we are. We bite as part of our mating rituals. We mark what is ours. Tasting our mate bonds us," Adam defends.

I get perfectly still. "What?"

Jack sits down and rubs his face. "G.J., I know you are not ready for this yet, but Adam is right. We mark our mates, bite them, and draw blood, so we have their taste."

"So if you bite each other, are you mated? I am sure that is not what you mean to say, right? I mean if I get into a scuffle with someone and they bite me that doesn't automatically make me their mate, right?" Alarm curls up my spine.

"G.J., you are pack now. It is our way," Jack says like that explains anything.

"So… in the car… when Adam's teeth hit my head?" I ask.

"He didn't leave a mark," Hamilton says quickly.

"She removed it," Adam shoots back.

"This might be the reason I was the only girl here. You

folks have scared them all off. Do you really think you can dictate when and with whom I fall in love with a snap of the teeth?" I ask Jack.

"I am your Alpha. You are now pack. We accepted you as under our protection. You are the one who chose to challenge for dominance. That took you from adolescent to Gamma. When you beat Luke, you established yourself as Beta of this pack. These were all things done by you and your actions. We have no females because of many reasons," Jack says.

"I know Alpha and Beta, but what is Gamma?" I ask.

Jack blows out a breath and begins to explain. "The hierarchy of the pack defines your role. When you can speak, eat, mate, and so on. I am Alpha of this pack, but I am Alpha of the territory council of Alphas as well. There are other packs around the world, but they have other leaders, and we don't see a need to challenge each other for dominance. I have no interest in trying to keep a wolf in Europe in line." He checks to see if I understand. I nod, he continues.

"The Beta of my pack is only Beta of this local pack. You will learn how to deal with them. But each of the Alphas of the other local packs in this territory have their own Betas to help them govern their own wolves. I only get involved if there is some kind of trouble. A Beta is a second in command. They make wolves follow the law. They carry out my orders. They keep the peace. The Beta is second only to the Alpha. We have not had a Shaman or a Seer for some time. They are the only other wolves who are equal to the Beta. Next are the adults who are old enough to challenge for dominance. These are all Gammas. The level of Gamma you are depends on whom you have challenged and beaten in a fight. Sometimes wolves don't choose to fight and just submit. They are still Gammas but will always remain submissive. There is nothing wrong with that. The next class down is the adolescents. They can play fight amongst themselves and establish a micro hierarchy, but it does not affect whom they will be when they begin to challenge as an adult, and it holds no sway within the actual pack. A wolf has to make the decision for himself as to when he is prepared to begin challenging adults. For the most part, eighteen is when the issue gets forced. It usually takes years to fight enough to be Beta. But Luke accepted your challenge, so you leap frogged everyone else. Usually, he would have sent you down to the lower Gammas to have them submit to you. But he wanted you to submit to him and made a really poor judgment call." Jack's face is grim.

"So, if someone challenges me I can do that?" I clarify.

"That all depends on if they have gotten Luke to submit. He is still the highest-ranking Gamma. After you beat him, I am pretty sure no one is going to get past him for a while. But if someone does get past Luke, you will have to accept the challenge, or if Luke gives it another go." Jack smiles, the humor in his eyes sparkling. "At the same level as the adolescents is the vagabond. The vagabond is a wolf who changes packs a lot and may choose to stay and fight his way into Gamma or chooses to move on. We don't currently have any, but they have come through from time to time. After that, level comes the pups and the Omega. The Omega is both the least important of the pack and the most. They never want to fight and always choose to submit. But they are the first to make any situation better and know it takes some compromise and submission for us all to get along. Wolves tend to be aggressive, and the Omega counters that. Some wolves look down on the Omega, but there is honor in every wolf."

"When you say pups do you mean women give birth to puppies?" I ask with a "please don't say yes" look on my face.

"Shifts for full-blooded werewolves use to happen in the womb. But, it has been generations since we have had a full-blooded were," Jack explains.

"Yikes. So a baby stays a baby now?" I'm confirming what I think he's saying.

"None of the werewolves today are full-blooded. Cubs are still hard on women. We have not had a shaman to help bring the women through the birthing process. That is one of the reasons there are no women left," Jack says with sadness.

"Wait. You know you will kill your mates with babies, and you are trying to marry Aunt Celia?" I'm horrified.

Jack looks at me really hard. "I love your aunt."

"I'm worried you will love her to death," I exclaim.

"That is not your concern." Jack is trying to use his voice of authority, but I don't care.

"Bologna. She is my only family. I will be damned before you kill her with your offspring." I'm beyond outraged.

"G.J.." Jack rolls my name out on a growl. "I will not harm Celia. I have Adam. I have no need for another child. Although this is none of your business, I could not even consider your aunt until I found out she does not wish to have children. She and I have discussed it. I will not ever hurt your aunt. She is precious to me."

"So that leaves me. I am the one you plan on playing Russian roulette with," I say, my ugly sarcasm out on display.

"G.J.," Adam says quietly. "You are the only one who will survive. You can heal."

I look at Jack. "How did this happen? I am not even sixteen yet. I have no intention of being on Teen Moms. And who is to say I will want to be with any of you? If I don't, then what? I have to because I can? Is that how this works in your mind?"

"I remind you that I am your Alpha. That means you do as I say," Jack starts and continues after stifling my objection, "and I protect you."

"Protect me how?" I am so skeptical.

"You are a Witch, not a wolf. All women have the choice to breed or not to breed under our pack law. No one will force you to breed with them," Jack says. "I cannot stop them from trying to win you, though." Jack smiles. "And even without your special skills, you have what most wolves are looking for in a mate, even at this age."

"Are you saying I am naturally bitchy?" I jibe.

Jack laughs. "No, but you are big and built sturdy. You have a naturally strong will that attracts most Alpha males. I can see all kinds of challenges in the future."

"Big and built sturdy? Well, that has to be in a love song somewhere," I quip.

"And you have fantastic legs," Adam adds helpfully.

"What do you know about her legs?" Hamilton asks annoyed.

"Sleep shorts, brother, best thing ever invented," Adam says.

"Let me see," Hamilton says.

Adam runs out of the room.

"Wait. What? Adam you stay out of my drawers," I call after him, but he is already running back with a pair of my sleep shorts held up in front of his face. "You are a pervert," I tell him.

"I am buying you long johns," Jack tells me.

"Get her a parka," Hamilton snaps.

"Are you going to start wearing those around now, too?" I ask Adam, referring to my stolen G.R.I.T.S. shirt.

"Nah, but I wouldn't mind sleeping with them," Adam says.

"Shut up, Adam," Hamilton growls.

The doorbell rings, and Adam jogs off to get it. Jack says, "Tonight I will start working with you on the history and laws. It will be a crash course, so make sure you are ready to pay attention. Luke will help with what Beta means till you get settled in."

"Can I join you?" Hamilton asks.

Jack looks surprised. "Of course. It might help G.J. if she had a study partner. One who understands the rules." There is a threat in there, but I'm fine with Jack keeping Hamilton in line. Somebody has to.

Nat comes in, followed by Adam. "Hey, look who is less broken. I heard about your Aunt's house. It's what is on everyone's mind today," Nat says.

"Anyone think they did it?" I ask with little hope in my voice.

"Nobody I have crossed paths with, but I haven't been out much," Nat says. "I'm glad you weren't home. Do these guys have any suspects they want me to check out?"

My brain flashes through all that has happened since I last saw her. Nat sits quickly.

"Big day, huh?" Nat makes light of the images. "Well, at least I don't have to keep *that* from you anymore."

"Thank you, Nat. As usual, you have kept our secrets well. You have our thanks and respect," Jack says.

"It's what I do. Don't worry about it," Nat dismisses his praise. "So Beta, wow. When you do something, you go big. How'd you manage that?"

"She made Luke submit. We had claimed her as one of us. He underestimated how powerful G.J. is and wanted to prove his dominance. He has been bored lately anyway." Jack chuckles. "Every wolf is going to try to take him now. I bet he gets challenged quite a bit for a while. He will enjoy the workout."

"I didn't even think about that." I look down, feeling bad for having stepped into this situation. "Me and my big mouth."

"You didn't understand. I tried to tell you both, but Luke kind of sucked you in," Adam explains.

"How's that?" Hamilton asks.

"Your dad threatened to kill G.J. because she started to figure out what you were," Adam informs him.

"Explain," Jack commands.

Hamilton appears stunned. And Adam doesn't know where to start, so, as usual, I'm the fastest mouth around. "Hamilton lost his temper at the table, I guess. I tend to help him along with that. Anywho, his eyes got all glowy, and I asked him what he was. Hamilton left. But Luke said I had broken the law."

Jack growls.

"I told him you would not approve," Adam chimes in. "But then he asked if I was challenging him."

Jack growls louder.

"Adam said no, but I said I would, so he would leave Adam alone. Then he came at me," I explain as if the rest is history.

"My dad tried to kill you?" Hamilton's face goes pale. "God, I didn't know how it happened."

"Yep. I guess it runs in your family. If it makes you feel better, you got a lot closer than he did," I add in mock encouragement.

Hamilton growls.

"Do you have to poke him like that, G.J.?" Nat asks.

I shrug.

"He threatened both you and Adam?" Jack is controlling his voice with what looks like a good bit of effort.

I nod. "He was on a roll."

Jack sits back, lost in thought.

Nat stares at Jack and says, "Wow."

Jack shoots her a look, and she shakes her head, letting him know she won't tell whatever it is.

"I was wondering, Nat? Can you find out from Aunt Celia who this P is?" I ask my psychic friend.

Jack sits up alert.

"G.J., that is an invasion of privacy," Nat admonishes. "Sure."

"You have a devious mind; I am going to like having you as my Beta." Jack smiles.

"You think P had something to do with your aunt's house?" Nat asks.

"We need to check it out. Aunt Celia thinks it had something to do with him, so it would be good if we knew what P is all about," I say. "It may not be P though, so let's not put all our eggs in one basket.

"Good point. Adam, Hamilton, now that things have died down, go see if you can track down anything that might be useful," Jack orders. "Take a few of the other boys."

I stand up.

"Where are you going?" Hamilton asks.

"I told you, I'm going to go close those circles," I announce.

"The hell you are," Hamilton objects.

"Man, do you have a problem talking to her." Nat shakes her head. "She just challenged a grown werewolf—your dad and second only to Jack—and won. What about this girl makes you think dictating to her is going to get you anywhere?"

Jack asks, "What circles?"

I bring him up to speed.

"Change in plans. You boys stay with G.J.. Help her get things back to normal in the woods," Jack modifies his previous order.

"I am perfectly capable of handling this on my own. Besides, Aunt Celia said I wasn't supposed to be alone with him." I nod toward Hamilton.

"Someone may be trying to kill you. I only control the pack. You are under my protection. Therefore, you will accept it when given," Jack instructs like he is explaining how to bake to a two year old. "Besides, I told your aunt while you were in my house, so I am still keeping my word. I believe she told you no woods."

I stick my tongue out at him. What? I'm fifteen.

"You should join the debate team," is Nat's dry observation.

"Are you coming?" I ask her.

"Me? Walk in the woods? On purpose? Pass," Nat rejects the invite.

After I show Nat where my new digs will be, she heads back to her house. The boys and I spend the afternoon looking for circles and fixing them. We find four of the vacant kind and one of the ones Drake mentioned. The difference is so great I can see what he means. One is a light touch, and the four are dark and heavy.

Chapter Twenty-One

Monday has us back at school. Hamilton and Adam always have practice in the morning, so since I'm mended up, I'm back on the bus. Only this time I have a huge letter jacket boy practically sitting on top of me. Since we are so intimate, I ask for his name. Kevin is very nice and is determined to walk me all the way to my locker along with Chris and another boy named Hank. There are so many people around me Drake can't get to his locker. I know this has to be Jack's doing, so I plan on chatting with him later.

After first period ends, Ms. Stontz asks me to stay after class. As soon as everyone is gone she says, "G.J., how are you dear?"

I remember I had seen her by Aunt Celia's during the fire. "I am as good as can be expected. We were lucky we weren't home when that happened."

"You have had a good bit to deal with lately. How are you handling everything?" she asks gently.

If she only knew. "What is that saying? If something doesn't kill you…" I begin the well-known phrase. "I am going to be a professional body builder any time now."

Ms. Stontz hoots then grows serious again. "I have been contacted by someone who said we may have a similar outside interest."

"What?" I'm a bit taken aback. "Who?"

She just smiles. "I was told you have a natural talent. I can help you learn more about how to control it. If you would like, you can join me and some of my friends. We can work with you, but please keep our identities to yourself. And Nat, of course. I am sure you are not prepared to keep things from her yet. But you will be soon, with our help."

"Are you Wiccan?" I ask in a hushed tone, leaning in to keep confidence.

"Yes, dear. We are but we choose not to practice publically. There are too many people who would miss use our talent."

"Can I just make sure about something?" I inquire.

"What is that?" Her face is open, inviting the question.

"Is Mrs. Ackers in your coven?" I have my face squished up and if she says yes, it will hurt physically.

"No, dear. Our group is about a positive experience with the world around us. We are very low key. Sara's mother tends to want more of the spotlight than we are comfortable with." Ms. Stontz intimates in that way that lets you know she thinks very poorly of that kind of person, but is just too nice to say so.

"When do you want to start?" I ask, eager to learn anything that will make me less of a Dyson when it comes to sucking up everything around me.

We make plans to meet in the evenings at a local bookshop that is near the coffee house.

Chapter Twenty-Two

So, my life for the next few weeks is full. I meet with the coven every night, and Jack holds class for Adam, Hamilton, and me. Homework takes on a whole new meaning. I spend every waking hour working on something and maybe a few that I should have reserve for sleeping. Boys strew around our house like lost piles of laundry waiting to be folded. Being part of the pack means there are men everywhere. I barely get outside anymore, and if I go anywhere, I have a beefcake brigade. I actually have to go to the coffee house, saying I'm meeting Nat for some girls only talk and sneak out of the bathroom every night in order to keep my promise to the coven. Jack has his boys all over the place. I can't go two feet without tripping over one or another of them. The good part about being packed in all the time gives Sara less direct access. She never stops the verbal attacks but seems more edgy about using her gifts on me. She is, however, glued to Hamilton every chance she gets. Fine by me. Those two can have each other.

The ladies of my coven are super nice, and I'm learning a ton. I have more books with old script than the Long Hall

at Trinity College in Dublin. Some of the language takes
me a minute or two to translate from old English to my
southern dialect. The way I phrase the workings the coven
is teaching me makes even the stuffiest of the ladies giggle.
But it always seems to work. I really never have had an issue
with the workings, but I don't want to scare them off. So, I
don't show off what I can do until I've been working with
them for a month. They go crazy. All of these women can
direct power, but none of them can hold it and make things
happen with a power that doesn't have something to do with
the element we are channeling. I think I'm going to have
to put up a dam to control all the gushing they do over me.

I guess I'm some kind of myth, like a unicorn. They were
just sure no true Witch still existed on the planet. When
they practice, I don't draw as much energy as I did when
Sara and her mom tried to pull power. After explaining what
happened that night in front of Jack's house, Ms. Stontz
says that is because her coven only pulls a small amount
of power, and they do it gently. "The Ackers believe the
more power you can pull the stronger practitioner you
are. There really is no need to wipe out nature in order to
enjoy its gifts."

Wow, that needs to be on a bumper sticker.

I tell her I have been closing their circles, and that makes
everyone get very quiet. Apparently that isn't something they
can do. Nor have they heard of anyone closing a circle and
healing the ground. They gush again. I'm going to get a big
head if this continues.

****

That night, Jack begins talking more about the history
of the pack. Apparently, the "no women in the pack" is
because Witches were the ones who taught the shaman how

to carry and heal after birth. The shaman were singled out and killed over the past few generations. Jack looks at me.

"Jack, to quote Prissy from *Gone with the Wind* 'I don't know nothin bout birthin' babies.'" It is only right for me to let him know I'm not prepared to save his race.

Hamilton throws his hands up in the air. "Why would you put that on her? She doesn't know anything."

"Why don't you do it? What have you ever even thought about when it comes to women or how our bodies can give life? You think because I come with the equipment I got the manual? We have the same health classes. Unless you failed, you know what I know. Why don't you take this on? The only firsthand experiences I have that you don't are cramps and some other unpleasantness. But if you would like, I could sock you in the gut a few times over the next few days to help you catch up. The only birthing video I have seen that even comes close to the real thing was Jim Carey coming out of a fake rhino's behind in an Ace Ventura movie," I rant.

"Great flick. Was that number two?" Adam puns.

"Shut up, Adam. Thanks, Jack. No pressure. Just the next woman's life is in my hands. Really, I only turn sixteen next week. What am I supposed to do? I am not even good with Band-Aids because I have never needed them. And you are going to drop this on me?" My eyes definitely have a curse word in them. Actually, it's a phrase.

"G.J., you are just one possibility of some help. Do you really think we just sit back and let the women we love die?" Jack's deceptively calm, but I can tell he's not happy.

"No way can she do this," Hamilton adds.

"How do you know what I can or can't do?" I turn on Hamilton.

"You just said you couldn't," Hamilton returns as if frustrated.

"So. I have never tried it. I bet I can do a lot of things I've never tried. I have never ridden a bicycle, but I bet I could figure it out."

"You have never ridden a bike?" Adam asks.

"No, but I bet I can do it," I say not sure what my point is anymore.

"So, now you are saying you can do this?" Jack asks, closing one eye as if he is just as confused as I am.

"No, but just because I am freaked out does not mean I won't try," I yell at the men.

Jack puts his face in his hands and rubs. "It has been a long time since I have talked to a teenage girl."

"Trust me, she is worse than most," Hamilton commiserates with Jack.

I narrow my eyes at Hamilton. "Okay, so I promise to help everyone I can, *if* I can—except someone dumb enough to mate with you. I think it is best for your species."

Hamilton grumps, "You are going to regret that."

Adam chuckles. "Well, that would put a damper on things. I thought the Bro Zone was bad."

"What?" I shoot Adam a look.

"Adam," Jack uses his warning voice. "I think we are done for tonight. Boys, if I can talk to you for a minute. G.J., I am sorry if I upset you, but this is part of our history. I need you to understand all that we know. Like it or not."

I nod, huffing out to settle down, and kiss his cheek. "Goodnight, Jack. I'll do what I can. Even for bonehead's poor stupid mate."

Adam holds his arms wide. "Goodnight, sis."

I roll my eyes but let him wrap me up and sniff my neck. Jack explained that contact is important for wolves, so I endure the smelling snuggles to a point. Hamilton moves in for his turn. I'm stiff as a wood plank until he's done. I would be somewhat okay with it if he didn't have this ridiculous look on his face every time he's done. It's like he takes that as some kind of submission and it rankles.

****

Ms. Stontz is so tickled I was born on March twenty-first. Apparently, it's a big deal for the Wiccan faith. Some ancient Germanic goddess of spring who liked white rabbits is celebrated that day. They call it Ostara. It sounds a whole lot like Easter to me, but I don't argue with her. She explains, "This was where the word 'east' most likely originated. The east is where the sun rises. The Sun God and Mother Nature come together, and in nine months, there will be the birth of a new year. This holiday calls for decorated eggs, but there are two different kinds, raw and hard-boiled. Raw symbolizes fertility and the four elements. The shell being earth, the membrane air, the egg white water, and finally the yolk represents fire."

"Interesting theory, but the membrane is what actually locks out air; the shell is what is porous." I can't leave scientific facts alone.

She ignores me and continues, "Hard-boiled is the idea of prosperity and good fortune."

We spend the next week decorating the eggs and cleansing all the ladies' houses. This calls for patchouli candles and planting herb gardens. I plant my herb garden at Jack's, but I'm fairly sure my clothes reek from the candles at the other ladies' houses, so I don't have to actually light one at home. I also throw eggshells around the outside garden. I used to do that back home anyway. This is to promote new life and good health in your soil, which I can agree with for logical reasons. The ladies have some big event in the woods they want me to be a part of, and I have to admit I am curious.

Now, I know this is rubbing up against my Christian upbringing, but I'm pretty sure this is what half of what we do as children at Easter time is related to, this tradition, and not the rebirth of Jesus. If you think about it though, what better time for God to show us renewal than during a time when other cultures would understand and relate? So, I get the big plan here and can move forward with a clear conscience. It is also interesting that Easter is chosen as the first Sunday after the full moon following the vernal equinox. In my mind, that somehow connects all parts of my life. My lunar-cycled friends balance with the Wiccans and my favorite carpenter's big day. I have always liked Easter, and this makes me feel even more connected.

*****

Aunt Celia loves my decorated eggs and helps me put them up all over the house. "You are getting really into the holiday this year, G.J.."

"I have discovered all kinds of new things about it," I reply, being intentionally vague.

"Have you given any thought to your birthday?"

"Nope. Honestly, I don't know what to say. If I could have a few more hours in the day, that would be great, but since that won't happen unless the earth's rotation slows, I don't really need too much." I'm more focused on hanging my egg than the conversation.

"I know. Let's have a shopping day. We can get you some new outfits and go get our nails done," she suggests. "Your hair is coming back in. Maybe it's long enough to get styled."

"Styling my hair at this point is gluing it down with gel, so I don't get confused with a q-tip. I am pretty sure a haircut would set me back a spell." I rebuff her attempt to get me away from my workload. Softening, I continue, "That sounds real nice, but I am not sure I have time for all that."

"What? G.J., it's your birthday. You can ease off the schoolwork for a day. I'm worried about you, kiddo. You are too young to be working so hard." Aunt Celia's concern is about to get too intrusive, so I derail her.

"Are you going to marry Jack?" Wham. No more talk about what I'm up to.

She slants her eyes at me. "Does it bug you that I am not married to Jack?"

"Well, I think you love him."

"I do."

"And I know he thinks you are made of all that is perfect in this world."

She blushes and shrugs, unable to deny it.

"So, if you finally have it right, why not show the world this is the real deal? You are committed. Just seems silly to me."

"You're okay with it? You don't think six husbands is maybe one too many for a person to have had? I feel like a big punch line. I don't want Jack to feel like just another one in the string of men I have married. He is really special, G.J.. I don't want to screw it up." She's kind of flinching, as if my judgment will hurt.

"Well, all the other guys asked you. Why don't you ask Jack?" I suggest.

Aunt Celia looks at me blankly. "But he's already asked."

"Today?" I question.

"No, a while ago," she says, giving what I'm saying a good old-fashioned ponder.

"Well, you said no then. The basic rule of contract law is offer and acceptance. If that offer is not taken as is, the counter offer is actually the possibility of a whole new contract," I instruct, dusting off my civics lessons.

"I hadn't thought about it that way." She smiles. "Are you thinking of law as a future?"

"No, just one of my many hobbies." I smile back at her.

She wipes her hands on her pants and says, "Excuse me a second."

I'm not there for the big moment, but Jack lets the whole house know he has been bit by a happy bug with all the racket he makes. Goodness that man can roar. If I didn't know he's a wolf, I would have gone with lion as my guess. He is so excited he wants to fly to Vegas and get it done right then. Aunt Celia says this is the last time she is going to do this, and she wants to do it right. So she needs at least three months to plan. The big day is set for the third week in June.

Chapter Twenty-Three

Their engagement announcement preempts my birthday party. It's not a big deal. I don't need much. Everyone is there, all my testosterone tikes in their swollen-armed glory: Drake, Gus, Nat, and all Aunt Celia's friends. The adult pack seems extra happy. Apparently, while Jack is unmated none of them can take a new mate, so this is a huge deal. This proves to be more unsettling the more I think about it. If all these men are now in the market for mates, I just moved up my timetable for needing to know how to make sure women can survive having little ones. Once again, I put myself in the middle of a mess by opening my large mouth. I mull over wiring my jaw shut just to give myself a break for a while. But if I bottle everything I have to say up for a time, I will explode like a Coke in the freezer.

My friends leave around ten pm, everyone catching a ride with Gus, who has another "engagement" to attend later tonight. What high-school kid has things start at after ten pm? Gus must have a very different life than I do most of the time. But I have things to do myself tonight. I go out back to try to sneak off into the woods to meet up with my coven. But just as I'm halfway across the lawn I hear, "You haven't been outside much lately."

Turning, I confront Hamilton. "Nope, sure haven't. I have a lot to study these days."

"We're studying the same things. Adam says you barely come out of your room unless you are meeting Nat for coffee." His voice is low.

"My only break." I drop the last word, hoping the conversation will follow.

"But you aren't," he says.

I just look at him. "Not what?" Now I am as still as if I am perched on a knife's edge. I look right at the boy, telegraphing him to not go anywhere near this subject.

But this is Hamilton so he has no earthly idea what a hint looks like; needless to say he wouldn't recognize one if it slams him in the face. "You don't go meet Nat. Every night for weeks, I have gone to the coffee house. You aren't in there. Your guards are outside waiting like you tell them to, but you're not in there. You don't show up until it's time to meet Jack. What are you doing, G.J.?"

"Why are you following me?" I ask strategically defensive.

"Not the point. What are you doing?" He's moving closer to me.

"Stop," I say, holding up my hand.

Hamilton stills, but he's watching me carefully.

"Look, I am doing what I am supposed to," I say, trying to end the conversation, but knowing this dog is on my scent, and he isn't giving up until I'm treed.

"You look wasted. Your light doesn't go out until two or three in the morning. You are up before Adam and he has morning practice. What is going on?" he asks.

"Stalk much?" I look at him like he just told me he likes to wear pantyhose, and let's face it; nobody likes to wear panty hose.

Hamilton doesn't respond. He just stands there quietly waiting for the inevitable, me to start talking.

"I am..." I sigh. "I found a coven. I am working with them to learn how to control what I can do so I don't turn space alien if confronted with power again," I confess. "I am also going through every book they give me to try to help the pack have young."

Hamilton laughs. "Man, I thought," He cuts himself off and shakes his head, "why is that such a secret?"

"Because the coven does not want anyone to know they exist. They have their reasons. So, I have to keep it a quiet. Please, Hamilton. If Jack finds out, he will track these ladies down and do full background checks on all of them. I made a promise. Please don't tell," I beg, looking up at the face that always seems to scowl at me.

"What happens if you're with them and something goes wrong?" Hamilton asks.

"I'll handle it. This isn't really your concern."

"*You* are my concern," he challenges, beginning his low growl.

"How's that?" I shoot back. Drake had been right. I'm now used to that rumbling noise that used to scare me so bad I almost needed fresh pants.

He does that hard staring thing he loves so much and says, "You are my... Beta." He bites out the last word.

"Great, then as your Beta I am telling you not to tell Jack." I play my trump card.

His growl gets louder.

"I have to go. Tonight is a big night." My eyes lock on his, and I add for good measure, "I am trusting you with this, Hamilton. Please don't make me regret it."

He stops growling and walks back into the house.

****

M s. Stontz is at the clearing when I arrive, along with a few other ladies. "G.J., happy birthday dear. Goodness isn't that dress lovely? Green suits you. Come help me place candles and draw the circles. We are only waiting on Stella and Tracy."

I take the salt and walk the circle, stopping just before it is closed. Ms. Stontz sets the candles at the four corners representing the compass points. Once the other women arrive, we place all of our offerings in the circle. Most of the women have clay pots with soil and a large seed inside it. The idea is for the seed to be blessed and have healthy and happy growth as a sign of what will happen in their lives this year. Other women bring some of their eggs they've decorated for fertility. Tracy is hoping to get pregnant, so that makes sense for her. A white rabbit is also placed in the circle as a gift to the goddess of springtime since it is one of her favorite things. I have to admit it is so cute. With everything in place, I take the salt and close the circle.

As we light the last candle, the troubles start. I feel power crash into me. My head slams back, and all I can see is the sky. I am trembling, and words are rolling out of me. Words I barely recognize and only hold a loose translation of from my minimal Latin. Our coven doesn't practice in Latin. What is happening to me? The women close to me scream and try to get me to stop whatever it is that I am doing, but there is no stopping the energy I am sucking into me. The chant I am repeating seems to be echoing, and I realize there are other people in the woods. I feel them. All of them. They have set up a circle around our clearing and trapped us. They are trying to control me. They *are* controlling me.

"By the Goddess, what are you doing, Leslie?" Ms. Stontz screams.

"She holds power. Tonight is the night when light meets dark, when worlds collide. Tonight we are able to control both sides of the power. We can use her tonight to make the world what we want it to be. Look at her. She can feed us power all year long. I know she is the one."

My skin is on fire and tearing apart at previously unknown seams. Mrs. Ackers laughs. "She will make everyone fear us. You stupid petty women only think about a happy life or some hope for offspring. She can swing the balance to us."

"G.J., fight it. Use what we taught you and let the energy go," Ms. Stontz coaches.

My head is still back, and power erupts from my mouth, shooting like a laser at the sky.

"NO," screams Mrs. Ackers. "Girls repeat after me. Glory Juniper Gardener, I bind the power you hold to you; I bind it to your spirit, body, and mind."

"Leslie that will kill her. You can't," Ms. Stontz yells. This makes some of Team Ackers pause.

I hear a howl. I think about my pack, and I wish I had not told Hamilton to keep this secret.

Sara speaks then. "Mom, if she's dead, how can she hold power?" Thanks for caring Sara. Amazing that mental sarcasm is still available while I'm going through this moment.

"Don't worry. She is just a container. If we bind the power to her, we can keep her in the basement freezer. She'll keep," is this crazy woman's answer.

What is worse is it seems to satisfy some of her coven because they begin to repeat the binding. Like electrical tape is winding around me, holding in the power so those seams that I mentioned before can't burst and give me any release.

"You are crazy. Do you think we won't tell anyone about this?" Ms. Stontz asks. I am not sure why people feel the need to give the bad guy a good reason to kill them.

"I know you won't. When the ritual is over, you will be too. G.J. will have sucked the life force right out of you. Everything in this circle will be gone. And G.J.'s troubled past will make her just another sad case of a runaway. No one will care," says Mrs. Ackers. That woman takes maniacal bitch to a whole new level.

I have to make this stop. I concentrate on my own thoughts and try to block what they force into me. What can I do? I don't want to steal the life from these women who have become my friends. A woman screams and then a gunshot fires. My eyes fly open. My wolf is standing, head low and growling. Another shot rings out, and he's hit. I see his body absorb the impact of the bullet pushing past his beautiful fur and into his flesh. He yowls in pain and lays in spasms. I run, not sure how my body is doing it, until I smash into the circle they have created.

The women of my coven are weakening as my body continues to draw in all the energy it can reach. I'm trapped. My wolf lies dying, and I'm trapped.

"Keep going, ladies. I will keep an eye out for any more wildlife. Don't get distracted," the insane Ackers woman shouts.

My fury is burning up some of the energy, and I use the reprieve to think. The other coven has switched to binding the power to me, so they have stopped using my voice as a conduit. "Ms. Stontz, get the salt, break our circle, get in, and re-draw it."

For how drained she has to be, she and the rest of our coven hustle. I guess that is what people mean by "if their life depended on it."

"G.J., you too," Ms. Stontz calls to me.

I shake my head. If I am in there, the magical line the other coven has on me will cross our circle, and my friends will not be safe. The rabbit in our circle stops moving. I have already drawn the life out of it. "Close it," I command, and she does, sealing them in and me out.

The power draw drops dramatically. Human beings are like generators, and I am embarrassed to say that like a junkie, I want more. Our circle is solid, though. But the other coven put their circle outside a line of trees. Trees have roots. Roots break the bounds of a circle. I drop to the ground and put my palms flat, feeling for the root systems around me, following energy lines, and connecting with them. The trees creak and sway as they pick up one of their coven and have her break the circle.

"No,"' Mrs. Ackers shrieks. "Sara, quick. Go draw the line."

Sara stands there, unwilling to move.

"You stupid girl, do as you are told," her mother yells.

I run for the edge of the circle while they have their debate. I escape. But my troubles are far from over. As soon as I'm out, Mrs. Ackers shoots me in the stomach. If I thought holding all that power hurt, I can tell you a bullet wound is nothing to slouch at. I grasp my stomach where the bullet went in, and blood oozes through my fingers. "There goes your battery pack," I say to the woman still holding the gun on me.

"Pity, and after all that trouble too—getting the girls to get pieces of your hair and skin, trying to get you to stand in the circle on the stage, so we could bind your mind and make you do all kinds of horribly embarrassing things, and burning down Celia's house to hide the fact that we had gone in and taken so many of your things. You could have been a treasure. But now you are just a big waste of time."

Her tone fills with such so much hate that I wonder if she practices that when alone in her car.

"Why?" Although curious, I am also stalling her.

"At first it was simply to prove you never cross an Ackers. You started it with hitting Sara in the face. We would never let such a thing stand. I was going to help the girls learn a few things by teaching them some dark rituals they could use on you. They never could get the rites to work. Which was when I figured out it was *you* pulling all of the power back and *you* closing our circles." She tsks. "Then I saw what you did the other night." She stops and makes a weird noise by sucking in through her teeth. "You can't do something like that and not pay. Besides, Sara has a thing for that Calhoun boy and swears you are keeping him from her. You are just in the way."

My wolf whimpers, bringing me back to the fact that I can't just stand here all night. I have things to do. I take the bullet I've been pushing out of me and healing while the woman has been yammering on, and throw it in her face. The trees are still mine to command, and they wrap up the women standing closest to each. Mrs. Ackers fires another shot, this one at my head. I stop the slug in midair. "You are the perfect example of why there should be sanity tests to buy one of these things." Then I drop the bullet to the ground and fling the gun from her hands off into the woods.

I no longer care about this crazy nitwit. I go to my wolf. Falling to my knees, I put my hands in his blood-soaked fur. He licks my wrists and whimpers in pain. He has lost so much blood, and I mentally curse the evil woman for being such a loudmouth. I focus everything I have on taking away his pain while removing his bullet and healing his wound.

I hear someone shout my name, and my healing wolf growls and leaps.

Chapter Twenty-Four

That is it for me. At least as far as full consciousness goes for a while. I fade in and out and see snippets of things, but when I come to, what has happened has a very *Wizard of Oz* feeling to it. Like Dorothy, I'm not sure what is dream and what is reality. I have always wondered why they didn't call that character Dottie and always liked that name. I recall my wolf licking my face. I remember being carried. I remember Jack yelling. I remember Adam and Hamilton's faces, but I can't place when I last saw them. I remember Aunt Celia crying and cleaning up the side of my head.

Memories start regaining their order. I am in my room at Jack's house, and he sits propped in a chair with his eyes closed. "Hey," I croak. If this keeps happening, I am going to have to make a deal with someone to sponge out my mouth from time to time while I am out.

Jack's eyes snap open, and he is fully alert, like sleep and wakefulness are just a switch he flips inside his eyelids. "About time, fix it so I can go get your aunt. I won't have her see you like this anymore."

"I'm fine, Jack. Thanks for your concern." There is my sarcasm on the loose again.

His chest rumbles, and I decide it will be better if I fix my head before I try to take him on. He seems very pissy, so I heal myself up right quick. Still hurts like the dickens, in case you are wondering.

"What happened?" I ask.

"I would know what happened if you had stayed with any of my wolves. But you trotted off into the woods by yourself when someone was trying to kill you. Why don't you start with how that could have happened?" Jack crosses his impressive arms in a show of manly intimidation.

"I found a coven who's helping me learn some actual witchcraft. They wanted to remain anonymous. We were meeting up to do a spring ritual. It's kind of a big deal," I explain. "Only Mrs. Ackers showed up and well… that chick ain't right in the head. Her coven tried to kill all of us. After I escaped their circle, everything kind of went black." I'm not giving up my wolf to Jack. He won't take too kindly if one of his men did not confess all this while I was out.

"Leslie Ackers?" he asks.

"Yes, sir. Oh, I forgot. She confessed to burning down Aunt Celia's house to hide that she had burgled it."

"G.J., some hikers found her this morning. She was mauled by a wolf," Jack says, trying to lead me to confess more.

"Do other wolves besides you all live around here?" I ask, doing that non-answer thing I've picked up from these folks.

Jack narrows his eyes. "Murder is a serious crime, G.J. The human law should have handled Leslie."

"Right, I am sure the cops would love to have seen the bullet I ejected from my body before I healed myself. Or should I have my secret coven come forward and explain how this other group of women was forcing me to draw the life force out of my coven? I have never been a Chuck Norris fan, but this vigilante wolf is a hero in my book. That woman has redefined menace for me, so I will no longer think of that cute little blond boy making mischief, she's now my mental picture." I finish, realizing two things—Adam and Hamilton are standing in the doorway like they had run from the other room, and I had neglected to tell Jack about me being shot. "She made me kill that poor bunny." I close my eyes, getting a flash of the dying rabbit. I hate pangs of guilt for things you really did not mean to do. It makes me feel twice as guilty for not accepting responsibility for it in the first place.

"She is worried she killed a rabbit?" Hamilton says, sounding disgusted.

I scowl at him.

"How many hits can that head of yours take?" Adam asks in his usual playful manner.

"'Takes a lickin' and keeps on tickin'.' No worries," I say cheerfully, letting everyone know I'm fine. "So, that is why I had the extended siesta. She must have hit me while I was..." I shut up just before I admit to having seen a wolf.

Hamilton makes one of his weird noises that sounds like "hmpf."

Jack stands and puts his balled fists on either side of my body as he leans down. "You, young lady, will stay with one of these two behind me every second of every day. You will not have secret meetings. You do not keep secrets from me. If Adam had not realized you'd left the party and gone to find you, God only knows what would have happened."

Adam and Hamilton exchange a look.

"You are also to start self-defense training, and I mean without using your hocus pocus. You are too valuable to be lost because you think you can take care of yourself. You will not take these kinds of risks. Got it? Never again." Jack is right up in my face.

"Okay, all right. I will keep some man-meat nearby at all times. Are you happy?" I shrink into my pillows. Jack stands to his impressive height. "If you are going to stay engaged to Aunt Celia, I suggest a mint before you go get her." Jack scowls. He is way better at it than I am. I put my hands up in defense. "I'm just sayin'."

****

So goes the rest of my school year. Ms. Stontz comes and introduces herself to my family. She says she won't reveal her coven, but in light of everything that has happened she can see how important it is for my family to know someone else in the circle. She tells Jack my coven didn't see what happened in the tree line because it was dark, and her view was blocked by the trees I'd moved to hold the other women. When they felt it was safe to come out, the other coven was gone and so was I.

Jack obviously has her followed and will do those background checks, but he's discrete, and I've kept my word. Sara moves in with her dad, surprisingly her parents were in the process of a divorce. There's a shocker. She's nicer to me now. Way too nice. Nobody likes a fanny kisser. I swear it's because Hamilton is trying to win Jack's approval by being the bodyguard most likely to drive me insane with lack of privacy. In doing so, if she makes any snide comments he acts like she shot the president.

I don't win the Governor's Science Award. That stings. Who cares about a robot that can sort trash for recycling? Okay, it's pretty cool, but next year I am taking Neil Larosso down at the science fair.

My self-defense training is going well. Adam is a good teacher, and I think Hamilton just enjoys playing my attacker.

He volunteers way too quickly when it's time to grab me. I guess it is good Jack has found a way for him to channel his violent tendencies toward me without me actually getting hurt. I enjoy getting to kick his butt, on the rare occasion I do. But I keep getting better, so soon I should be able to do it when he isn't letting me win.

Nobody has challenged for Beta yet. I guess we'll see. The whole pack is coming for the wedding. I see no problems on the horizon there. *Right.* I get straight A's, but I have to argue with the PE teacher to get the B changed. Stupid dodge ball. Drake is still harassing Nat; that is fun to watch. Jiminy Cricket how clueless can a girl be that a boy likes her? Gus floats in and out. He always seems to be busy, but he flirts with the best of them and is always good for an ego boost.

Epilogue

The wedding is June twenty-first, which also happens to be the summer solstice. I help with the set-up and have the altar at the south side of the lawn. The summer solstice rite should be south-facing. Never hurts to encourage good vibes from every faith. The flowers are bright, and the bride's maid dress Aunt Celia chose is nice enough, but come on people, have you ever seen a good one, really? Five hundred people attend, and I am stunned at the size of this territory's pack. I get more than a few stares that go a little too far for what is appropriate for a sixteen-year-old girl. Nothing like being the only girl who can survive a mating to fill up a girl's dance card. For once, I am absolutely fine with being sandwiched between Hamilton and Adam all the time. These two I can handle.

The ceremony is beautiful, and Jack looks like he's going to burst he is so happy. Aunt Celia, well, she's just radiant. She's sparkling like a diamond. Mama would have loved to see them together. I still miss her, but I know she's here in spirit. Unfortunately, part of the day I have to sort of dance around the room, spinning from one man to the next, to get in all the sniffing that's required. I'm not sure what the other people at the wedding tell themselves to make that okay in their minds. Whatever it is that keeps them from thinking this is bizarre, I wish they would share, because I am totally creeped out.

My time as a Beyblade ends, and I catch up with Nat, who is doing her best to ignore Drake as he looms over her. "Still not used to the sniffing," I say as we watch Jack and Aunt Celia take the floor for their first dance.

"Dude, be glad you don't know what they're thinking. Some of these guys need to get out more," Nat informs me, which doesn't make me feel any better.

"So it *is* good to not hear someone's thoughts all the time," Drake prompts.

Nat just gives him a dirty look.

"Speaking of... I know P had nothing to do with the fire and all, but I still want to know who it is. Do you mind finding out?" I ask.

"Ehh...for you, gorgeous, anything," Nat says as she slaps my cheek.

We look at the head that holds the information as Aunt Celia goes up on her toes and whispers something to Jack.

"Ooh, that's awesome." Nat says.

"What?" I say as Jack's horrified face turns to mine.

"Your aunt Celia has a bun in the oven," Nat says, and those words completely rob me of breath.

I am never painting another fertility egg in my life. The spring ritual must have been over cast.

About the Author

K.W. Benton has long been a daydreamer who has finally decided to put her wild thoughts on paper. She started taking mental adventures from a young age and was always one to love a good story. Family is number one in her heart although some of the most important people are family by choice. She is the mother of two and a wife of one. In raising her children, she discovered it was difficult to teach them to reach for their dreams if not leading by example. She has been blessed with good friends, hilarious family, and great love. She adores Jane Austen, spicy food and a good snuggle. Her favorite place to be is with the ones she holds dear.

Made in the USA
Charleston, SC
10 August 2016